ACKNOWLEDGEMENTS

I'd like to thank those who have aided me in the preparation of this novel. To my mother and editor, Barbara, for her always insightful input. To my father, Derek, for passing his love of video games onto me and answering many of my science and tech questions related to the book.

To my beta readers who provided very valuable comments on earlier drafts: Claudia Pileggi, Julian Russell, Karine Weber, and my sister Carolyne.

I'd also like to thank my high school film teacher Ancil Deluz for his insight on the relationship between entertainment and society.

ARCADIA

For Nana

"Entertainment has nothing to do with reality. Entertainment is antithetical to reality."

– Michael Crichton

PROLOGUE

The tires screeched as Miller rounded the bend, another stretch of desert road looming in his headlights. He watched the speedometer tick past eighty and felt his heart pound so fast it hurt, an invisible vise tightening around his chest. Miller's mind, however, was more preoccupied with other concerns. His eyes darted to the rear-view mirror. The night was black and empty behind him.

For now.

He knew they wouldn't be far behind. There was no way they'd let him make it back to the city, he was too much of a liability now. He needed somewhere to get off the road and hide. But side-paths were few and far between, and they would undoubtedly check all of those within a twenty-mile radius. He swore under his breath.

Then, about half a mile up ahead, an oasis of light appeared at the side of the road. A lone red pickup was refueling at one of the pumps beneath an overhang with a big sign in cursive, neon red letters: Road Runner's Gas & Diesel.

A sense of relief started to come over Miller, but he knew he was far from out of the woods.

His rental car didn't even begin to slow until he whipped into the gas station, narrowly missing the tail end of the pickup and sharply coming to a stop in one of the three parking spaces in front of the convenience store. Without turning off the vehicle, he threw the door open. A quick glance over his shoulder as he stumbled out of the car yielded no sign of any pursuers, so he quickly slammed the door shut and made for the store entrance. He heard the driver of the truck shout "Watch your driving, asshole!" but he barely registered it as he grabbed the handle and swung the glass door open.

A chime sounded as he entered and the sales clerk behind the counter, a lanky man with long hair and glasses, looked up from his phone. "Can I help you, sir?"

"No, no, I'm fine," Miller managed to get out. His hands were shaking, his clothes were covered in desert dirt and dust, and there was a nasty cut on his forehead. He realized he was probably attracting unnecessary attention, but he didn't care at the moment. Crouching by a rack of potato chips, he cautiously peered out the front window.

The woman with the pickup was cleaning her windshield with a squeegee while she waited for the pump to finish. The road beyond her was empty. Miller took several deep breaths, trying to regain any semblance of calm. *Keep it together, keep it together*, he told himself.

Any progress he made vanished as a pair of headlights appeared off in the distance to the east, the same direction he had come from. His heart beat faster again and he felt the urge to retch. As the vehicle drew nearer, he could see it was a black sedan, a mid-2010s Chevy Malibu.

It was them. There was no mistaking it.

Miller felt himself sink lower to the floor. His eyes were now perfectly level with the bottom of the window.

"Excuse me, sir?" he heard the clerk say.

"*Shhh*," Miller hissed.

The Malibu was now approaching the gas station, appearing to decrease its speed as it did so. Abruptly, Miller ducked down so that his entire body was out of sight. He felt his chest heaving in and out with each deep breath. *Don't turn here, keep going. Keep going, you fuckers. Keep going…*

They might already be out there. He could picture the black car pulling into the spot beside his. Then the driver's door would open and–

He couldn't wait any longer. He had to look. Immediately, Miller poked his head up and took in the view outside. The Malibu was nowhere in sight. Looking to the right, he saw a pair of rear lights disappearing off into the night down the road.

A massive sigh of relief escaped him. He nearly collapsed to his knees. The bastards either hadn't seen him or had just figured he wouldn't have stopped here. He didn't have much time though, they might come back. Just as Miller headed for the door, the clerk suddenly appeared in front of him.

"Excuse me sir, what's going on?" he said.

"None of your business." *And you wouldn't believe me if I told you*, he thought.

"Sir, have you been abusing substances?"

"Have I…? *What?*" Miller could barely believe anyone would ask him that. Then he realized he must look like a crack addict right now. "Look, I need to get out of here."

"Sir, I don't think you're fit to drive." Out of the corner

of his eye, Miller saw the guy reaching his arm out to grab him.

In a flash, he whipped out the pistol he'd concealed in his jacket and aimed it squarely at the clerk. "*Get. The fuck. Back,*" he hissed.

The man threw his hands up. "Okay, okay, take it easy..."

"I said *back* goddamnit!" Miller barked.

The clerk finally clued in, taking several big, reverse steps toward the counter. Miller didn't waste another second. In a flash, he turned around, pushed through the door, and dashed to his car. He didn't stop to see if the woman with the truck saw he had a gun. Miller opened the driver's side door and scrambled inside, frantically fumbling with his seatbelt. He threw the car into reverse and gunned the engine. The sedan shot back out onto the main road and turned with a squeal of its tires. He shifted it into drive and revved forward, speeding off into the west.

Inside the store, the clerk wiped sweat from his brow as he dialed a number on the landline phone. After a moment, a voice answered with: "This is 9-1-1, please state your emergency."

Miller didn't pay any attention to the stop sign and careened straight out onto US-93's southbound lane. Fortunately, there was no one else out here in the middle of nowhere, not at this time of night. From here it was mostly a straightaway back to civilization. The damn rental didn't have automatic lane assist, so he had to keep one hand steady on the wheel as he pulled out his phone. Miller entered his passcode with his right hand, glancing up at the road every few seconds just to make sure he didn't veer off.

Swiftly, he opened up the dialer, went to recent calls, and tapped on Lewis's name. He brought the device to his ear, staring intently ahead at the endless stretch of asphalt while the barren desert passed in his peripheral. The phone kept ringing.

"Damnit Lewis, answer your fucking phone!"

His eyes darted around the landscape, taking in what he could see. The moon was a week away from being full, but there was still enough illumination to get a glimpse of the Mojave. It wasn't flat out here; there were hills and rises all around, even mountains off in the distance. He wished he could enjoy it, but he hadn't come here to play tourist.

A pre-recorded message of his friend's voice began to play. "Hi, you've reached Desmond Lewis at the *Technologist*. I'm sorry I was unable to take your call. Please leave a message and I'll get back to you as soon as I can."

Miller opened his mouth, prepared to speak, but an automated message began saying: "At the tone, please leave a detailed message…" He grunted and drummed his fingers on the steering wheel as he waited for it to finish its aggravating spiel. Finally, it ended.

The phone beeped.

"Alright Lewis, I want you to listen to me very carefully. I've stumbled onto something, and it's big. I don't know if I have much time before they find me, but if anything happens to me I want you, no matter what you do, to stay away from –"

It happened very quickly, so quickly Miller was surprised he was able to take it all in. A pair of headlights launched out at him from the left side of the road just up ahead. He jerked the wheel to the right as hard as he could. The highway was raised up here, and a guardrail separated the pavement from a steep hill that went down about twenty feet. The front of Miller's car plowed into the railing at an angle, the impact causing his thumb to press down on the End Call icon before the device slipped free from his hand entirely. The next thing he knew, there was a hideous screech of metal as the railing gave way, scraping along the side of the car as it kept going. The wheels lost contact with the ground, and for a moment the entire vehicle sailed through open air. Miller felt himself float upwards, suspended by his seatbelt.

Then the car hit the ground.

Because of the angle, the inertia compelled it forward, spinning and twisting end over end as it violently tumbled across the terrain. The airbags deployed and Miller squeezed his eyes tightly shut as glass cracked all around him and a horrible pain shot through his right leg. Finally, the wreck lurched to a halt on its side, then fell back onto its roof, wobbling slightly before remaining still.

Miller slowly opened his eyes. His face was covered in blood and he felt light-headed. Had he just blacked out? If he had, it mustn't have been for long. Coughing, he unbuckled his seatbelt and fell down onto the car's ceiling. His entire body was racked with pain, and it definitely felt as if his right leg was broken. All the windows were beyond repair, but not shattered. He was in no shape to break the glass himself, so he feebly reached into his jacket to pull out the pistol.

It looked like a Glock, he realized. He hadn't had time to thoroughly examine it when he'd grabbed it earlier. Checking the clip, he found he still had two bullets left. Flicking the safety off, he aimed it at the windshield and covered his ears with his free hand and other shoulder. Then he pulled the trigger.

The weapon roared and the glass pane fractured further

but didn't shatter. Only one shot left. Miller aimed again and fired. This time the windshield splintered into a thousand shards, which rained down onto the ground and *clinked* on top of each other. Keeping the weapon firmly in hand, he pulled himself forward, trying to avoid cutting himself in the process. It was no use. Miller clenched his teeth and wriggled his way out of the overturned sedan, wincing through the pain.

Once clear, he turned over onto his back and gasped for breath. The cold, desert night air stung his lungs, but he didn't care. He felt like he could lie there forever, staring up at the stars. There were so many of them, he realized, this far from the city where light pollution couldn't mask them. Infinite nebulas and supernovas waving at him from across the universe.

The sound of an engine brought him back to Earth. Grimacing, he looked to his right and saw a black Chevy Malibu pulling up to the opening in the guardrail his car had made. The headlights shone out from the top of the hill. He shielded his eyes, squinting to get a better look. The driver's side door of the vehicle opened and a figure stepped out.

Miller's blood ran cold.

What he saw shut the door and walk to the top of the hill was not human.

Whatever it was, it was clad in some kind of advanced-looking white spacesuit, like an astronaut's, but from within its helmet came an otherworldly blue glow.

No, he thought. *It's not possible*.

Slowly, methodically, the thing began making its way down the slope toward him. The blue light where its face should have been emanated outward, casting an eerie radiance on the dusty ground as it walked.

Terrified, Miller raised the pistol and squeezed the

trigger. It was useless; he was all out. He began pulling himself back along the ground, muscling past the pain in his leg. The creature was closer now, almost at the rear of the wreck. He heard slow, inhuman breaths coming from within the suit.

He couldn't move any faster. Exhaustion overtook him. The pain was too much, the air too icy, the shock of the crash finally catching up with him. Miller collapsed onto his back. The figure blotted out the stars above him, staring down and shining its blue light into his eyes.

"Please," was all he could muster. He wasn't sure if he wanted to be spared or for it just to finally all be over.

The monstrosity answered with a sharp kick to his chest. He felt his ribs crack and he lurched up for air. It hurt to breathe. The astronaut-thing lashed out with its booted foot, again and again, each blow harsher than the last. On the fourth savage impact, his ribcage gave in as a shard of bone skewered his left lung.

Miller lay back in the dirt, wheezing. He coughed and blood spewed from his lips. His entire body shuddered, bracing itself for the end.

The thing looked down and tilted its head, either out of curiosity at what were to be his final actions or admiration at its gruesome handiwork. Then it turned and left, trudging back toward the hill and the black sedan beyond.

Miller didn't watch it go. His eyes remained transfixed on the sky above him as he heaved and coughed blood once more. It was so awe-inspiring and beautiful that he immediately regretted not stargazing more during his life. Darkness crept closer and closer around the edges of his vision.

Slowly, the stars disappeared, and the sky dwindled to

black forever.

PART ONE

NEW GAME PLUS

01

Desmond Lewis stepped out of the car and took a deep breath of fresh night air. Beyond a railing to his right, the valley stretched off below and the brilliant lights of downtown Los Angeles twinkled in the distance. He gazed off toward the skyscrapers and up at the clear night sky. There were a few stars, but for the most part, it was an endless dark canvas that extended in all directions, making the world feel small. It brought a smile to his face.

Jenna slammed the passenger door shut and sighed, clearly psyching herself up. "How do I look?" she asked, inspecting her black dress.

"Absolutely terrible." He grinned. She laughed and rolled her eyes. "Come on," he added. "They're your parents. If anyone should be worried, it's me. I've never had a conversation with them for more than five minutes."

"That's why they don't annoy you yet."

Lewis turned to the front of the house before them. It was sleek and rectangular, complete with the right angles and copious glass panes of ultramodernist design. The house was two stories high and had a three-car garage. He'd often dreamed of owning a place like this here in Beverly Hills, but as a tech journalist, it seemed a bit much for his current paycheck.

Maybe one day, he thought with a smile. Then he turned back to her. "Alright, how do *I* look?" Lewis took a brief moment to examine himself. A 26-year-old African-American, he was tall and lean. He wore the tailor-made navy suit Jenna had given him for Christmas a few weeks ago paired with a red tie.

"Handsome," she said, then: "Wait." In a few brisk strides, she reached him and began adjusting his collar. He glanced at her turquoise eyes and light-brown hair while she worked.

"There." She kissed him. "Done."

They walked arm in arm toward the front door, edging past one of her parents' cars parked in the driveway. Lewis noticed a bumper sticker on the rear that read "Democrats for the Right to Life", which he recognized as a left-wing anti-abortion group. He realized he didn't know much about her parents' politics besides what she had told him about their stance on video games.

Lewis rang the bell and turned to Jenna. She looked tense. "Hey, relax," he said, massaging her shoulder. "Just remember, after we get through this the rest of the night will be more fun."

He kissed her on the cheek and turned back to the door. Their mutual friends had a surprise party planned for her back at her apartment. Lewis had done his best to keep it under wraps, but he had a feeling she'd already figured it out or at least expected something.

His phone vibrated in his pocket and he pulled it out. Jake Miller was calling him. That was strange. *What does he want at 8PM on a Sunday?*

Suddenly the door opened. Lewis swiftly declined the call and slid the phone back into his pocket. He could talk to Miller later.

Before him stood a man and a woman in their late middle ages. Lance Bateman was tall, tanned, and fit, with jet black hair that had turned gray at the sides. Not bad for someone in his early sixties, but Lewis figured it was dyed. His wife Patricia stood beside him about a foot shorter and her skin slightly paler. Her brown hair – certainly dyed – was cut to her shoulders. Lance wore a collared shirt and chinos, Patricia an expensive wool jacket over a white blouse and skirt. They each had warm smiles on their faces.

Lance shook Lewis's hand while Patricia hugged her daughter. "Happy birthday, baby," he heard her say as Lance gave him a firm grip.

"Desmond, how have you been?"

"Very well, Mr. Bateman."

"Oh please, call me Lance! Come on in."

He stepped inside, then felt a tugging on his arm. It was Patricia Bateman. "Desmond, you have to let me say hello!" She gave him a big hug and a kiss on the cheek. "How have you been?"

"Wonderful, Mrs.–"

"Oh good, good." She began leading them after her husband. Lewis looked at Jenna and she rolled her eyes. He nearly chuckled to himself.

They turned right and walked out into a large open space with a professionally decorated living room to the left and an open kitchen to the right. Fine art adorned the walls while flowers and framed photographs were positioned on various tables throughout the room. Lewis saw a portrait from ten years ago, a smiling 16-year-old Jenna sitting next to her younger brother James. Lewis had never met him, but Jenna had mentioned he was off at Duke playing tennis.

Directly ahead was a gigantic window that stretched the entire length of the area, interrupted only by a sliding glass door. It provided a full view of the back patio, swimming pool, and the L.A. skyline beyond. In front of the window stood a sleek, glass table that had been set for four.

Lance was already there, gesturing for them to take a seat. "The view's really something, isn't it?"

Lewis took it all in and nodded. "It's stunning," was all he could think to say.

"That's what sold us on this place," Lance said, sitting down. "We moved in just before Jenna began kindergarten."

Lewis took a seat across from Lance, his girlfriend to his right. Soft jazz played from unseen speakers. Red wine had been poured, and a bottle of cabernet sauvignon sat on the table next to a bright green gift bag.

"This is for you, sweetie," Patricia said, handing it across the table to Jenna.

"Thanks, mom." She pulled a video game case out of the bag. It was the latest *Mario Party*. "Oh, how sweet," she managed to say convincingly. He wondered if her parents realized she didn't own a Nintendo Switch.

"Well," Patricia said, "we just figured you might enjoy something fun and light, maybe as a break from all the shooter stuff you usually play."

She laughed. Lance laughed along with her.

"It's very thoughtful of you," Jenna said, putting it down.

Everyone raised their glasses in a toast to her birthday,

then they each took a sip.

"Oh, congratulations by the way on your latest win," Lance added, lowering his glass. "What do they call it again…a cyber-sports championship?"

"E-sports," she corrected.

"Right, right!" Lance said, giving himself a light smack on the head. "I keep forgetting." He turned to Lewis and chuckled. "You see, the rest of our family plays *real* sports."

Jenna wasn't amused. Lewis managed a smile and took a big sip of wine. He figured he was going to need it.

Patricia turned toward him too. "Desmond darling, has Jenna scared you off with all her crazy video games yet?"

He put the glass down and forced a laugh. "No…at least, not yet." He winked at his girlfriend and she rolled her eyes.

Patricia nodded. "Do you play a lot of games?"

"I used to," he replied. "Back when I was a kid and up through high school. Once I got to college, I just didn't have much time for them anymore."

"What kind did you play?" Lance asked. "I know Jenna is really big into the, uh...first-person shooters."

"*Battlefield, Tomb Raider, Assassin's Creed…* A bunch of the popular ones back in the day," Lewis said.

Lance chuckled. "I'm sure Jenna has mentioned a bunch of my rants about violence in video games…"

Lewis tried to keep it light. "I think she joked about it once or twice."

Lance nodded. He sipped his wine, then set it down again as a big smile came to his face. "So Desmond, if you don't mind me asking…what's your opinion on it?"

"C'mon, Dad," Jenna protested.

Lewis shrugged and gave an honest answer. "I mean, I don't really mind it, but I think it can get a bit excessive at times. I've never liked gore just for gore's sake."

"Exactly!" Lance said. "It's unnecessary, is what it really is."

"I think it's a lack of creativity," Patricia chimed in. "I think it's much harder to say more by showing less."

"Can we not get into this again?" Jenna sighed, putting a hand to her forehead.

"Come on, we'll keep it peaceful. It's an intellectually stimulating discussion!" Lance said, gesturing around the table to all of them.

"It's my *birthday*," she groaned.

"Then we'll keep it brief," he promised, then turned to Lewis. "I couldn't agree more with you, Desmond. It's just excessive and overwrought. There's so much blood and gore in all media today, and it just gets a pass because we've become desensitized to it. But video games are the ones that disturb me the most because the player actually participates in the violence – even if it's simulated!"

"It rewards people's bloodlust is what it does," Patricia added, after another sip.

"How many times do I have to say this? If people can't tell the difference between a video game and reality, then they already have serious issues. Besides, those games help people let off steam," Jenna countered.

"Maybe," Lance continued, "but teaching people – especially children and teenagers – that any form of violent release is a good way to cope with their emotions will perpetuate dangerous thoughts. Thoughts that one day might lead them to snap and–"

"Oh, for Christ's sake," she interjected. "You're not still on the whole 'video games make murderers' thing, are you? Because that shit is *so* 90s."

"Studies have proven that violent video games cause aggression."

"*Traffic* causes aggression!" Jenna shouted. "By that logic, everyone in L.A. has lost their mind!"

"Well, that's already debatable," Patricia muttered.

Lance shook his head. "It isn't a relic of the 90s, Jenna. It comes up whenever there's a new mass shooting, and every single time, everyone keeps ignoring it as a real problem!"

Lewis sat quietly and watched the shots volley back and forth, unsure of what to do.

"When was the last time anyone seriously considered it?" Jenna asked. "Honestly."

"Actually, quite recently," Patricia said. "Did you read that *Atlantic* article from, what was it, two weeks ago?"

Jenna nodded. Lewis did too, recalling when he had come across the article about a week and a half back. It was a thinkpiece with an axe to grind titled: "It's Time to Reconsider Video Game Violence." Penned by well-known writer Sylvia Fenster, it cited various studies over the years, including ones that Jenna had said were disproven, but the main focus was on a number of similar incidents over the past several months.

The first had been in Jacksonville at the end of August. A YouTube star of Let's Play gaming videos, much like the ones Jenna did, named Shane Dempsey had been shot and killed by his girlfriend Lola Hayworth, also a hardcore gamer. She then took her own life immediately afterward. In the weeks that followed, his fanbase claimed they felt she "had always looked creepy" and close friends of hers said she'd been on antidepressants. However, the police had found her extensive collection of almost exclusively obscenely violent video games, ranging from *Doom* to *Grand Theft Auto*. She also owned more controversial games such as *Hatred*, *Manhunt*, and *Postal*.

The second was Trevor Mann of Denver in late October, a 27-year old gamer who strangled a friend to death who had come over to play first-person shooters at his apartment. Mann had then pitched himself off his tenth-story balcony. Friends said he'd displayed no previous signs of aggression or violence and appeared happy in the weeks leading up to the incident. However, Fenster wrote, investigators discovered Mann was an avid player of horror games, especially some ultra-violent Early Access releases from the digital marketplace Steam.

The worst case occurred in Maine. An avid college student gamer named Dan Folsom had suddenly gone berserk, stabbing his mother and sister the day after Black Friday while he was home for Thanksgiving break. He'd then taken his own life, hanging himself with a belt. The father arrived back from gift shopping to discover the bloody mess. Both the mother and daughter were taken to a hospital, but only the little girl survived. "And that was just a Christmas miracle," Fenster wrote. She went on to argue that this disturbing trend was likely due to the increased violence of modern video games, which made "the concerns we were having a decade ago look trivial."

"That article was a cherry-picked propaganda piece written by a self-righteous twat with a thumb up her ass," Jenna shot back.

"Jenna, *language*," Lance said, appalled.

Lewis tried to suppress his smile.

"Video games haven't become particularly more gruesome in recent years, there have always been some explicit media that are outliers from the norm. Fenster cited no sources or examples of how they've supposedly gotten that much gorier in the past few years."

"She doesn't need to," Lance explained. "I think the recent killings by gamers are enough proof that playing too many violent video games takes a toll on your mental health. Now I'm not saying *everyone* who enjoys those games is bound to commit murder, but I think you can have everything in moderation – like drinking. A beer or a glass of wine once in a while is fine, but if you become an alcoholic, it'll eventually kill you. I'd say the same goes for gaming. Look at the perpetrators in those cases, they practically lived and breathed violent media!"

"So what, people like me?" Jenna said. "Because I play those games you think I'm going to snap and kill a bunch of people?"

"No honey, not like that," Patricia said, suddenly backtracking. "To be honest, we thought you would've grown out of it like James did. I mean, you are 26 now."

"Some of my friends at FF are just a bit concerned, especially with the article and all," Lance explained. He turned to Lewis, realizing his guest had been excluded from most of the conversation. "I sit on the board of Family First, in case you didn't know."

He raised an eyebrow. "Oh really?"

Jenna had mentioned it before. It was something Lance did in addition to his career as a hedge fund manager. Based in Los Angeles, Family First was one of the largest media watchdog organizations in the United States. Last year it had filed the most Federal Communications Commission complaints of "inappropriate" content on cable TV. They weren't known for being particularly fond of movies or video games either.

"I feel like we get a bad rap in a lot of circles," Lance said, clearly wanting to change the subject, even by a margin. "People seem to think we're all a bunch of crazy Christian fundamentalist conservatives, but that's not true. Violence in the media is actually a bipartisan issue. There's one woman at the downtown office who has a big Obama poster on the wall and the guy next door to her is the biggest Trump defender you'll ever meet. And aside from abortion, I'm hardly conservative at all. I supported Bernie Sanders until the end a few years ago, and personally, I think gaming promotes gun culture and breeds toxic masculinity. But, I recognize those are my own beliefs. This is much bigger than you and me and all of us. This is something both sides can and need to come together on."

"There are also people on both sides who play violent games," Jenna added.

"Exactly," Lance continued. "What I'm trying to say is that this doesn't have to be a political issue. It's a *social* issue, one that we all need to come together on."

"Can we please talk about something else?" Jenna said.

"Alright," Lance conceded. "After all, it is your birthday… We're just concerned about you, sweetheart."

Shortly after, they had filet mignon for dinner and the rest of the evening passed with banal conversation in the living room about Lewis's education and career. Then Patricia decided to share stories of her daughter's embarrassing childhood exploits in honor of her birthday, which Lewis thoroughly enjoyed while Jenna's cheeks turned bright red. Finally, at half past ten, the two of them said goodnight and headed back out onto the driveway.

"Jesus, I thought that would never end," Jenna said as she climbed into the car.

Lewis got into the driver's seat beside her, already thinking about the surprise party.

"I need a drink," she said. "Actually, more than one." She flashed a smile at him. "Good thing where we're going has a lot of those, right?"

"Where's that?" he said, trying to keep cool.

"Well, my place."

"Right, right," he said.

"Anything going on there I should be aware of?" she said, not even trying to hide her smirk.

"I guess we'll just have to see," he said, smiling.

As he started the car, he put his phone in the cupholder and saw he had a new voicemail message. It was probably from Miller. Whatever it was, it could wait.

02

Lewis turned the key and heard the familiar *click* as the door to her apartment unlocked. He looked at Jenna. "After you," he said.

With a heavy dose of sarcasm, she said, "Gee, I wonder what's in there..."

She disappeared into the darkness of the foyer and flicked on a light. Immediately, four people jumped out from various sofas, chairs, and corners and screamed: "SURPRISE!"

"Aww, thanks guys!" Jenna said.

Lewis could tell she wasn't even phased, but she did look happy, so at least there was that. He took a look at the familiar faces. There was Ricky Ramirez, his friend since UCLA and his current roommate, over by the kitchen. He'd actually met Jenna through him. It appeared as if he'd set up some kind of bar; Lewis decided he'd head over there first.

The others were mostly her friends, but he'd become closer with some of them since they'd started dating. He saw

Charlie Wong, a heavyset guy wearing a gray hoody and baggy jeans, Claudia Levine, dressed in all black as usual, and Pierre Koch, a lanky man who always looked intoxicated no matter what time of day it was. Jenna went over to greet them while Lewis headed to Ricky.

"How was the family dinner?" he teased.

"I need a drink," Lewis replied.

"I figured as much," Ricky said, mixing him a very strong rum and coke.

Lewis took it and glanced around the apartment. Jenna's parents had paid for it initially, but she now made enough through e-sports and promotional deals to afford downtown L.A. on her own. It was a decent size. There was the foyer, the living room, and the kitchen off to the left with a large window that had a good view of the city, and an office and a bedroom down a short hall to the right. The lights of several nearby buildings cast illumination through the window into the dimly lit kitchen.

"So, did they wax on about the perils of violent video gaming?" Ricky asked.

"You weren't kidding."

Ricky laughed and shook his head. "I've known the Batemans for ages. Jenna and I used to make jokes about her parents all the time."

"They got her the latest *Mario Party* for her birthday. Figured it would be more wholesome entertainment than the stuff she usually plays."

He chuckled again. "Classic Batemans. Not to knock on *Mario Party* though, that shit's fun."

Lewis nodded. "I'll admit they made sense about some games being gory for no reason and that it's not a partisan issue, but they just don't seem to be that well informed. The

Atlantic op-ed only added fuel to their fire."

"Yeah, I read that too," Ricky said. "Weird shit. I looked into some follow-up articles, ones that went into more detail on those cases. Some of it's really sad, especially the family that got stabbed. I mean, Jesus."

"The kid must've had a lot of issues."

"That's the thing though. Apparently, he was a bit socially awkward, but that's it. Good grades, a small but solid group of friends, no clear signs of depression, no history of violent tendencies…"

"Strange," Lewis noted.

Ricky glanced out the window. "It's a bit suspicious that so many gamers have started doing crazy shit recently. Like, why now? And the only common thread between all of them is that they played violent games?"

"I mean, that was kind of the point of the article."

"Yeah, yeah, but…you know what this reminds me of?" Ricky was always comparing things to the plots of movies, books, or games, or just coming up with conspiracy theories of his own, mainly just for fun. "*Polybius*."

"*Poly*-what?"

"*Polybius*, man! You know, the urban legend?"

Lewis shook his head. It didn't ring a bell.

Ricky gave an exasperated sigh. "Okay supposedly, there was this arcade game that popped up around Portland called *Polybius* back in the 80s. One day, the machines just started appearing in some suburbs. Nobody knew where they came from, but you know, it was just a game, so people didn't have anything to be worried about; they just started playing it. Then, slowly, they became addicted. Huge lines began forming in front of these things, people going nuts just to play more and more.

"Then they started having *night terrors*. We're talking next level bad dream shit here. People couldn't take it. Some of them killed themselves. Others went into intense therapy. And then one day, all the *Polybius* machines disappeared. Most people don't know where they went, but some...some say they saw them being wheeled away by the Men in Black, put in the back of unmarked white vans and then – *boom*. Gone, never seen again."

"So it was all one big, fucked up psychological experiment?"

"Well, so the legend goes. It's pretty much confirmed to be fake, no trace of anything like it exists. People didn't start talking about *Polybius* until the early 2000s. *But...*" He raised a finger. "Life can imitate art just as art imitates life. If you're some twisted, high-level CIA bureaucrat looking for the next MKULTRA and you stumble across this shit online, I mean bingo, am I right? What a perfect way to test brainwashing! You've even got a well-worn scapegoat: violence in the media. People will connect the wrong dots in the big thinkpieces, and people like Jenna's parents and their Family First pals will lap it up and run with it. Meanwhile, *nobody suspects a thing.*"

Lewis nodded. "Interesting. Doesn't explain why all the M.O.s are different in these cases though."

"True, true," Ricky admitted. "But if you could make a game with psychoactive effects, it'd probably affect everybody differently."

"Fair, but I'd rather not joke about this. Especially after what happened to that family."

"No, no, no, of course not," Ricky said, backtracking.

Charlie made his way over to the bar. "Hey guys," he said. Lewis realized he looked far more tired up close with heavily pronounced bags beneath his bloodshot eyes. "Can you whip up something for me, Ricky?"

"Sure, what can I get you?" he asked.

Charlie rubbed his face and gave a dismissive flick of the hand. "I don't care. Just something that'll fuck me up fast."

Ricky nodded. "Double vodka-cran it is."

"You alright, Charlie?" Lewis asked.

He nodded. "Yeah, yeah. Just got back from Vegas, feeling a bit tired, that's all. It was a big weekend."

"What took you there?" Ricky asked, pouring in the vodka.

"Oh, just took a little time off. There was some stuff there I'd wanted to do for a while." He rubbed his forehead.

"Sure you're okay?" Lewis asked.

Charlie said, "Yeah, yeah, I've just been having a headache lately. I think it's something with my neck."

Lewis realized he hadn't even started on his rum and coke yet. Taking a sip, he turned back to Ricky. "Can you whip up something for Jenna?"

"Sure. G&T's always been her favorite." As Ricky poured, Lewis glanced back at Charlie. His hands were shaking. Before he could decide whether or not to make a comment, Ricky handed him Jenna's drink. "Here you go."

"Thanks," he said, and made his way over to where his girlfriend chatted with Claudia and Pierre in the living room.

"… but I don't know," Claudia was saying. "It just seems super gruesome and not really that scary."

"I think that's what I like about it." Jenna gave a brief laugh, then saw Lewis's outstretched hand with the gin and tonic.

"For the birthday girl," he said.

"Bless you," she said, snatching it from his hand and

bringing it to her lips.

"Oh, I've gotta get one of those," Pierre said, moving off toward the kitchen.

"Also," Claudia continued, "I just don't really think it's that original. I mean why all the secrecy if your product is just another glorified rip-off of *System Shock 2*?"

"What's everyone talking about?" Lewis asked, glancing between them.

Jenna lowered her glass, having drained half of it already. "This new sci-fi horror game beta."

"But it's not your typical beta," Claudia added. "They're calling it 'Select Access.' Only people with some degree of prominence in the gaming world have been given it. I guess they gave it to me because I'm a developer, and they obviously sent it to Jenna because she's, well, *her*." Claudia smiled and gestured as if she was introducing a member of a royal family.

Jenna finished the last of the G&T and wiped her mouth. "Aww, thank you." She looked at the empty glass. "I don't think there's enough liquor in the world to make me enjoy an evening with my parents. Be right back." She headed toward the bar.

"Go easy!" Claudia called after her to no reply. She chuckled and shook her head.

"So what is this game, again?" Lewis asked.

"It's called *Rogue Horizon*. Basically, it's in the future, and they've lost contact with this exploratory ship in another solar system. Then, they get there and find it all banged up and drifting into a black hole."

"Damn, I hate when that happens."

"So, they send your character to board the ship, and basically the crew has been infected with some alien parasite and it's all gone to shit. It's basically every sci-fi horror game since the late 90s, but they definitely try to play up the black hole element – and the VR."

"I've never played a horror game in VR," Lewis noted. "Is it really that much scarier?"

Claudia nodded. "It is at first, but just like with anything, after a while you start to get used to it. This one's way gorier than most, but gore doesn't equal scares in my book. It's just more disturbing than anything else."

"What is?" Charlie said, walking over to them nursing a half-empty vodka-cran.

"*Rogue Horizon.*" She turned to Lewis. "Charlie's been playing it too."

He chuckled. "Yeah, a lot of it actually. I thought it was kind of dumb at first, just a cheap blood-fest, but I don't know…there's something about it that I just started finding really compelling. I've almost finished it now."

"So for this secret beta, do you have to send feedback or…?"

Charlie nodded. "Yeah, they ask you a survey at the end of the game. They're planning a big public reveal sometime soon, but they didn't specify when."

"Who's the publisher?" Lewis asked.

"Some indie company, I forget the name," Claudia said.

Jenna came back over, downing the rest of her second drink as she did so. "Still talking about the game?"

Claudia nodded. "Des says he's never played a horror game in VR before."

Jenna's eyes widened as she turned to her boyfriend. "Really? Then you *have* to play this one."

"I'm sure there are better ones to start with," Claudia objected.

Jenna dismissed her with a wave of the hand. "Nah, he can handle it. Right, Des?" She playfully punched him in the arm.

"I don't know." He took another sip, then winked at her. "It might be too scary for me."

Two hours and several drinks later, Lewis and Jenna bade Ricky and Claudia goodnight and closed the front door behind them. Pierre and Charlie had left earlier.

"That was great," she said, putting her arm around his shoulder and giving him a peck on the cheek. "But you can't keep surprises for shit."

"What gave it away?"

"When you asked for my keys earlier today and wouldn't tell me why. Also, I saw a to-do list on your desk last time I was at your place."

He put a hand to his forehead. "Ah, shit."

Jenna laughed. "Don't sweat it, I had a really good time. It made up for dinner." She wobbled slightly and nearly toppled over, but he caught her arm. She laughed again.

"You should probably drink some water and go to bed," he suggested.

She chuckled and shook her head. "Not until you play the game!"

He glanced at his watch. "Babe, it's after 1AM. That's a terrible time to play a horror game."

"It's the *best* time to play a horror game." She was drunker than he realized. "I haven't been playing it as much because I've been focusing on FPSes for the championship, but I've wanted to play it. It's really, really compelling. There's something about it…" She put a hand to her head.

"Here," he said, walking to the kitchen. "Let's get some water." He retrieved a glass from the cabinet and filled it with water from the refrigerator, then handed it to her.

"Thanks," she said, drinking it. "But I'm not going to bed until you play it."

"I've got to go to work tomorrow."

She put her arm around him and gave him a mischievous grin. "You really are afraid, aren't you? Besides, it's my birthday. I command you." She kissed him.

Lewis sighed. Had he been even slightly soberer, perhaps he would've told her he'd play it tomorrow evening. Lewis let her lead him to the office, which she had set up as her gaming station. It was also where she recorded videos for her YouTube channel. There was a PS4 hooked up to a 40-inch 4K TV and her Alienware 17 laptop sat on the desk, complete with its glowing keyboard. An Oculus Rift headset was plugged into it, two Touch controllers resting a few inches away.

Jenna sat him down in her plush leather chair, which was designed to make long gaming sessions comfortable, and pressed the power button.

"Are you sure about this?" he asked.

She gave another playful smile. "Only one way to find out."

Then she helped him slide the VR gear over his head.

03

Stars. Everywhere.

Up, down, left, right. No matter where he turned, he found himself suspended in a twinkling void. Then, as he lifted his head back up again, he saw a logo fade in from the blackness. ROGUE HORIZON it read in giant, silvery sci-fi font letters. An eerie soundtrack began playing in the background. Then the phrase "Press Any Button to Continue" materialized below the title.

"Let me guess: you're still stuck at the main menu, aren't you?" he heard her voice say from right beside him. It was weird knowing she was right there even though his eyes saw nothing but vast, dark space where she stood.

"No, no, I got it," he said, hitting the B button on one of the Touch controllers. He held one in each hand.

Suddenly, the logo disappeared and he was engulfed in total darkness. The star field began to fade in once more, a swell of chilling orchestral music growing louder. Ahead of him lay an enormous black hole, its circular rim glowing red as nearby stars, planets, and even light itself were swirled into its inescapable vortex.

He drifted closer and closer, but the gaping maw of the gravitational singularity barely grew larger. Then he realized he was rapidly approaching a lone object, stranded in the abyss. No, not an object – a ship. A big one. It was roughly rectangular in shape and appeared to be several hundred feet long. The closer he got, the clearer the damage to its exterior became. It was battered with large dents along the side; several compartments were torn open and leaking cargo into space.

Finally, he came to a halt with a perfect view of both the ship and the black hole beyond. The words "New Game", "Load Game", "Options", and "Extras" floated into view before him.

Lewis smiled. This was going to be fun.

Using the controllers, he selected "New Game" and was immediately presented with some slots in which to place his save. The first was already taken and labeled "Jenna", so he selected the open one below it and entered the name "Des." After confirming the creation of a new save file, the screen blackened again.

For a moment, there was silence. Then he began to notice an electrical hum, emanating from all around. Gradually, the world faded in.

He sat against the wall of some kind of transport vessel, strapped in by a large safety harness that reminded him of the ones from rollercoasters. The compartment was dark save for a single strip of harsh white LEDs running along the ceiling. The walls and floor were steel gray. Looking down, he saw his character was wearing some kind of white, metal spacesuit. There was a similarly suited figure seated to his right and another on the row of seats on the opposite wall.

"There it is," came a voice over the loudspeaker.

Lewis leaned forward – his character tilting his head as he did so – and looked to the right, toward the cockpit. It was open, and he could see the back of the pilot's chair and a figure working the sleek, futuristic controls. The instruments of the holographic dashboard glowed green. Beyond the pilot was a large front window, through which Lewis saw them approaching the ship first seen in the menu screen. The black hole gaped off in the backdrop, streams of light swirling around its rim as they were drawn into its dark maw.

A gruff-sounding female voice appeared in his right ear. "Alright team, you'll enter the *U.S.S. Montana* through a medical dock. It seems to be one of the few airlocks still accessible. The ship is drifting closer and closer to the singularity. We estimate you only have six hours before the gravitational pull is inescapable."

"Roger that," said the man strapped in next to him. He spoke with a Southern drawl.

"Your mission," the commander continued, "is to search for any survivors and figure out what the hell happened. Operation Rouge Horizon was meant to study black holes, but we lost contact with the expedition two months ago. Foul play by the Colonial Federation is suspected. Be cautious."

Lewis saw through the cockpit window that they were pulling up alongside the massive vessel, which utterly dwarfed their own craft. Soon, the transport came to a stop. There was a *hiss*, then a *click,* and suddenly his harness slid upward like a gull-wing door. Without him having to move, his character got to their feet. The two other astronauts – he guessed they were all space marines – did the same.

The one across from him spoke with a British accent.

"Lasky, Rogers, on me." The man's name popped up above his head in Lewis's display: Smith. He turned to his right. The other teammate read "Rogers." That meant he must be Lasky.

Smith lead them to a door at the rear end of the transport, Lewis moving with the Touch controllers' analog sticks while turning his head with the Rift. This was going to take some getting used to.

"Connor, what's the status on the airlock?" Smith asked.

"Ready," the pilot responded. "You're clear to proceed."

Smith punched a code into a transparent keypad next to the door. With another *hiss* it retracted upward into its frame, revealing a white chamber beyond. Smith and Rogers moved forward, Lewis following. Once they were all inside the ship's airlock, the door closed behind them.

"Sergeant, rules of engagement?" Rogers asked.

Smith turned toward him. Lewis realized they all had helmets on even though they were in oxygenated areas. It was probably easier for the development team not to have to create faces that spoke if this was still in beta. Or maybe it was meant to be an artistic choice.

"We don't know if there are any hostiles aboard. Stay close and watch your six. All damaged compartments have been sealed off by the ship's computer system. Our access to the decks is limited, but we should be safe unless structural integrity is compromised."

The other door opened up. The team moved forward, stepping out into an eerie medical reception area. The lights were dim and flickering, and the walls were covered in blood. Lewis saw a red trail leading off down the hall, going through an open doorway to the left. The desk was abandoned and the waiting chairs all sat vacantly. The music in his headphones became creepier.

Lewis couldn't help but crack a smile. "Could this get any more cliché?" he joked, but there was no reply. Jenna must've gone to bed already. He hoped she'd had some more water.

It was slightly unnerving though, knowing he was alone in a dark room well past midnight playing a horror game. *Relax,* he told himself. *It's not that scary. Or original.*

Just from the aesthetic he could tell the game desperately wanted to be *Dead Space* or the most recent *Prey*. He remembered when he'd first played *Dead Space*, all those years ago. What had he been, sixteen? All of his friends had long since been playing all the big M-rated games, but Lewis had only played a bit of *Call of Duty* by then. Horror had never really suited him because, if he was honest with himself, he hadn't liked getting scared. The game's Necromorph enemies did give him nightmares, but that had been well-crafted tension with carefully placed jump scares. This whole thing was starting to feel like a cheap knockoff. They were already on the ship with little to no explanation, and they probably weren't going to get much more. The body count would probably kick in any minute now. Why go to all the effort of having a secret beta given to only a select few if the game wasn't that revolutionary? Maybe it would come into its own later.

"Shit," Rogers said, shining a flashlight beam around. A pistol suddenly appeared in Lewis's right hand, and he realized he could aim it around by moving the Touch controller. Of course, this had been a VR feature for a while now, but it was still impressive to him. At least the game had that going for it, but he sensed that was its central gimmick.

"This way," Smith said, leading them forward. He had his own flashlight and pistol out. "Keep a lookout for any life signs."

"Something's not right here," Rogers drawled.

No shit, Sherlock, Lewis scoffed to himself.

The group edged down the corridor, approaching the door where the blood trail snaked in. Smith put up his hand and they stopped. "Lasky, scope it out."

Lewis sighed. Of course they were going to make *him* do it. Nudging the analog sticks forward, he watched his character take several steps toward the blackness where a jump scare undoubtedly awaited him.

He shone his flashlight into the room. The beam danced across the floor, illuminating a horrifically mauled corpse. Lewis walked closer. The dead man lay on his back, dressed in what looked to be a gray flight suit. His intestines were torn out and lay around him in disarray. Blood was everywhere, splattered across the floor and walls. The eyes, Lewis noted, were gone too.

It was disgusting. Something about it just felt wrong, but he couldn't place it. It was something about the detail. There was a kind of strange, glossy sheen on the corpse – the blood and the entrails gleamed in the glow of his flashlight.

He turned his head, looking all around the chamber. It appeared to be a conference room. But the walls, the big table, the ceiling fan, even the projector screen didn't feel as fleshed out. They felt like objects or environments in a game, as they were, but this corpse felt somehow more *real*.

Whoever had made this had seemingly put more effort into the body than the rest of the level design. Maybe the gore detail was supposed to be a selling feature. Some people would buy a game like this just for that alone.

He wondered if Jenna would be one of them.

"Sweet Jesus," Rogers muttered.

"This doesn't look like an accident," Smith said, leaning closer to the carnage.

You don't say, Lewis thought.

"What kind of person would do this?" Rogers said, to which Lewis rolled his eyes. Christ, why were people in horror fiction always so slow to realize that monsters were running around?

Smith started to back up. "I don't know, but I don't like it."

He had just made it to the door frame when suddenly a bald figure appeared behind him. They wore a similar flight suit as the dead man, but their skin was ghastly pale and covered in glowing blue veins. The eyes were black as coal with tiny red pupils. The teeth were pointed and razor-sharp. Like the corpse, this model was rendered with a higher level of detail. It seemed to stand out from the rest of the objects in the game, as if its horrific image were meant to be uncannily real.

Time seemed to slow down as the thing took hold of Smith and sunk its teeth into the side of his neck. Smith started screaming, his blood spewing everywhere. Lewis felt unable to move as he watched the creature's claws dig through its victim's abdomen and begin pulling out a tangle of innards. In fact, he realized his character was actually incapable of motion by design. He jerked the Touch controllers, nudged the analog sticks, but nothing happened. Even turning his head had a delayed reaction, everything happening in slow-mo.

They wanted him to watch.

It was awful. Smith was now on his knees, his own intestines mixing with that of the corpse's on the floor. The monster pulled upward on the helmet, one bare and sharp-toed, glowing-veined foot planted on the helpless man's shoulder. Its claws were stuck fast into Smith's neck. He could hear the man choking on his own blood.

Why aren't we shooting? Lewis briefly thought.

This whole scene had just been a few seconds, but already it felt like a surreal eternity.

Then the zombie-thing tore the head off and a geyser of blood erupted into the room. Things started happening faster, much faster now. Rogers was running past him, screaming, "Go, go, *go!*" and Lewis turned to follow as the horrible creature *screeched* after them. A second door opened at the other side of the conference room and a moment later, both of them were sprinting down another darkened corridor.

A noise came from behind them, sounding like a banshee. It drew closer and closer even as they ran. Closer and louder and–

No.

Lewis pressed the Start button. The game paused, a series of options floating before him as the rest of the world froze and blurred. He took a deep breath in and then exhaled, placing the Touch controllers back on the desk. The Rift headset joined them a moment letter and Lewis found himself alone in pitch blackness.

As a chill shot down his spine, he felt around for the desk lamp and cursed under his breath until he found it. The bright white LED light flashed on and nearly blinded his eyes, but he adjusted it away from him, blinking several times.

Lewis had played violent games before, but something about this one troubled him. It was the focus, he realized. The gore was the star of the show. But not just any gore. It was unnerving, gratuitous violence that somehow got under his skin unlike anything he'd ever seen or played.

He glanced at a digital clock sitting on the desk. It was nearly two in the morning. That probably wasn't helping either. Shit, why had he let Jenna talk him into this at such a late hour? He had to get to work in the morning. Rubbing his forehead, Lewis got up, turned off the lamp, and stumbled his way to her bedroom. Sleep was all he needed now.

The forest was dark. The only sounds came from the chirping of crickets and a soft breeze that rustled through the treetops.

Lewis walked forward, careful not to trip on the uneven ground as he reached the side of the road. Here there was light, or at least more of it. Several lampposts lined this lonely stretch of asphalt that snaked off deeper into the wilderness.

The scene was unsettlingly calm, and as he turned to the left, he saw why. A late 90s Ford Explorer lay upside-down in the middle of the road, badly battered and windows smashed. About twenty feet from the vehicle was a black woman and her child, huddled on the shoulder of the lane.

Lewis cautiously ventured closer. "Excuse me? Are you hurt?"

The woman paid him no attention. She was holding the boy very tightly. He kept looking back at the car, but she pointed to the heavens and directed his attention upward. "Look," she said, "look up there."

The boy did so and Lewis followed their gazes. Far beyond the treetops was a twinkling sky, serene and instantly calming in its majesty. He felt his shoulders loosen up and inhaled a breath of fresh air. Much better.

"Everything's gonna be alright," the woman said. "Everything's gonna be alright…"

She kept saying it over and over again and Lewis looked

back down at them. Both mother and son refused to take their eyes off the stars. Tears poured down her cheeks, but she never looked anywhere but up, repeating the same words as if saying them many times would make them come true.

"Everything's gonna be alright."

Lewis looked ahead, down the road, and immediately shielded his eyes. There was another vehicle that had spun off the road, its rear end pressed up against a tree as a single high beam shone out across the pavement. The other front light was smashed to smithereens along with that half of the car's front. It was also an SUV, an old red Chevy Trailblazer.

As he watched, the driver's side door swung open and a figure climbed out. Lewis immediately felt the pressure returning, the strain on his shoulders, the goosebumps on his skin.

It wasn't a man, at least he didn't think so. It looked like an astronaut, but the suit appeared way more sleek and advanced than what NASA had today. It was white, metallic, and covered in blood. Through the helmet's glass there was not a human face, but an ethereal blue luminescence.

The otherworldly thing began stumbling toward them, picking up speed as it walked out onto the road. It gave off an aura of pure evil. Lewis could feel it in his bones. Then, in the same instant, he realized it wasn't coming for him. It was after the woman and her son.

Lewis turned back to them and crouched down, trying to shake her arm. "Excuse me, ma'am – *you need to get out of here.*"

She wouldn't listen and the boy didn't seem to notice him, either. They were still stargazing and she kept muttering over and over, as if stuck in a loop, the same four words: "Everything's gonna be alright, everything's gonna be alright…"

Lewis looked back toward the advancing menace. He could hear its strange, inhuman breathing. The blue light from within its helmet cast a glow on the ground before it.

"Please, ma'am, you need to get away from here," he said.

It's going to kill you, it's going to finish it. Leave. Leave now.

But he couldn't even bring himself to speak the words. He stood up, backing away like a coward as the monster advanced. He didn't want to look–

A hand roughly grabbed his shoulder and spun him around. He found himself face to face with Jenna, wearing an evening dress. She stared past him with a blank expression, blood smeared all over her face and clothing.

Her lips parted and she spoke, very softly:

"*Arcadia awaits.*"

Lewis bolted upright. He took several deep gulps of air as he looked around the room. It was Jenna's place, just as it always looked. He glanced at the clock on the nightstand beside him: 4:46AM. He flopped back onto the sheets, feeling calmer.

Jenna turned over and placed a hand on his chest. "Are you okay?" she asked.

"Yes," he breathed, though he scarcely believed it himself.

"Don't worry," she said, nuzzling closer. "It was just a dream."

He put his arms around her and felt her lips brush against his cheek.

04

Lewis got up at 7:30, even though he felt like shit. Morning sunlight glinted through the blinds, and he could hear the sounds of traffic outside on the street below. Jenna was still asleep. Quietly, he got dressed and made his way to the kitchen to make himself a quick breakfast.

Then, with his satchel in hand, he was out the door, locking it behind him, and making his way to the elevator. A few minutes later, he pulled out of the parking garage in his blue Ford Fusion sedan out onto 4th Street. It took him nearly 45 minutes to get to Marina Del Rey thanks to traffic on the 10, but the 405 had been mercifully less congested.

When most people thought of tech in California, Silicon Valley immediately came to mind. But over the past two decades, a large number of computer and software companies had set up in the Los Angeles area, particularly along the coast from LAX to Santa Monica. Now, as the 2010s drew to a close, the area known as "Silicon Beach" was widely considered to be one of the largest tech hubs in the world.

And it was here that the offices of the *Technologist* were located on the 10th floor of 400 Admiralty Way, which gave a stunning westward overlook of Marina Del Rey's harbor, a sea of sails fluttering in the wind beneath a cloudless blue sky.

Lewis didn't stop to take in the sights out the window as he exited the elevator and briskly made his way through rows of cubicles toward his own. While he walked, an overweight Korean man came up beside him.

Lewis glanced at him but didn't stop moving. "Hey, Donnie. Have a good weekend?"

"Richter's called an emergency meeting for 9," he said. "Apparently something bad's happened."

"Well, that is what an emergency usually implies." They were almost to his desk now.

"Word's already going around the office."

"What are they saying?"

They'd arrived. He slung his satchel over the chair and took a seat, making sure the multicolored, meticulously-laid out post-it notes plastering his desk were still in order. He began taking out his laptop. He hated running late.

"Des."

"Yeah, sorry it's been a hectic morning," he said, wiping the sweat from his brow.

The look on Donnie's face was serious, stone-cold.

"It's about Jake. They're saying he's dead."

A surreal, icy sensation overcame him. Lewis blinked. "*What?*"

Donnie nodded. "Apparently it was some kind of accident. But the police got involved and…" He put up his hands. "I'm just waiting for Richter to give us the full details."

Lewis put his hand to his head. The phone call last night. He could have answered, but he didn't. Now he'd never get another chance to speak to his friend again.

"When's that meeting?" he asked.

Donnie glanced at his watch. "In about three minutes."

Lewis nodded slowly. Every other concern he'd had about getting work done today had vanished in the blink of an eye.

Somehow, they crammed all 30-plus staffers into the conference room. The beautiful day outside failed to reflect the glum mood on this side of the glass. Valerie Richter, a tall woman in her late 40s, stood at the head of the long table.

The Editor-in-Chief's ordinarily stern expression was replaced today by a softer one as she adjusted her rectangular-rimmed glasses and looked up at them to speak. "I'm sure by now most of you have heard what's happened. Last night, just after 8 o'clock, Jake Miller was involved in a single-vehicle accident on US-93 in Nevada. He swerved off the road, the car tumbled, and although he managed to pull himself out of the wreck, he died from injuries sustained in the crash."

She took a moment to look around at each of their faces. Lewis stood at the back of the room next to Donnie, his arms folded across his chest as he intently listened to every detail.

"I know it's hard to stamp out rumors, so I'll just tell you what I know regarding the police investigation. About five minutes before the crash, Jake pulled a gun on a gas station clerk" – a round of whispers began circling the room – "who then called the police," Richter continued, speaking louder now. "According to him, Jake didn't try to rob the store or anything. He appeared as if he had gone crazy or was on drugs, and he immediately fled in his car. The clerk called the police, but by the time they found him he was already dead.

"Now, we all saw Jake around the office and can agree he was a good writer, but we don't know much about his private life. And that's because it's none of our business and it's going to stay that way.

"His girlfriend said he went to Vegas for the weekend to take some time off. They're not sure if he tried some drug and had a bad reaction – they haven't got the toxicology reports back yet – but regardless, I don't want any of you spreading seditious gossip around the office or to anyone else. This is a tragedy. Jake was a good man, and if any of you shuffled off this mortal coil, heaven knows what skeletons we'd find in your closet. So show some damn respect for the dead."

The room was silent.

Afterward, Lewis stumbled into the bathroom and splashed some water on his face. Everything felt strange and he was terrified of what he was about to do next.

He pulled out his phone, dialed voicemail, and went through the prompts to get to New Messages. Then he took a deep breath and brought the device to his ear.

A synthetic voice announced, "You have. One. New message. First message."

Lewis had no idea what he expected to hear. He now knew the call had come just minutes before his friend's death, if not closer. He feared the recording may have captured the accident itself, the sound of tearing metal and broken glass followed by Miller screaming in his death throes.

But he knew he had to listen to it, even just once.

Miller's voice filtered into his ear. "Alright Lewis, I want you to listen to me very carefully. I've stumbled onto something, and it's big. I don't know if I have much time before they find me, but if anything happens to me I want you, no matter what you do, to stay away from–"

There was a squeal of tires, then sound abruptly cut off. Lewis pressed the phone closer, but the next noise that greeted him was: "End of new messages. To replay your messages, press…"

He tapped the number before it finished. This time, he paid attention to each syllable, hearing Miller string together the words but being unable to accept their meaning.

I've stumbled onto something, and it's big.

I don't know if I have much time before they find me.

If anything happens to me, I want you, no matter what you do, to stay away from–

And then, there it was. The most frightening bit. Lewis replayed it a third time just to be sure he had heard it correctly.

Right before the tires squealed, as Miller swerved the car toward what would be his death, Lewis heard another sound approaching. It sounded like the revving of an engine getting closer, another vehicle speeding toward him and causing his friend to abruptly alter his course.

He started shaking. The phone nearly dropped from his hands, but then his entire body tensed up.

There was no doubt about it.

Jake Miller had been murdered.

"All I'm telling you is, they've ruled it an accident." Valerie Richter threw up her hands and leaned back in her chair. "I tend to trust the police with these things, they've had more experience with them than I have."

"But you heard it," Lewis said, pointing to the phone. It lay on the desk between them, the sunlight from the window reflecting off its black screen and dancing along the wall. "He says he's stumbled onto something, a conspiracy."

Richter sighed. "I know this might be hard to accept, I really do, but what we just listened to were the ramblings of a man who may have been on drugs."

"Jake wasn't a conspiracy theorist. Maybe he was running from someone."

"Out in the desert? What's he running from, Area 51? This isn't the *X-Files*, Des."

"But you can hear the other car, the one that rams him off the road!"

"I didn't hear that," she said, leaning in closer as he played it again. They both listened very carefully at the end. To Lewis, it was unmistakable. He could hear the roar of an engine growing louder a split second before the tires screeched as Miller swerved.

Richter sat there for a minute, completely silent. Lewis exited from voicemail and waited for her response. Finally, she nodded.

"I'll admit it does sound like *something* else is there, but that could just be our ears playing tricks on us. There was no sign that the car had been rammed off the road."

"But if Jake swerved to avoid it, and *then* tumbled off the road..."

Richter shook her head. "Sometimes, when our friends die we want there to be a villain. It's easier to put the blame on some malevolent force than to accept that in real life, sometimes things just happen without reason. I don't know why Jake pulled a gun on that clerk, I don't know why he thought there was a conspiracy after him. It probably has something to do with drugs, which is sad. I hate to see good people turn to substance abuse, but then again I didn't know much of his personal life outside the office."

"And what about this voicemail?"

"If you want my advice, delete it. It'll save you a lot of trouble from the police, and the last thing we need is a scandal. I can guarantee you that they wouldn't find anything out and this would just slander one of our writers. We're an up-and-coming digital magazine. We can't take on *Wired* if people think our journalists are drug-laden conspiracy theorists. I want this quiet and respectful. It's what Jake deserved."

Lewis nodded solemnly.

"A lot of people have left early today. I'm not expecting much work to get done, other than my tribute piece that goes live at noon on our front page. You should take the rest of the day off."

"Thank you," he said.

As he passed through the door frame on the way out, he heard her say, "And Des?" He turned around. She forced a grim smile. "Take care of yourself."

"Thanks, Valerie."

He packed up his belongings but didn't leave immediately. Lewis stopped by Miller's cubicle, just a row away from his, where several flowers lay on the desk. He took one last glance around it, still taking in the fact that he would never see his friend sitting here again.

Papers and file folders were scattered about. He wondered how Miller had been so productive when he never seemed to be organized. They'd even made jokes about it from time to time. While Lewis's sticky notes were neatly arranged on the wall in front of his desk, Miller's were stuck all over the place at haphazard angles.

It almost brought a smile to his face, but then his eyes passed over one note posted next to a calendar and his blood ran cold. Making sure no one else was looking, he reached over and grabbed it, turning it over in his hands to be sure it was real.

It was teal blue and bore a single word in red sharpie, which had been circled in the same color:

Arcadia.

05

He called Jenna on the way back to his and Ricky's place in Santa Monica, informing her of Miller's passing, but excluding the part about the voicemail. She told him how sorry she was, that she'd only met him twice but he'd seemed like a good guy, and that he should come over to her place again tonight unless he needed to be alone. He thanked her, said he'd be glad to, and agreed to be there for dinner at six.

Lewis spent the afternoon sitting on the sofa scouring the corners of the Internet. The word "Arcadia" had a number of meanings, from the traditional image of a pastoral utopian society to the Tom Stoppard play to the Duran Duran off-shoot band from the 80s. Nothing gave him a lead.

He put his laptop on the kitchen counter and decided to pace around the apartment, mulling over the possibilities in his mind. Ricky wouldn't be back until later, so he had plenty of time to himself to think.

Jake Miller had not been a drug abuser. Lewis had known him for only about a year from work, but they'd really hit it off. On more than one occasion when they'd been out drinking, Miller had drunkenly stumbled over to Lewis, grasped him by the shoulders and said, "I just don't get the druggies, man. Who could need more than booze?"

Having never so much as touched a gram of marijuana in his life, even when offered in college, Lewis had agreed. He realized that if any of his friends were to try out an experimental substance, it would probably be his girlfriend. He knew Jenna occasionally did drugs, and he had spent an evening helping her recover from a bad trip on MDMA she'd gotten from some creep at a party, but she was far from an addict. Jake Miller would've been the last person to drop acid out in the desert.

So then what the hell had happened? What explained the paranoid, frantic voice that had spoken to him through the digital void? To Lewis, the sound of the distant, revving engine was key. There had to have been another car. Maybe it was just a near hit and run with a drunk, who fled the scene for fear of getting a DUI.

But that was just too coincidental. Miller was telling him about something he'd uncovered, and he just happened to have an accident at that exact moment? He had said: "I don't know how much time I have before they find me." It seemed that whoever *they* were had found him a lot sooner than he'd hoped.

And then, that final warning.

If anything happens to me, I want you, no matter what you do, to stay away from–

Away from what?

Sighing, Lewis sat down and massaged his temples. Miller hadn't said anything strange in the past week. It had only been briefly last Friday that he'd mentioned he was taking off to Vegas for the weekend. Lewis hadn't thought anything of it, but now his mind mulled over every recent interaction he'd had with the dead man.

Miller usually told him about the stories he was working on. What had he been writing lately? Lewis remembered him talking about something to do with virtual reality, but it hadn't been a singular game or console.

He closed his eyes, thinking back to last Wednesday. The image began to take shape: Him and Miller standing in the coffee lounge. Lewis's hand holding a glass of water – he hated coffee – and Miller drinking an espresso. Lewis telling him about his upcoming article on Silicon Beach vs. Silicon Valley. Miller talking about research into this new VR place. What term had he used to describe it?

Theme park. A virtual reality theme park. Lewis had only heard of them in passing, so the phrase stuck out in his memory.

"What do you do at one of those?" he recalled asking.

Miller laughed. "Well, I guess 'amusement park' would be a better term for it. A theme park implies all the attractions are set around one unifying concept, but at this place, you can do pretty much anything."

"VR rollercoasters?"

"Through volcanoes or across the moon. You can go anywhere. But they do so much more at this place too. You can climb a rock wall and your headset will make it seem like you're scaling Everest. And forget laser tag; the deathmatches they have can be set in any time period or environment. Medieval sword clashes, World War I trenches, sci-fi space battles, you name it."

"So do you run around wearing an Oculus Rift or…?"

Miller shook his head. "Much more advanced. Yeah,

there are headsets, but you also have haptic feedback suits for the rest of your body. You can 'feel' a virtual object when you touch it; it's really cool."

The conversation had changed topics after that. Miller hadn't even mentioned the place's name or where it was located.

Lewis got up from the sofa, retrieved his laptop from the kitchen countertop, and sat down in the living room again. He Googled "virtual reality theme parks" and got a number of results. It was evidently a growing trend, with many companies creating their own similar attractions around the globe, from Dubai to China. The first prominent one in the U.S. had been The Void, which was based in Utah with a few satellite locations around the country and abroad to showcase their technology. Now they had competitors springing up elsewhere across the States.

Lewis scratched his chin. Virtual reality was one of those overdue bits of the future that had always seemed just around the bend. The concept was older than most people thought, dating back to the mid-20th century when the Sensorama was released in 1962. Developed by Morton Heilig in the late 50s, it showed a 3-D film with sound, smells, and fans to create wind effects. As computers rose to prominence in the 1970s and 80s, the idea of immersive simulations grew ever more popular. It became a staple of science fiction; writers everywhere saw the future of humanity living in cyberspace, where the lines between virtual reality and actuality became increasingly blurred. In the 90s they started seeing it as the future of all video games, yet at the verge of the 2020s, standard console and PC gaming were still going strong.

Of course, the past decade had seen great leaps in VR popularity, mainly pushed by the Oculus Rift and competing headsets such as the HTC Vive. But the fact remained that they were still too expensive to go mainstream.

At least, not yet.

Lewis realized he was getting off-track. If someone really had killed Miller, it probably had nothing to do with a virtual reality amusement park, but it was the only lead he had to go on.

Except...

Taking out his phone, he pulled up the contact for Miller's home number and tapped the call button. Julia would probably be there. He realized he should've done this earlier, but the possibility of a murder plot had imposed a monopoly on his thoughts all day.

The voice that answered was quiet, detached. He heard a sniffle, then, "Hello, Des."

"I just found out. I'm sure you've heard this from a lot of people today, but I'm terribly, terribly sorry, Julia." Lewis had only met Miller's girlfriend a few times before, but she'd always seemed nice enough. She'd been dating Miller since college though, so if he'd told anyone what he was investigating, it would have been her.

She sniffed again. "Thank you. I really appreciate it." She took a deep breath. "I just don't know what to believe. The police think he might've been on drugs, but I told them he *never* would've done that, not even in Vegas."

"I didn't believe that story for a second, either," he said comfortingly. "But I need to ask you something: Do you know why he went there?"

"I don't know." He could picture her at the other end of the line, sitting by a box of tissues, her eyes red from hours of tears. It sounded like she was starting to accept it, but he knew the scar would never leave her. A memory swam into his mind, but he swiftly pushed it away.

"He just started acting strangely," she continued, her voice soft. "This past week, there was something about him… I can't even place it. He just seemed on edge, paranoid even. How was he at work?"

"I didn't notice anything out of the ordinary," Lewis told her. "But he would have shared more with you."

"He didn't tell me he was going to Vegas for the weekend until Thursday. I asked him why, but he wouldn't let me know. Just said there was something he needed to get to the bottom of."

She blew her nose. "You're gonna think I'm crazy," she said, with a brief laugh. "But I don't think it was an accident. Something's not right about all this. I mean, it just doesn't make sense. I think he got caught up in something. Going to Vegas was one thing, but then why was he all the way out there in the desert?"

Lewis sighed. "I'm sorry, Julia. I really don't know. But I don't think you're crazy. I'm trying to figure out what he was after. Do you remember when he started acting differently?"

"I'm not sure, exactly." He could hear her wiping her nose again. "I mean, there was the…but no, that wouldn't make sense."

"What wouldn't?"

"Well, Jake kept talking about this game. Kept saying it was really violent and disturbing, but he'd played lots of messed up games before. I mean, you knew him, Jake loved video games."

"What was it called?" Every muscle in Lewis's body tensed up. *No fucking way,* he told himself. *There's no way he was playing it, too. How the hell would he have it? It was only sent to prominent people in the gaming industry.*

Of course, Miller was the *Technologist*'s video game specialist. Not so much a reviewer, but he wrote pieces about new gaming technology and the future of the industry. That had been why he was researching VR theme parks.

"I don't know, he wouldn't say. But he got really obsessed with it."

"How so?"

"He was playing it all the time. I mean, he'd never let me see it–"

"Julia, do you know his desktop password?"

A pause. "Yeah, why?"

"I need you to go onto his computer and try and find this game. Please, it's very important."

"Um, okay. Wait, do you think it has something to do with his…?" She didn't want to say the word *death*.

"Maybe. I'm not sure."

"Okay," she said. There was another brief pause. "I'm at his desk now. Booting it up."

Lewis got up and walked over to the window. It was late in the afternoon, the buildings of Santa Monica casting long shadows on the streets below. He could see cars on Wilshire traveling toward the waterfront, probably heading to the pier before sundown. Keys clicked over the phone as Julia put in Miller's password.

Then, after another few seconds, she said, "Alright, I'm in. Where would it be?"

"I need you to put *Rogue Horizon* into the search bar."

"Okay," she said. More typing. Then, "There's nothing there."

Lewis took a deep breath. "Can you look around the desktop for any strange programs. Icons you don't recognize?"

"I'm sorry, gaming was always Jake's thing. Aside from Word, Chrome, and the Recycling Bin, I don't know any of these."

He nodded. "Thanks, Julia."

"Is that it?"

"Yeah," he said, rubbing his forehead. "It was just a hunch. If there's anything you need, just call me. And again, I'm really sorry for your loss. Jake was a great guy."

"Thanks," she said. She sounded distant. He could imagine her staring out a window, barely registering the conversation. Then she hung up.

Lewis tossed his phone back onto the couch and continued pacing. He massaged his temples and took a deep breath, trying to stay focused.

If Miller had played *Rouge Horizon*, why wasn't it on his computer? He shook his head. He was getting too paranoid, seeing connections where there were none. There were plenty of other games that could've disturbed his friend. It was just that that damn horror beta was stuck on his mind. There was something about the scene he had played last night that had really gotten under his skin.

And of course, the dream.

He hadn't had a nightmare like that in years. He could still see Jenna standing there, all covered in blood and whispering the words: "*Arcadia awaits.*"

It couldn't be a coincidence he had heard that in a dream and then seen it again on a dead man's desk the next morning, could it? Where had the word come from and how had it worked its way into his mind?

Lewis sat down again. No, this had nothing to do with the game. He'd had a strange dream. Maybe he'd seen

Arcadia somewhere else recently, that's how it got in there. Who knows why Miller had had it on his desk anyway? It may have been something from another article, long ago. After all, the desk had been in complete disarray. Miller had never been very organized.

He was reading into things too much. No, this "Arcadia" word wasn't the key.

And yet Miller had circled it in red. It had to be significant.

He grabbed his laptop and opened up Google Maps. He found US-93, following it north away from Vegas and into the desert. There was really nothing out there, yet Miller had been heading south. He must've been coming back from somewhere.

Slowly, he typed the word "Arcadia" into the search bar.

A waypoint appeared. Lewis blinked. "You've got to be fucking kidding me."

The first result, located out in the middle of the desert over an hour north of Las Vegas, was a compound labeled with the now-familiar name. There was a link to a website. Cautiously, he clicked it.

The page it directed him to looked like something from an 80s sci-fi movie. And there in the middle of the screen, in glowing metallic blue letters, was digitally inscribed:

ARCADIA

Virtual Reality Amusement Park

Lewis went over the entire site with a fine-toothed comb. There were only three tabs other than the main page: About, Experiences, and Tickets. The first gave a fairly typical public relations spiel:

An oasis in the Mojave Desert, **ARCADIA** is the future of virtual reality entertainment. Take to the skies, dive beneath the sea, or visit worlds beyond your imagination. With our advanced **NEBULA** headsets and haptic-feedback suits, you'll experience thrills and excitement unlike anything else. Whether you've come to Las Vegas for business or pleasure, be sure to escape to **ARCADIA**.

The Experiences page was more illuminating. Lewis saw the names of dozens of virtual reality games. Many bore alliterative titles such as *Aerial Adventure*, *Deep Dive*, and *Everest Escapade*. Visitors could find themselves immersed in the cockpit of a Vought F4U Corsair during a dogfight above the Pacific in 1942, evading deep sea predators at the controls of a submarine in the Mariana Trench, or dangling off the side of the world's highest mountain with one hand.

There was just one thing Lewis didn't get. The graphics on these games were good and the photos of Arcadia itself – sleek black corridors lined with neon blue LED lights – made it look like a fair amount of coin had been put into its construction.

So why had it been so hard to find?

It hadn't come up in the top search results for "virtual reality theme park", or "Arcadia", or really anything. Maybe it was just new and they were still working out the kinks, trying a soft rollout. From what he gathered on the website, it had only opened about half a year ago in the summer of 2018.

On the Tickets page, bolded text informed him that Arcadia was all booked up for the next six months, but that they would be opening up advance reservations "soon." Lewis scratched his chin. Maybe it was already immensely popular in certain circles, and they were purposely trying to keep a low profile to manage demand. He'd have to ask Jenna or some of her gamer friends if they knew of it.

The only clue as to who owned the place was a little strip of text hidden at the very bottom of the page:

ARCADIA and all games displayed on this page are © Andromeda Virtual Systems 2019

Googling them yielded a less flashy corporate site prominently displaying a shot of the main Arcadia building – which looked like a large, black, modernist warehouse – with a gorgeous Mojave Desert sunset in the background. Something about the photo was both breathtaking and eerie at the same time.

The CEO of Andromeda Virtual Systems was a man named Victor Zhao. The photo of him on the About page showed an attractive Asian man in what appeared to be his late thirties, sharply dressed in a gray suit. Lewis couldn't help but think his smile made him look a tad conceited. Zhao's bio read that he used to be a game developer with "years of experience" in the industry, but his name didn't ring any bells to Lewis. He had founded AVS in 2016 with the goal of "creating the next level of immersive entertainment."

Lewis's phone rang. It was Jenna.

"Hey, are you on your way over?"

"I'm leaving soon."

He could sense some uneasiness on her end of the line. "Are you okay?" she asked after a moment.

"Yeah," he said.

She sounded concerned. "You sure? It's pretty shocking to lose a friend like that."

Lewis nodded, not taking his eyes off the screen. "It's…been an interesting day."

The face of Victor Zhao smirked at him from cyberspace.

06

The only sound in the dark corridor was the exhalation of oxygen inside his helmet. Lewis danced the beam down the hallway, watching it illuminate the white floor and overturned medical gurneys. A red exit sign glowed far off in the black distance. His right hand held a shiny, blocky pistol, which he aimed ahead as he advanced forward.

It had been like this for several hours now. Rogers, his other teammate, had been crushed in half by a closing airlock door a little while back. The game's designers had put significant detail into having his lower half jettisoned into space while still tethered to the upper half by a long knot of intestines. After that, the blood and guts probably should've stopped bothering Lewis, but the game kept finding ways of advancing its carnage.

The plot was secondary to the scares, which were secondary to the gore. Right now, he was heading down yet another darkened passageway to retrieve yet another item relevant to the shoestring story, so that he could somehow activate the emergency thrusters of the ship and propel it away from the black hole – or something like that. But all he could think about was the next gruesome spectacle the game had in store. It egged him on, simultaneously terrifying and exciting him with the prospect of horrors greater than those he had already witnessed.

His in-game character finally reached the end of the hall. No monsters. Yet.

There had been some bullshit explanation about a meteorite that had hit the vessel and leaked an extraterrestrial contaminant, but Lewis felt the writers had come up with it on the fly. The plot was thin, and it was clear that whoever developed this game was only interested in the derelict spacecraft as a violent haunted house they could toy with.

Lewis moved his Touch controller and watched his digital hand press each of the four buttons on a keypad, inputting a code he'd found elsewhere on this deck of the ship. The door clicked open and Lewis whipped out his pistol again, aiming it into the pitch black of the next area.

Something between a hiss and a groan slithered out from the abyss. Lewis held the gun up, ready to strike.

An infected crewmember stumbled out, clearly in a more advanced stage of the virus than previous enemies. His head was still pale white, hairless, and covered with bioluminescent sapphire veins. But his face was elongating into a distorted, lizard-like snout. His black eyes were larger and more animalistic, with the once beady red pupils having grown to dilated slits.

Lewis didn't think twice. He fired, the shot echoing in the tight corridor.

The bullet hit the abomination in the chest, red blood spurting forth from the wound. The creature reared back toward where it came from, critically damaged. Lewis swapped his weapon for a crowbar he'd gotten back near the start of the game and lunged after it. Swinging the metal instrument, he connected the hooked end with the injured monster's face.

Blood splattered the wall as Lewis struck again and again. The thing collapsed to the floor. Lewis kept swinging his Touch controller, which vibrated with each impact as he smashed the thing's head open and it finally stopped moving.

He took a deep breath and then bent down to search the corpse for supplies, yielding a med-kit and three spare bullets. Merely reaching his hand for them added them to the inventory. Standing up, he aimed the flashlight down the corridor. Nothing else lunged out at him, but there appeared to be only one way out about a hundred feet forward.

Lewis replaced the crowbar with the pistol and slowly edged forward through the doorway, keeping the flashlight aimed ahead. A hovering display popped up above the weapon when he looked at it, showing he only had eleven shots left even with the ammo he'd just collected. He swore under his breath, continuing on through the hallway. The beam lanced through the shadows, revealing blood splattered across the walls, ceiling, and floor. It had a shiny, surreal texture that he didn't like. It made the hairs on his arms stand on end, goosebumps blanketing his skin.

Then there was a strange noise, a sort of ethereal moaning. It had surfaced now and then throughout the game, so he knew it had to be an effect. It intertwined with the soundtrack, a set of minimalist, drawn-out notes from a digital synthesizer that were surprisingly effective.

Stay focused, he told himself. *It's just a game. You can turn it off at any time.*

Then why hadn't he already? Christ knew how long he'd been sitting here in Jenna's office, hogging her computer after dinner. She was the one who actually needed to play this thing, it was her job. But even though playing a violent horror game after the loss of a friend was probably the last thing he should be doing, she'd let him have at it anyway, gave him his space.

Why *was* he still playing? What did he honestly think he was going to find here?

His beam cast a glow onto something on the floor and he stopped. It was a dismembered corpse, the arms and limbs scattered among the viscera like a twisted art project. He swallowed and took another deep breath. The dead woman's face was staring up at him, upside down from this angle. She was rendered in shockingly high-res detail, there was no question about it. It was like seeing a PS4 game character in a PS3 game environment. The eyes were locked on him, the mouth agape in an endless, silent scream. It looked so *uncannily* real...

"No," he said, nudging the controls back. His character took several reverse steps. He realized his hands, gripped tightly around the wireless Touch controllers, were shaking. *What the hell is wrong with me?*

Then the entire ship shuddered. The metal groaned and it felt as if gravity was listing to the right.

The flashlight went out. Why had it gone out? Right, because the plot had demanded it – one of those big scripted moments, he realized as the overhead lights suddenly flickered back on brightly. He started to look left and right, but it was a delayed reaction again, his character moving in slow-mo.

Something big was about to happen and the game wanted

him to see it. As if the damn body hadn't fucked with him enough. He gazed ahead. The door at the end had the letters AIRLOCK emblazoned in red above its frame. They wanted him to go outside, probably a spacewalk sequence. Yeah, he could handle that. He realized he was gently nodding to himself, his in-game avatar repeating his actions in the digital realm.

He nudged the analog sticks on the Touch controllers forward.

Nothing happened.

Lewis spun the knobs in all directions. Nothing changed. He was stuck.

Then came the breathing.

It drifted into his headphones from some distance behind him; in and out, in and out through a respirator. It reminded him of Darth Vader. Slowly, he turned his head around and his character's body did the same.

Way back through the door, past the dead body of the mutated crewman, at the other end of the corridor he had just come from, was an astronaut. It stood there in a sleek white outfit, the kind of thing NASA would have a few decades from now, maybe more. Normally, seeing an astronaut figure would've been a sign of relief, another non-player character ally to assist him in fighting off the unnatural. But Lewis sensed immediately that this was not a friendly face. In fact, it had no face, just a bright blue glow shining out from within its helmet.

Lewis tensed up. *It's the dream again. None of this is real, none of this can be–*

The lights shut off. Blackness engulfed him and he couldn't see anything, swinging the VR headset around in the darkness of Jenna's office, trying to catch a glimpse of something, anything. Even the blue glow had vanished from view.

Then the brightness returned, flickering for only an instant. There it was, the astronaut, standing right in the door frame he had entered this stretch of corridor through. Even in this light, he couldn't make out the origin of the blue glow behind the glass. He wasn't even sure if the being had a face at all.

Instinctively, he pulled the analog sticks back. This time, his character responded, slowly backing away from the extraterrestrial menace. The thing just stood there, watching him. Then–

Blackout.

Lewis pulled the entire controllers back harder as if it would make a difference, his character reeling backward into the dark as he braced himself for what was about to come.

Flash on.

Lights everywhere.

The astronaut stood right before him, shining its horrifying blue glow into his eyes, its breathing now deafeningly loud in his headphones, its outstretched arm mere inches from his face–

Lewis screamed.

The thing walked forward now, continuing to reach for him as it did so. The palm of its white-gloved hand split open and a reddish black appendage – more like an insect's leg than a tentacle – snaked its way out.

He realized he was still screaming but didn't stop. This wasn't like the games he played when he was younger. The TV screen had protected him then, an impenetrable barrier beyond which the animated world could never hurt him.

This thing appeared to be mere feet from him, the enemy

rendered in a higher level of detail than its surroundings. The monster was so real he could have touched it.

The spider-tendril kept extending, getting closer. Blood poured through the gap in the creature's palm it had torn open. He felt time slowing down, certainly a scripted effect, as his character stumbled back through the open airlock door. The tendril was getting closer, the breathing of the creature louder and louder.

His eyes darted to a panel with green and red icons on its touchscreen surface: green for open, red for close. Lewis's left hand sailed through both physical and virtual space as he forced the Touch controller toward the imaginary spot. In the game world, his fingers made contact with the CLOSE icon and the door abruptly slid shut on the tendril.

The severed appendage dropped to the floor and writhed around. Then it twitched and went still in a puddle of black blood. He heard the thing outside cry out – a noise that sounded like a cross between a banshee and a *Tyrannosaurus* – and stomp off back down the hall.

Words flashed in the center of his vision:

CHECKPOINT REACHED. AUTO-SAVING YOUR PROGRESS.

Then they vanished.

Breathing a heavy sigh of relief, Lewis paused the game and pulled the headset off. He was startled to find Jenna standing across the desk from him, looking worried. She'd turned the lamp on.

"Everything okay?" she asked.

"Yeah, yeah," he said, barely believing it himself. "Just a very freaky game. You played much of it yet?"

"You should probably get out of this room for a little bit. You've been cooped up in here for hours."

Lewis glanced at the analog clock on the wall. It was past 10:30; he'd been playing since just after 7:45. "That's a good idea." He put all the gear down on her desk and followed her out to the living room.

Once they were on the sofa, he leaned his head on her shoulder and she began running her fingers through his short hair, massaging his scalp. "You're becoming like Charlie." She forced a laugh. "He's become obsessed with that game lately, too."

"What's he say about it?" Lewis asked, staring at a cubist painting hung on the opposite wall.

"Not much. He mentioned it was really disturbing him, giving him nightmares. He'd called to ask if I'd experienced the same thing."

He looked up at her. "And have you?"

"I'm worried about you," she said, gazing down at him with a sad expression. "I think you should take a break from it. At least give yourself some more time after Jake's death."

Jake.

The voicemail message played in his mind again. He heard his friend's final warning, followed by a revving engine and a squeal of tires. Then nothing.

At that moment, it hit him.

Lewis launched to his feet, whipping his phone out. "Hold on a sec," he said, frantically typing into the Google search bar.

"What are you doing?" she asked, more concerned than incredulous.

There was no website for *Rogue Horizon*. He guessed that would defeat the purpose of a secret beta. His hopes shot upward momentarily as he spotted a gaming forum that mentioned it, but when he tapped the link, he found the page no longer existed.

"Des," she said, touching his arm.

Lewis barely noticed, dashing back around the corner to her office. He slid around the desk and crouched in front of her laptop. The pause menu was up on the screen. He exited to the main menu and scrolled to Extras, then found the option for Credits.

They were short and to the point, just a slow text crawl against a view of the derelict vessel and the black hole beyond:

DEVELOPED BY
GALACTIC GAMES

Lewis turned his attention back to the phone in his hands, typing in the two words as fast as he could.

Luckily, there actually was a website for Galactic Games. Unluckily, it was little more than a space shuttle logo and the tagline "Games that are out of this world" with a black background. There was no location for a headquarters, no About section, no Contact, nothing.

"Des, what's going on?"

He looked up. Jenna was standing there in the doorway drenched in blood from head to toe. A troubled look rested on her face.

Lewis blinked several times and shook his head.

Now the blood was gone, but her expression remained.

Very calmly, he said, "I was just curious about something. That's all."

07

Lewis opened his eyes.

It was dark, sometime after midnight. City lights filtered through closed blinds, illuminating segments of the ceiling. The distant sounds of cars drifted up from the street below. Jenna was somewhere behind him on the other side of the queen mattress. He could hear her slow, rhythmic breathing.

Lewis felt restless, as if he had been tossing and turning. It didn't feel like he'd gotten very much sleep.

Then he froze. He heard a sound coming from beyond the open doorway to the hall. Something was out there. Every muscle in his body tensed up and he listened carefully.

Nothing. Somewhere a clock ticked. He exhaled softly and closed his eyes.

It came again, a footstep. Then another. He was sure of it.

Lewis squeezed his eyelids tighter. *Don't look, don't look, don't look...*

It was coming closer to the bed. He could hear the

inhalation and exhalation through its respirator, could imagine the blue glow blanketing the sheets.

Open your eyes.

He looked at the last second before the footsteps arrived at his feet. A shadow stood there, its shape taking form as it lunged for him out of the blackness, its white-gloved palm split open and pouring blood.

Lewis turned and violently shook Jenna's arm. His head turned back to face the menace–

The creature was gone.

His girlfriend groggily stirred awake beside him. "What's happening?"

"There was…" He blinked multiple times, stupefied.

No, he hadn't just woken up. That couldn't have been a dream. He continued staring at the space where the apparition had been.

Jenna leaned over and kissed his shoulder, then gripped his hand tightly. "It's just another nightmare," she said. "Go back to sleep."

He knew he'd been fully awake the entire time.

The atmosphere in the office that morning was full of unease. Lewis felt odd sitting at his desk and found himself frequently gazing out the window off to his left. Several hundred words of his latest article were sitting up on his screen, and he had his notebook from the interviews ready beside him, but the words just weren't coming out of him today.

He minimized the document, found the website for Arcadia – this time searching for "Arcadia Virtual Reality Amusement Park", and even then it was the fourth result – and located a phone number under the Contact section of the

Tickets page.

After several rings, a woman's voice answered. She sounded sour. "Hello?"

"Hi, is this Arcadia?"

"Yes."

"My name is Desmond Lewis. I'm a reporter for the *Technologist*. I'm working on a piece about virtual reality theme parks, and I was wondering if I could book a private tour."

"We don't give those."

Lewis massaged his chin. "Well, is there any way I can get tickets to come out and see it? It looks really great from the website, and I'd like to see how it compares to–"

"I'm sorry, sir. But tickets are sold out for the next six months."

"Huh. I find that a little odd since you don't advertise anywhere."

"We are quite well known on the virtual reality circuit, and currently have more demand than our small facility can handle. We've begun construction on an expansion."

"Okay, how can I get an interview with Mr. Zhao?"

A pause. "Mr. Zhao does not do interviews."

Lewis picked up a pen and tapped the end of it gently against his desk. Was he really going to go this far? At this point, he saw no other option.

"Got many e-sports champions swinging by? Because I know for a fact that Jenna Bateman wants to visit your place."

He could hear another voice somewhere in the background and pressed his phone tighter against his ear. The woman on the phone took a while longer to respond. "I thought you said you were a journalist, not a spokesman for Ms. Bateman."

This answer surprised him. Did people think Jenna had a spokesman?

"No, but I am her boyfriend. To be honest, I'm kind of writing the article as an excuse to get her into your place." He was going on the fly now, saying whatever came to mind first. "She'd wanted to go but saw the tickets were all booked up on your website." He laughed. "I promised her I'd do this as kind of a birthday gift for her, try to use my press badge to slip ahead of the line."

There was no response.

"Look at it this way: You get a photo of Jenna Bateman playing your games on the front of your website, which, let's face it, is a little sparse at the moment, Jenna gets to visit a VR theme park, and I get to write my damn article. Everybody wins."

After a few moments, the voice said, "As it happens, I've been informed that Mr. Zhao is somewhat of a fan of Ms. Bateman's. He'd like to meet her in person. How soon can you come?"

Lewis blinked. "Uh…" He glanced at his calendar. *Why not make it a weekend trip to Vegas?* "How does Friday sound?"

Another bit of muffled conversation. Then: "That works just fine. I'm putting you and Jenna Bateman down for a special tour at 9AM Friday. Mr. Zhao will greet you in the lobby. See you then."

She hung up.

Lewis sat back in his chair, stunned. Until thirty seconds ago, Victor Zhao had been but a smug-faced photograph, the leader behind an enigma. Now he was going to personally give Lewis a tour of his secretive VR park. And he was a fan of his girlfriend.

Things were getting stranger by the minute.

"Just to be clear, it's a what exactly?" Richter asked, sitting at her desk.

"A virtual reality amusement park. The equipment they have there allows for more advanced games and experiences than just a standard commercial headset."

"I think I've heard of these before. And you think this is what Jake was looking into?"

Lewis nodded.

Richter sighed and leaned back in her seat. "Des, I know his death must be hard on you but–"

"I'm not investigating anything," he said, putting up his hand. "Just…just…trying to finish what he started. Out of respect for him."

Richter raised an eyebrow. "Sounds like a wild goose chase to me."

"Why would he have done drugs at a VR park? It's clearly unrelated to what happened."

"No, but it is in the same vicinity where he died."

"You think there's a connection?" Lewis said, suddenly excited.

"No," she replied. "I think *you think* there's a connection, and you're using a business trip as an excuse to look into it further."

He sighed and rubbed his temple.

She frowned. "Des, you're one of the best writers we've got at this paper, and you've been here less than two years. I know you've got good instincts, but this just seems far-fetched."

"There's something very weird going on, Valerie," he

said. "It's bigger than Jake, bigger than Arcadia. I've got a hunch – an unproven hunch – but I think it's tied to something spreading across the country."

His boss chuckled. "Now that's a fucking hook!"

"If I'm right, you'll have a huge story on your hands."

She shook her head. "It's not like in the movies, Des. The stereotypical editor, always sending their best writer off to get the scoop no matter what… We're not yellow journalists, we're tech reporters. I want Jake to rest in peace, and for us to heal and move on with our lives. I'm worried that this little investigation of yours is going to hinder that."

"Just give me the weekend," Lewis said. "I'll know by then if I'm right or not."

"And if not?"

"I'll go back to my other article. Life will go on. And we'll have closure knowing his death was really an accident."

Richter considered it for a moment. "Fine," she said, raising a finger. "But only for Jake."

"Thank you." He got up and left her office, closing the door gently behind him.

Now on his lunch break, Lewis stepped outside into the brisk January air of the parking lot and made his way toward his car. As he did so, he took out his phone and decided to call Charlie. Jenna had mentioned something last night about him having hallucinations and horrible dreams. If the past two nights were anything to go on, Lewis figured it might be beneficial talking to someone in the same boat.

It rang a few times, but Charlie picked up just as Lewis opened the car door. "Hello?" came the voice. It sounded tired, breathless.

Lewis gazed off at the fluttering sails of the marina. "Hey Charlie, how's it going?"

"I can't talk right now. They're watching me."

He paused for a second. "Excuse me?"

"They're everywhere. They're gonna get me."

Lewis sat down in the driver's seat and closed the door. "Charlie, hey, what's going on?"

"Someone's trying to get into my fucking house, man! They're gonna get me!"

"Okay, okay, just stay calm." He slid the key into the ignition and turned it to the side, the engine roaring to life. "Have you called the police?"

"They're everywhere, man. They've got fucking eyes everywhere!"

"Who's they?" Lewis said, throwing on his seatbelt.

"I'll tell you everything, man. Just please, for the love of God, help me!"

"Okay, I need your address."

"329 Cedarvale Lane, Pasadena."

Shit. That was at least 40 minutes away. And that was if he somehow avoided L.A. traffic. "Charlie, I'm on my way, but it's gonna take a while. You need to call somebody closer."

"I can't talk." The phone went dead.

Lewis's pulse was racing. He put the gear into drive and tore out of the parking lot.

08

His hands gripped the steering wheel tightly as he cut off a Mercedes SUV doing 80 miles per hour, sliding into the new lane and applying more pressure to the accelerator. Google Maps said taking the 405 up to just north of the city and turning onto the Ventura Freeway east was the fastest way to get to Pasadena. There'd been traffic on the 405, but he'd driven along the shoulder lane to get past it.

Lewis glanced at his phone, sitting in the cup holder beside him. Current ETA was still twelve minutes. That wasn't good enough.

Making sure there were no cops around, he sped up until he was going just shy of 85 miles per hour. Three minutes later he whipped down the off-ramp for Exit 25C, applying the brakes as his vehicle shot out into a road.

His phone rang just as he swerved onto Fair Oaks Avenue and raced south. He pressed a button on the steering wheel and the call went to the car's Bluetooth speakers.

"Hello?" Heavy breathing on the other end. "Charlie?"

"Jesus Christ man, they're here. They're at my fucking doorstep," he rasped. Distantly, Lewis could make out a knocking on a door. "What do I do?"

"Charlie, just stay put and hide. I'm almost there."

"Shit, I gotta go."

The call ended. The light ahead of Lewis turned from yellow to red.

He slammed on the brakes and abruptly came to a stop, earning a blaring honk from the car behind him. Lewis breathed in and out, gripping the steering wheel tightly with his left hand. He waited for the light to go green again, then slammed the gas and flew through the intersection.

The Ford Fusion came to a halt across the hillside street from 329 Cedarvale Lane. Cautiously, Lewis stepped out of the car. Sunlight streamed through tree branches, casting shadows of leaves down on the sloping asphalt as they rustled gently in the breeze. He squinted up at the empty, periwinkle blue sky. It was a beautiful day; he was surprised not to see anyone outside.

A few cars were parked in front of houses or in driveways up and down the street, and in front of 329 was a FedEx truck. Lewis looked past it to the house itself. It was an average sized lot for the neighborhood, a bungalow painted grayish-green with white frames around the windows. The curtains were all drawn shut. Since it stood on a hill, Lewis could see that the left side of the house went down farther than the right. It might even have a basement, a rarity in the Golden State.

The front door stood ajar.

Lewis walked across the street and up the stone path to

the entrance, a strange feeling coming over him. Something about the whole scene felt off. It wasn't until he got to the door that he understood why. At first, he was about to gently rap on the wood and call Charlie's name, but he looked down just as he began extending his arm.

Blood pooled around the doorstep, a dark crimson trail leading off into the dimly-lit interior of the house.

Immediately, Lewis took several steps back. He pulled out his phone and rapidly dialed three digits.

"9-1-1, what's your emergency?"

"I'm at 329 Cedarvale Lane, Pasadena," he said. "My friend called a few minutes ago from inside the house, saying someone was trying to get in. There's blood around the front door and a trail of it going into the house."

"The door is still open?"

"Yes."

A moment's pause. "I'm dispatching a squad car to investigate. They should be there in about five minutes. Please stand by, and step away from the house."

"Please hurry," he said, and hung up.

Suddenly, a cry erupted from beyond the door.

Lewis froze. He wasn't sure if it sounded like Charlie or not.

Then a voice: "Hello? Is someone there? Please help!"

"Charlie?" he called out.

"Dear God, please help me!" It sounded like they were in pain.

Lewis looked around. Nobody else was around to assist.

Slowly, he edged toward the door and softly pushed it open. Directly in front of him was a wall with a coat rack. To the right was a living room and to the left was a dining room and a corridor branching off deeper into the house. The blood trail went that way.

"Hello?!" the voice called.

Lewis moved closer, one careful step after the next. He wished the police were nearer, but if Charlie was hurt, he might need his help right now. Around the corner, he saw that the short hall emerged into an area with a breakfast table and what appeared to be an open kitchen off to the left; Lewis wasn't sure, he couldn't see all of it yet. At the back was a sliding glass door leading out into a small backyard with a BBQ and a brick patio. Daylight shone through the glass, illuminating the table and the body of a man lying on the floor in a pool of blood.

He was still alive, dressed in a FedEx uniform, clutching a wound in his abdomen, and looking pale. He feebly reached his arm out toward Lewis, blood dripping from his fingers. At first Lewis, frozen in shock, thought he was going to beg for help again. Then the words escaped his lips: "Watch…out…"

A large shape lunged out from behind the corner, moving like a wraith. Lewis saw a kitchen knife slash through the air and somehow caught the large arm that wielded it, the blade mere inches from his face. For a moment it remained there, slightly wobbling as the attacker was unable to overcome Lewis's determination. Then the assailant grabbed his shoulder with their other arm, turned, and threw him toward the kitchen.

Lewis tumbled to the floor. His shoulder hurt, but the pain vaporized in his mind's frantic resolve to figure out what the fuck was going on. He spun over onto his back to get a good look at the maniac.

The silhouetted, hulking figure stepped into the light, brandishing the steel blade. Charlie appeared torn between fright and rage as he raised the knife. "Get away from me," he said, stepping closer.

Lewis raised his hands. "Jesus Charlie, put the knife down!" He blinked multiple times, half expecting the man to disappear. But he stayed there, his hair mangled and his shirt drenched in the delivery man's blood.

"You're not gonna hurt me anymore!" Charlie shouted, then lunged for him.

Lewis scrambled to his feet and dove behind the island countertop of the kitchen. He surfaced on the other side just as Charlie swung the blade across. It cut across his left forearm and he jumped back.

Charlie snorted like a bull, narrowing his eyes. He edged to the right, then the left, unsure of which way around the counter would best bring him to his target.

Lewis raised his hands. "Charlie, it's me. Desmond. You called me." Very slowly, he began moving his right hand behind him to pull open a cupboard door and feel around inside it.

Charlie shook his head. "Not gonna get me, not gonna get me…"

Moving with surprising speed, he slid around the island corner on the left and lunged for Lewis, whose fingers had just curled around a drinking glass, which he hurled at Charlie. His assailant brought up his arm to cover his face just before the projectile hit his elbow and shattered.

Lewis ran around the other side of the island, running toward the hall, the front door, and safety. He remembered the blood on the floor a split second too late. His feet slipped out from underneath him and he crashed face-first to the ground.

Get up, get up.

He'd just managed to get back to his feet when Charlie grabbed him by the shoulder, opened a door beside him, and violently shoved him in. Lewis suddenly felt himself briefly soar through the air, then tumble painfully down step after carpeted step, his entire body battered from every angle as the world spun around him.

Then it ended, pain jolting through his body as he sprawled out onto smooth flooring. Wearily, he glanced back up. It was dark down here, save for the light drifting down from the top of the staircase. A darkened figure descended like a hawk down the steps, blocking out the light. He could see a knife wielded in the attacker's hand.

Lewis was lying prone. He pressed his palms onto the cool, hard tile and forced himself back up in spite of the pain. Behind him stood a maze of radiators, heaters, and boxes. Directly in front of him was a door.

He threw it open, slid through, and slammed it shut just as Charlie reached the bottom of the stairs. Lewis turned the lock into place just as he heard the pursuer yell and the knife blade stuck its way through the wooden door. Lewis jumped back, feeling as if his heart were in his throat. On the other side of the barrier, Charlie roared and stabbed the knife through several more times. He began aggressively jiggling the knob, and when that didn't work, resorted to kicking. The door shook violently in its frame.

Lewis looked around, trying to remain calm. Light shone into the room from a small window near the ceiling, which appeared to be at ground level outside. There was a tiny bathroom off to the right, a bed to the left, and an assortment of gaming equipment on a desk before him. There was also a sofa behind him next to the door. He recalled a comment Jenna had once made about Charlie living in his parent's basement, but other concerns quickly overrode the thought.

Diving for the sofa, he pushed it from one end with all

his might to slide it in front of the rattling door as fast as he could.

"They're everywhere!" Charlie screamed from the other side of the cracking wood. "Make it stop! Make it stop!"

The door broke just as Lewis took a step back, but his assailant had barely enough space to get his arm into the room. The knife swung through the air wildly while its wielder shrieked in rage.

Lewis turned back, looking from the desk to the window. He had no other choice.

Pushing aside the monitor for Charlie's Alienware desktop, he scrambled up onto the desk and reached for the window sill. He fumbled with the latch, but he couldn't get it to slide across. It appeared to be stuck.

He swore under his breath.

Charlie delivered one powerful kick after another to the door, the couch shifting forward with each blow.

Lewis looked left and right. He had only two choices for a hiding spot: the bathroom or under the bed. But as soon as Charlie figured out he was under there, there'd be no escape. He leaped off the desk and dashed into the bathroom, sliding around behind the door.

He heard several more crashing noises, then heavy footsteps as Charlie stormed his way into the room. "I know you're in here," his voice boomed. "You're not gonna get me!"

Lewis leaned around the door to look at the sink counter, searching for a weapon. The metal soap dispenser looked heavy enough. He inched back into the crevasse between the door and the wall, squinting through the tiny gap by the hinges.

He saw Charlie bending down to look under his bed.

Now was his chance.

Lewis slipped out, snatched the dispenser, and swiftly returned to his hiding spot. Through the gap, he watched as Charlie spun around toward the bathroom. Red anger swelled in his face, the knife trembling in his hand.

"I won't let you hurt me," he hissed.

Lewis's heart was pounding so quickly he wondered if Charlie could hear it. His hulking figure stomped closer, a growl rising in the back of his throat. He had to know Lewis was behind the door.

It was now or never.

Lewis raised the soap dispenser. It weighed at least a few pounds. As Charlie entered the bathroom, he swung around and smashed it against the man's forehead. Charlie reeled back, the blade nearly slipping from his fingers, as he clutched the bleeding gash above his left eyebrow with his other hand. Lewis didn't hesitate; he gave another adrenaline-powered swing, this time stronger. It connected with the center of Charlie's face with an audible crunch.

Charlie fell back against the counter, both of his hands clasping his broken nose. The knife clattered to the floor, but for some reason, Lewis didn't think to grab it. Fight or flight instinct had chosen flight, and he found himself dashing past his attacker, past the knocked-aside couch, and out the door. He swung around the pole at the base of the steps, using his momentum to launch himself up the stairs.

Somewhere below, Charlie bellowed in anger and came thundering after him. Lewis climbed the steps on all fours to reach the top faster. It sounded like his pursuer was right behind him. He reached the top landing, scrambled to his feet, and slammed the door shut after him. There was nothing to block it this time; it would only momentarily slow him down.

Lewis stepped back from it and was about to sprint for the front door when something caught his eye off to the left. The delivery man lay still in a pool of his own blood, his open eyes gazing emptily at the ceiling.

He wanted to grimace, to turn away, but his shock was interrupted by a tremendous crash as Charlie smashed through the door. His inertia carried him straight over to the slick trail of red, and he slipped in the same liquid that had stained his shirt. Lewis didn't wait for him to get back up. He ran straight down the hall, skirted the corner, and dashed through the front door and out into the daylight.

A police car had pulled up beside the FedEx truck and two officers were climbing out, one male and one female. They spotted Lewis and immediately drew their guns.

"Hold it right there!" the man said, aiming his pistol at him and stepping closer onto the lawn.

"Put your hands up!" yelled the other.

Lewis did so, realizing his jacket must have blood on it from when he slipped and fell in it. Also, frantically running out of the house where a 9-1-1 call had emerged had to look a bit suspicious. He gestured back toward the house with one hand.

"The killer's still in there," he said.

"Just get on your knees and stay put," the female officer said. Both of them were coming closer now.

Lewis did as he was told. Suddenly, they froze in their tracks and aimed their weapons somewhere past him. "Hey freeze!" the male officer barked.

He threw a look over his shoulder. Charlie stumbled out the front door and stormed toward the three of them down the stone path. His eyes were deadlocked onto Lewis in a menacing glare, his mouth contorted in a snarl. His face was badly banged up from the soap dispenser and blood seeped from each nostril.

"Sir, drop the knife and put your hands up!" one of the officers shouted.

But Charlie didn't stop. Lewis twisted around and fell on his backside and began scurrying back as the attacker drew nearer. His intent was evident in his eyes even before he raised the knife up high. He lunged forward, his mouth open in a scream.

A sharp *crack* resounded behind Lewis off to the left and Charlie's body jerked back, a red geyser sprouting from the center of his chest. His charge became a stumble and he collapsed onto the grass a few feet down the hill from Lewis.

For several seconds, Charlie lay there, his widened eyes staring off blankly. Words escaped his lips, barely louder than a whisper: "*Arcadia...awaits...*"

And then he went very still.

09

The room was cold and grey. A single strip of fluorescent lighting hung from the ceiling and the only amenities were a steel table with three chairs, two on one side and one on the other where he was sitting. On the wall before him was a mirror, which he knew was a two-way.

Lewis brought the glass of water up to his lips and took a sip. His fingers weren't trembling anymore; that was a good sign. Detectives had been in and out all afternoon asking questions and then more questions as others outside the room analyzed new bits of evidence collected from the house.

Everything backed up his version of events, so there was no question of him having committed any sort of crime. Charlie, in some kind of hyper-paranoid trance, had stabbed the FedEx delivery man at the doorstep and dragged him all the way to the back of the house, where he had bled to death by the time the police arrived. Given the phrases he'd used on the phone with Lewis, as well as his cries while assaulting him, the cops guessed that Charlie thought the delivery man and Lewis were agents of some conspiracy out to get him. Once he'd brought the man over to the kitchen table, he'd waited around the corner for the next "enemy" to come through. That just happened to be Lewis, and in his delirious state, Charlie must not have recognized him.

The only real question that remained was why.

Lewis had made phone calls to Jenna and Ricky, letting them know that he was alright, and one to Richter explaining why he wouldn't be back from his lunch break today. He'd been alone in here for about fifteen minutes since the last officer had asked a few questions.

The door behind him opened again just as he finished the last of his water. He put the glass down on the table as a lean Latina woman in her early thirties sat down opposite him, placed a thick folder on the table, and extended her hand.

"Special Agent Sara Gonzalez, with the L.A. Field Office." She flashed an FBI badge, then returned it to her suit jacket. "Mr. Lewis, I know you've had a terrible day and have already been over this many times, but I just have a couple of extra questions."

Lewis spread his hands, tired. "Fire away."

She slid a notebook out of the file, opened it to a new page and retrieved a pen from her inside jacket pocket. Without looking up, she said, "Do you know if Charlie Wong was on antidepressants?"

"I can't say for sure, but I don't think so. Were any found at the house?"

She shook her head. "None so far. Did he have any known mental health issues or emotional difficulties that you were aware of?"

"No," Lewis said. He'd only known him a few months, but everything Jenna had said about Charlie described the antithesis of the man who had just tried to kill him. "If you don't mind me asking, why is the FBI interested in this case?" He was pretty sure he already knew.

She paused for a moment and looked at him. "Over the past six months, there have been several instances across the country of people with no prior mental illness issues, who weren't on any medications with severe side effects, who inexplicably committed murder-suicides. The only common thread was that they were all known for playing violent video games, just like your friend Charlie. My bosses want to find out why."

For the first time all day, Lewis felt relieved. "I read the *Atlantic* article."

She scoffed. "That barely scratched the surface. I've seen the detailed police reports, the files on all the investigations. We're noticing some patterns. I was in L.A. this week for some other business, so the timing of this case is great."

"What kind of patterns?" he asked.

"I just need answers to a few questions, and I'll let you know if any spring up," she said, forcing a smile at the end. She seemed like someone who only resorted to politeness as a necessity.

Lewis said nothing. Everything he'd said to the authorities up to this point had been strictly about the events of the day. He hadn't mentioned *Rogue Horizon* or Miller or Arcadia to anyone at the station. But if the feds were looking into this across the nation, then maybe they would believe him.

"Had you noticed a change in Mr. Wong's behavior recently?" Gonzalez asked.

He thought for a moment. "Yeah, actually. A couple of nights ago he was at my girlfriend's birthday party. He looked exhausted, but said he'd just gotten back from a busy weekend in…Vegas," he said, just now remembering. He couldn't believe he hadn't seen the connection before. "His eyes were bloodshot and he just looked drained, like he'd been flying halfway around the world."

"But Las Vegas is barely a two-hour flight."

"Exactly. I don't know what he got up to in Vegas" – *although I have a pretty good idea where he went* – "but something about him just seemed off. He talked a lot about this game he'd been playing. It was a kind of secret beta, he probably wasn't even supposed to talk about it. He said it was both disturbing and oddly compelling."

"Did the game have a name?" Gonzalez rapidly jotted down notes.

"*Rogue Horizon.*"

"*Rogue Horizon?*"

"Yeah, it was some sci-fi VR horror game."

"Would that be played on a PC?"

"Yes."

She scribbled something out of view, then looked up. "And that was the only thing out of the ordinary?"

Lewis thought it was an interesting coincidence that one of the lead investigators in a nationwide FBI case just happened to be in L.A. when the latest gamer snapped and went homicidal.

"Yeah," he said, thoughts flooding his mind. He recalled his conversation with Ricky, the same evening all of this had started. The *Polybius* urban legend, clandestine test projects like MKULTRA. Few organizations would have the gall – or the funding – to pull off something like this save for the three-letter government agencies.

"We looked through the games on his computer and his

consoles. There was nothing with that name. Maybe he deleted it."

"Has that name come up before in your investigation?" he asked.

"No," she said, writing something in her notes. "But that doesn't mean it's not relevant. Maybe some people can buy the explanation that video games drove these people to commit murder, but violent interactive media has existed for decades."

"You think something else is going on." It was a statement, not a question.

She looked up from her notes. "That's what I'm trying to find out. Is there anything else you can tell me about *Rogue Horizon*?"

Lewis bit the inside of his lip. He wanted to tell her everything – the dreams, Arcadia, Miller's message – but he just couldn't trust her yet. A compromise wormed its way into his mind. "I'm afraid that's all I know right now, but I have a bunch of friends who are fairly big in the gaming world, including my girlfriend. She might know some other people who played it. Is there any way I can contact you if I hear anything else?"

Gonzalez fished a business card out of her jacket pocket and tossed it across the table to him, then stood up and put her notebook back in the file. "Call me if you learn more about the game. Even seemingly tiny details could be important."

As Lewis walked into the main lobby of the Pasadena Police Department, a cop approached him and pointed to the front entrance. "Your girlfriend's here waiting for you Mr. Lewis, she just stepped outside to take a call."

"Thank you," he said, heading for the exit.

The sun was getting low in the sky as he walked down the front steps, a late afternoon breeze gusting through the air. He had a great view of the magnificent architecture of Pasadena City Hall, just a block south down Garfield Avenue. Jenna stood in front of her parked Tesla Model 3, still talking on her phone.

She spotted him and said, "Oh, he's here now. Gotta go." Then she hung up, ran over to him, kissed him, and gave him a bear hug.

He took a deep breath and embraced her tightly. "It's been a long day."

"I'll fucking bet." She leaned back and looked at him. "Come back to my place tonight. We'll have a nice, relaxing evening. I'm going to make penne alfredo, absolutely no meat or red sauce."

"That's probably for the best." Neither of them were vegetarians, but he could live without meat for a couple of days after what happened. As they walked toward her vehicle, he said, "Who were you calling?"

"Claudia," she said, after what seemed to Lewis like a moment's hesitation. "I was just letting her know what had happened. She said she's talked to Charlie's parents."

"How are they taking it?"

"They're devastated. They were both at work when it happened. Had they both been at home, I wondered if he would've killed them too."

"Jesus," he said as he climbed into the car. He thought about that college student in Maine who'd stabbed his mother and sister.

"I just can't believe what happened," Jenna said, putting the car into reverse.

Lewis looked out the window up at the sky. "Me neither," he said. He didn't know what to believe anymore.

10

Sitting in the kitchen, Lewis gazed out the window at the cityscape. He checked his watch: just after 7:30. Jenna probably wouldn't be back for another ten minutes or so. She'd realized she was out of ingredients for penne alfredo and was determined to make that dish tonight, even when Lewis said he'd be okay with just ordering pizza. But when Jenna had her mind made up, nothing could stop her. He did admire that when she made a plan, she stuck with it.

Part of him felt a pull toward her office and the game that awaited, but he was able to override the urge with a better idea. Standing up, he went to one of her cupboards and withdrew a glass and a bottle of Glenfiddich. Then he poured himself a three-finger scotch, placed the bottle back where it belonged, and returned to his seat.

Lewis hadn't even had time to take a sip when the cordless home phone rang in its charge port. He was surprised she even had one of those in this day and age. The caller ID displayed a local number but no name .

Out of curiosity, he answered it. "Hello?"

"Desmond, is that you?" It was Lance Bateman, her father. Lewis remembered Jenna telling him she'd just gotten the phone installed; she must not have put in all of her contacts yet. Or maybe she just didn't want to put her parents in. Either way, he realized picking up the phone had probably been a mistake.

"Yeah, yeah... Sorry, I've had a rough day."

"I heard. Jesus, that's terrible. Jenna told me when I called earlier, said she had to rush off to the police station." He sounded genuinely concerned. "In fact, I was calling to check in and say how sorry I am to hear what happened. I wasn't sure if you two were back yet, or if you'd gone to your place. Jenna hasn't been answering her cell phone all afternoon."

That struck Lewis as odd. "Thank you, Mr. Bateman. I really appreciate that." He took a big swig of scotch.

"Hey, like I said, call me Lance!" There was an awkward pause. "God, she wouldn't tell me anything. I had to watch it on the local news."

Lewis realized he hadn't checked any media outlets since leaving the station. "What's the press saying?"

"Well, at first it was just 'Pasadena man kills FedEx driver,' but then more details started coming out. They mentioned he was shot by the police trying to kill someone else who had arrived at the scene, so I guess that was you, and... Jesus, did they shoot him right in front of you?"

Lewis nodded, then realized Bateman wouldn't see the gesture. "Yeah," he said. "Yeah, they did."

"That's terrible."

He shrugged, taking a sip of scotch. "Beats the alternative."

"And of course, they're talking about his video game habits."

Here we go, Lewis thought. He imagined Jenna listening and rolling her eyes.

"I mean the guy sounded like your stereotypical gamer: overweight, lived in his parent's basement, clearly had social issues…"

"Charlie was a nice guy." He looked down at his drink. "At least he had been."

"See that's the real tragedy of it all. Violent games can corrupt the weak minded, even if they're good people at heart."

Lewis sat up. "You know Lance, I think this time you may be right."

There was a chuckle from the other end. "Wow Desmond, that's…I think you're the first of Jenna's friends to ever agree with me on this." He laughed again, trying to lighten the mood. It was thoughtful of him, Lewis decided.

"I wouldn't say violent games are bad across the board," he clarified, "but I think maybe in a few cases they can be dangerous. Have you ever argued that some developers deliberately try to impact people's sanity?"

Bateman paused. "Well, some of my friends at Family First might take that stance, but I feel their rhetoric can be a bit alienating. Reverend Thompson once told me he thought game companies did the devil's work, but I'd say that's a tad extreme." Another chuckle. "I'd say it's carelessness, really. Developers add more blood and gore to make more money because they think that's what sells more. And sadly, it does. They're corrupting society by catering to people's baser instincts and desires and getting filthy rich off of it." Lewis imagined him saying all this while standing on his patio with its breathtaking view of L.A.

The voice on the phone continued. "The video game industry has been larger than Hollywood for some time now. I remember reading an article last year that said *Grand Theft Auto V* had made over $6 billion, and it's still selling. *Avatar* made $2.7 billion nearly a decade ago, and no movie's come close to that since!"

There was another pause. He heard Bateman take a breath. "Sorry, I get easily worked up on this subject."

"No worries," Lewis said, taking another swig of Glenfiddich and feeling it burn his throat on the way down. He wondered when his girlfriend was getting back.

"Anyway," Bateman continued. "Is Jenna around?"

"No, she's out doing some last-minute grocery shopping."

A pause. "Do you mind if I ask you a question? It's kind of an odd one…"

"I've been asked a lot of odd questions today. Ask anything."

"Have you…noticed a change in Jenna's behavior recently?"

Lewis thought for a moment. "I can't say that I have."

Silence. Then, "It's just…I don't know…maybe she's been fine with her friends, but she's been acting strange recently to her mother and I, just within the last couple of weeks. I can't place it exactly, but she just seems…different lately." A pause. "Does she play a lot of the same games Charlie did?"

"Some of them, I guess."

"It's just…her mother and I are so worried she'll wind up like him, like Charlie. She rarely talks to us anymore and I'm afraid that one day I'll turn on the TV and see that she's killed somebody." He sounded like he was holding back tears.

"I don't think you have to worry about that, Mr. Bateman. Then again, everything seems pretty strange to me right now."

"Perfectly understandable. Sorry for rambling. And please, call me Lance."

The call ended. Lewis sat there for a moment, deep in thought. Then he got up, walked over to Jenna's office and flicked on the light switch. He sat down in her chair and booted up the computer. He knew her password and was quickly into the system, opening up the game from its desktop icon of a black hole. He slid the Oculus Rift over his head and found himself floating in space, the silver sci-fi letters of the title appearing before him in giant letters.

He pressed a random button to continue, tapped his foot impatiently as he flew through space toward the black hole and the damaged starship, then quickly selected "Load Game." He was disappointed to see that the two save files, labeled "Jenna" and "Des" respectively, did not report game progress or total play time.

There was another way to see how far she was, of course. He could simply load her file: if he recognized where she was, he knew roughly how many hours she'd played, and if he didn't recognize it he would know she'd gotten ahead of him. He reached out his Touch controller, highlighting her name. All he had to do now was press a button, and he'd load her save. His hand hovered there, the cursor wavering slightly in digital space.

Somewhere, distantly, he heard the front door opening. "Des, I'm back!" she shouted.

Quickly, he exited the game, closed her laptop, and placed the VR gear back where it'd been on her desk. Then he turned off the light and ducked out of the room.

They sat on either side of the bar counter, eating their dinner and not saying a word. After keeping it pent up inside him all afternoon, Lewis decided to speak his mind.

"I think the game made Charlie do those things."

Jenna nearly choked on her food. She coughed a couple times, then drank some water. "Excuse me, *what*?"

"*Rogue Horizon*. He was having hallucinations, bad dreams. Somehow, it drove him insane, and he killed that guy and nearly killed me too." Lewis's tone was remarkably calm. He'd thought about it for so long it didn't even sound strange to him anymore.

"You don't know the game caused those nightmares," she said, stabbing penne with her fork.

"That's what you told me."

"No, that's what I told you *he* told me. I thought he was crazy when he said that, and I laughed it off on the phone with him. Even he chuckled and said, 'Yeah, you're probably right. It's something else.' I told him he never got enough damn sleep." Jenna ate the penne angrily, already spearing more. "You're starting to sound like my parents," she said, covering her mouth with her hand as she chewed.

Lewis folded his hands in front of him, looking at the table. "I've been having strange dreams too…and some hallucinations."

She looked up, a softer expression coming across her face. "Des, you found out a friend of yours died yesterday and today another friend tried to kill you. Anyone having the week you've had would probably be messed up too."

"This started Sunday evening, before I knew Jake was

dead. The same night I started playing the game."

"Strange dreams can happen at any time."

"This wasn't just any strange dream. I saw the glowing blue astronaut and I hadn't even gotten to that part of the game yet!"

She looked confused. "What glowing blue astronaut?"

"You know, the one from the game? It's in this spacesuit, but you can't see its face because there's this blue light coming from inside its helmet." She didn't appear to be following. He raised an eyebrow. "How far have you gotten?"

Jenna looked away and brushed a strand of her light brown hair back from her face. "Not that far." She took a sip of water. "I really need to play more of it."

"Right now, that's the last thing I'd recommend."

"Des, video games don't have side effects that cause psychosis. They've proven this many, many times."

"It's not a side effect. Somebody *designed* that game to do this."

She sighed. "Look, I know you've had a really bad day, but–"

"No, I'm dead serious. It's the only thing that makes sense."

"Des, video games affect everybody differently. Maybe you and Charlie got bad dreams from this one, but I can guarantee that whatever caused Charlie to snap had nothing to do with it. He was probably going through something we just didn't know about, something that took a terrible toll on his mental health."

"You weren't there, Jenna. That wasn't the Charlie I'd met before. Something had scrambled his mind; it was like he was trapped in a nightmare and was lashing out at it in the real world."

Red color flushed through her face. "You sound like all those nimrods who say video games rot your brain – which, fun fact, they don't! Many studies have shown they actually have a positive effect on cognitive development. And anyway, both of the major political parties in this country have used games and other forms of media – comic books, movies, TV shows, you name it – as scapegoats for violent crime because they don't want to confront the real, complex issues of mental health, because they understand it *even less* than they do entertainment!"

"I know that. I believe you, honestly. But *this game* specifically–"

"My parents once told me I spent too much time on the 'PlayBox 360', okay. I had a fucking *Wii* back then! For years, they and people just like them have blamed their children's actions on video games instead of taking credit for their own shit parenting!" Her face was completely red now, seething with rage.

He didn't say anything. This happened from time to time.

"You know, when I got the diagnosis, they blamed it on me having played too many first-person shooters. As if *Call of Duty* causes fucking borderline!"

He tried to keep his eyes from wandering to the red lines on the insides of her forearms, as they always tended to do whenever this topic came up. He reached forward and took one of her hands into his.

She bit her lip, looking away. "Shit, why did I bring that up? Why do I always make things about myself? I mean Jesus, you nearly died today and–"

"Whoa, whoa, whoa, take it easy," he said in as soothing a tone as possible. "I'm fine. It's fine. You're fine. You're one of the strongest people I know, okay." When she'd first told him she had BPD, about two months into the relationship, she admitted she was scared because several people had left her after finding out in the past. Lewis wouldn't have dreamed of it.

They were silent for a few moments, him holding her hand and her looking anywhere but at him.

"We're going to Vegas this weekend," he said, trying to sound cheerful.

She returned her attention to him. "Really? What for?"

"A business trip. It was planned before all this happened. I was going to tell you, and then…"

She nodded slowly, looking down at her food.

He continued, "There's this place outside the city. A virtual reality amusement park, called Arcadia. I'm writing a piece on it. It looks really cool and–"

Jenna furrowed her brow. "This doesn't have anything to do with Jake, does it?"

He paused for a moment. "To be honest, I'm not quite sure." And that was the truth. "The people there are big fans of yours," he said, shifting the subject. "They specifically asked if I could bring you along. They're giving us a private tour and everything, which they usually never do."

She laughed. "You son of a bitch."

"What?"

"You used me to get backstage access, didn't you?"

He shrugged. "Maybe it helped a bit."

Jenna shook her head. "Normally, I'd probably be a bit pissed but after everything you've been through this week…fine." She turned her fork over in her hand, watching the light glint off the silver. "So, what exactly do they do there?"

"That," he said, "is a very good question."

11

Before climbing into bed with Jenna that night, he decided to call his parents. He always tried to check in at least once every week to see how things were. David and Gabrielle Lewis currently lived upstate in San Jose. He had taken Jenna up there for a few days at Christmas last month; a good time had been had by all. Lewis walked to the kitchen and put his palm on the window, his other hand holding his Galaxy S9 to his ear.

His father picked up on the third ring. "Hey Desmond, how are you?"

"Not great…" He relayed an edited version of the week's events from Miller's death to his brush with death in Pasadena, keeping anything to do with Arcadia and *Rouge Horizon* out of the picture.

His father was silent for a good long while.

"Well, shit," he finally said.

Lewis laughed. His dad had never been averse to the art of swearing. "Yeah, it's…it's been an interesting week."

"What do you think made this guy Charlie lose his marbles?"

He played a game possibly designed by the government to make you kill people. "I have no idea. Probably something personal, maybe a mental health issue he was keeping hidden. Perhaps he was on antidepressants and they just didn't work the way they were supposed to. They're still investigating it."

"I'm truly, terribly sorry. Your mother is out walking Lucy, but she'll be back soon. Do you want me to call you when she's here so you can tell her in person?"

Lewis smiled at the memory of Jenna hugging his family's dog, an old German shepherd, on Christmas morning. Lucy had really liked her; he always took it as a good sign when his dog was fond of someone. Lucy had absolutely hated meeting one of his college girlfriends, and about a month after that Lewis had found out she'd been cheating on him.

"Nah, that's okay," he said, snapping out of the reverie. "Just let her know I'm alright."

Alright. The word took him back to the dream of the woman and the child by the wreck of the car, gazing up at the stars as she tried to comfort her son with a soothing tone and a single phrase, repeated over and over.

Everything's gonna be alright.

He wished he could believe her.

"You should take the rest of the week off too. Today's not enough," Richter's voice said over the Bluetooth speaker in his car. He was stuck in westbound traffic on the 10, his Ford Fusion sitting amidst a sea of stationary vehicles.

"Jenna and I are still flying to Vegas tomorrow

afternoon," he said. "The tour at Arcadia is too good of an opportunity to pass up."

"I already lost one writer in the past week, I don't want to lose another."

"So you do believe there's a connection?"

"Between Arcadia and Charlie? I don't know what to believe anymore. If what you say about this game is true…" The traffic had barely inched forward in the ten minutes it took to fill her in on the *Rogue Horizon* part of the equation. "I mean, you have no evidence Jake Miller played it," Richter said.

"No, but I heard the phrase 'Arcadia awaits' in a dream, and then out of Charlie's lips as he lay dying. We both played the game. I don't know if Jake heard those words too, but him having an accident a few miles from a place called Arcadia seems pretty suspicious. Not to mention Charlie had also just got back from Vegas; he probably went out there too."

"But since you've played it, wouldn't *you* be at risk of going postal too?"

"I don't think so. I didn't spend as much time with it as Charlie did. And if the game was enough to have the complete intended effect, whoever made it wouldn't need to lure players out to Arcadia. There must be something else that goes on out there."

"Jesus… How sure of this are you? I mean, what if we've got the wrong Arcadia? What if this place has nothing to do with it?" she asked.

"I have no clue. We start back at square one. But think of it this way: if I'm right, you are going to have one *hell* of an exclusive story."

"I mean, yeah, but if you're right and there really is some top-secret government project… You shouldn't mention this to anyone else. How much does Jenna know?"

"Enough, but she doesn't believe me."

"Good. Keep this quiet…and Desmond, stay safe."

"I'll do my best."

The call ended. He was glad he used WhatsApp, but even though the call had been encrypted, he knew that if who he thought was behind this was truly behind it, they would have other ways of keeping tabs on him.

A car honked behind him, jolting him back to reality. He looked forward. Not a single vehicle was moving. He sighed.

Just another glorious morning in L.A.

Ricky was playing video games, his PS4 hooked up to a 32-inch LCD screen in one corner of the small living room. He immediately paused it and got up as Lewis entered the room.

"Hey man, Jenna filled me in on everything after you called. That's some fucking crazy shit." He gave him a hug.

"That's one way to put it, yeah," he said as Ricky patted him on the back. He turned to the TV. "What are you playing?"

"The latest *Black Ops,* getting ready for the *Call of Duty* championship this year. I'm still pissed they removed the campaign mode. Fucking cheap bastards, charging $60 for a game with no story."

"I think Jenna's been practicing that one a lot."

"Yeah, *CoD* is her shit."

Lewis sat down on the couch and sighed. He needed to get everything off his chest, all of it, to someone who would understand. Richter had the right idea of not telling people, but nearly every rule had an exception, and he'd been friends with Ricky Ramirez long enough to trust him with his life.

"There's some stuff I need to tell you."

"Yeah man, sure," his friend said, sitting down in a chair opposite him. "Anything."

Lewis noted how people would go out of their way to treat you extra kindly following a brush with death. "It's a long story, and it's already gotten pretty weird." He filled him in on everything from Jake Miller's voicemail, to the dreams, to Arcadia, to the website of Andromeda Virtual Systems, to a highly detailed rundown of the events at Charlie's house.

When he was done, Ricky sat back in his chair. "Whew. I have heard some crazy shit in my life, but that takes the fucking cake."

"You believe me?"

"Of course I believe you, man. It's just fucking nuts, that's all. But it explains a lot." He scratched his chin. "This *reeks* of *Polybius*. What did I tell you?" He laughed. "And that was just supposed to be a joke…Christ."

"We don't have the full story yet, but it's definitely looking that way."

"And this Victor Zhao guy," Ricky said. "I swear I've heard that name before."

Lewis leaned forward. "You have?"

"Yeah, yeah… It was from a while ago, like five years back or something, when I was working at EA the summer after junior year at UCLA. Now, people like Jenna's parents are always going off about video games being 'murder simulators' and what not, but one time there was this dev making a game where you literally played as a serial killer.

"Like, there wasn't even much story, it was just kind of a sandbox thing. And it was really in-depth. You had to choose your M.O. and be consistent with it, had to stalk similar types of victims. And you would drive around the city following these people, observing their habits. The graphics weren't great at this stage, but a lot of detail had been put into the gameplay. The AI of the people you stalked was pretty advanced; they were all randomly assigned habits and paths around the city they would take before returning home at certain times of the day.

"And then you had to kidnap them and choose how to kill them, how to arrange the body, whether you wanted to make it ritualistic or whatnot... Like, it was crazy how much fucking thought they had put into it. 'Disturbing' was the best word for it. The team tried to get EA to back it and publish it, but all the execs were just like, 'No fucking way. Are you people insane? A *serial killer simulator*?' It was going to be called *Bloodlust* or some shit. But the lead dev's name was Victor Zhao or something like that, I swear."

"Did you ever see him? Would you recognize him if I showed you a photograph?" Lewis asked.

Ricky shook his head. "I never saw the guy in person, just heard his name. Everybody thought he was a crazy fuck. After that, he vanished from the industry. I never heard of him again. Until now, of course, if it really is the same guy."

Lewis shook his head. "That's insane."

"What's more insane is how he went from a nobody to suddenly building a state of the art virtual reality theme park that nobody's ever heard of, yet is supposedly booked up until July. It just *screams* front organization to me. I bet the CIA is all over this shit."

"If he did try to make a serial killer simulator, it's no wonder they chose him to head up a project like this. Who better to make a twisted game?"

"I'll tell you what," Ricky said. "I've got a cousin who works in the Nevada State Police. Now, he's based up in

Reno, but we're pretty chill, and he'd probably be okay with doing some digging on Jake's death for me. He should have access to the case file if I'm not mistaken, since it was a highway accident outside of a municipality."

"Wouldn't it fall to a county sheriff's office then?"

"Yeah, but he can probably get access to their system."

Lewis massaged his temples. "I can't believe I'm really going out there tomorrow and doing this shit."

Ricky laughed. "Neither can I, pal. But you and Jenna do me a huge favor and watch your fucking backs out there, alright?"

PART TWO
VIRTUAL ACTUALITY

12

Sunlight brushed across the tops of the palm trees lining the Strip, bathing the sides of casinos in an early evening glow. The road was cast in shadow by the structures on the west side of the thoroughfare. A smile came to Lewis's face as he took in his surroundings.

The last time he'd been in Vegas had been for a trip the summer just before his final year of college, once he and all of his friends had turned 21. Lewis, the youngest of the group, hadn't come of age until a week before the trip. What little he remembered of the weekend had been very good; the rest was an intoxicated blur in his memory.

The rented black Corolla cruised past Planet Hollywood, Bellagio and its famous fountains coming up on the left. Lewis glanced over at Jenna, who sat behind the wheel. A pang of nervousness shot through him as he saw her briefly glance down to check something on her phone.

"Jenna!"

"What, I'm just quickly checking my–" Her eyes

widened and she looked ashamed for a moment, her attention returning to the road. "Right, sorry I forgot how big a deal that is to you. Especially after what happened."

"It's really just a safety concern, nothing personal." But they both knew it was very personal for him. "How far is it now?" he asked.

"With this traffic, no more than five minutes." She'd been here more often than he had for championships and conventions.

And she was right. Roughly four minutes later they took a left and pulled up the main tropical foliage-lined drive to the Mirage complex. Lewis could see a giant glass dome and the hotel itself, which had three wings going off so that it looked like a giant Y from the air. The large porte-cochère was split into two areas by a divider laced with jungle flora, one for taxis directly outside the sliding doors of the front entrance, and the other for valet parking.

Jenna pulled up into the parking area, and a hotel staffer opened the door for her. Lewis stepped out of the passenger side and took a deep breath of chilled air as he looked around. The temperature was in the low 60s, but it was expected to drop down to the 50s or even the high 40s this evening. He'd always found it interesting how the desert could be blisteringly hot in the summer and frigid in the winter. Vegas had even seen snowfall on exceedingly rare occasions.

The valet popped the trunk and pulled out their suitcases. "Thank you," Jenna said, handing him the car keys. She and Lewis pulled up the handles on their luggage and walked over to a path that cut through the divider and led straight to the entrance. Taxis stopped, giving them the right of way.

Lewis began feeling a strange sensation as he and Jenna strolled across the walkway. Once they reached the curb, he stopped and looked back. He could see nothing out of the ordinary, but he could have sworn it'd felt like he was being watched.

"Des!" He turned to see her gesturing for him to follow her inside. "Let's go!"

Taking one last look behind him, he joined her again and together they stepped into the indoor oasis.

Directly ahead was a tropical botanical garden beneath the glass dome, a walkway snaking through it. The area to the left led off into a vast sea of slot machines and gambling tables, while to the right the long reception counter stood in front of a glass aquarium that ran its entire length.

They checked in and received their keycards for a room on the 19th floor. As they walked to the elevators past the casino, Lewis felt the strange sensation again. A quick glance around yielded no apparent stalkers, but this did little to ease his fears. A professional would be highly skilled at blending into a crowd. He quickened his pace.

"Whoa, slow down," Jenna chuckled.

He pressed the button for the lift and tapped his left foot impatiently. The doors finally opened, letting out a businesswoman and a man in a Hawaiian shirt. Lewis and Jenna entered the elevator and he rapidly pressed the Close Door button.

"What's wrong with you?" she asked, half-joking.

Mercifully, the doors closed before anyone else could slip in and the steel box lurched upward.

Lewis breathed a sigh of relief. "Nothing. Travel sometimes makes me a bit anxious."

"I know you're lying."

"I just want to get to the room, that's all."

"Still lying," he heard her mutter under her breath, but the conversation ended there.

The room's window faced south. Lewis saw they had a clear view of the Coliseum of Caesar's Palace and the Eiffel Tower replica across the street. Further down the Strip, Lewis could see the sleek, modern architecture of the Cosmopolitan, and in the far distance, part of the Sierra-Nevada mountain range. He knew the sights would become even more breathtaking once everything lit up for the night, but they were still about an hour from sundown.

"What'd you say we go out on the town tonight?" Jenna's voice called behind him. "Vegas nightclubs are legendary, but I've only been to a few."

Lewis turned around. She was lying on the bed with her hands behind her head, staring up at the ceiling. "I'd like to, but…" He used the first excuse that came to mind. "I'm feeling pretty tired and I'd rather not be around crowds. There's lots to do here, why don't we just stay at the hotel for tonight?"

She propped herself up on one elbow and gave him an understanding look. "Okay, sure." It had, after all, been only two days since his near-death experience. He would be able to coast on that for a while longer. Lewis didn't want to tell her he was worried about them being followed if they left the casino.

Or worse.

Several hours and three drinks later found Lewis sitting beside her at a bar, staring at the wavy wooden paneling that undulated across all the walls around them. The place was called Stack and located on the Mirage's main floor, just out of reach of the smells of cigarette smoke and desperation that characterized the casino.

They'd had an early dinner at another restaurant, then played a couple rounds of low-stakes blackjack. Between the two of them, they'd made a small profit of $20 and had decided to celebrate their luck.

Sitting to the left of him, Jenna downed the rest of her third G&T and asked for another. "How much of this can you expense?" she asked with a grin as she turned to him.

"A fair amount. We shouldn't go crazy, but I'm sure my boss won't mind too much given recent events." And if he was truly onto something, the story he'd write in the aftermath of all this would pay enormous dividends.

He was starting to feel the buzz now, but too many thoughts weighed on his mind for him to enjoy it. Lewis's gaze focused on the wall as his mind shifted through information. The Andromeda website, Victor Zhao's smug grin taunting him, the delivery man trying to warn him as he lay dying in a pool of his own–

"Hey," Jenna said, nudging his shoulder. "You look bummed." She looked a little tipsier than he was.

He briefly smiled back at her, then picked up his glass and examined the remainder of his Blue Hawaiian absent-mindedly in the dim lighting of the bar. "It's just been a big week, that's all."

She leaned closer and whispered in his ear, "I know how I can cheer you up later if you're feeling up to it." He didn't need to look at her to know that she had a big grin on her face.

Lewis put his hand over hers on the counter and looked at her blue-green eyes, his lips forming a genuine smile this time. "That sounds–"

"Whoa, excuse me," said a man in a checkered shirt with a Texas drawl, nearly bumping into them. He sat down on the right side of Lewis. Both he and the blonde woman with him looked to be in their thirties. With his leather cowboy boots and Lone Star belt buckle, Lewis figured the only thing he was missing was a Stetson.

The bartender came over to the new arrivals. "Two whiskey sours," the man said. The bartender nodded and turned to the rack of liquor. The Texan couple turned their attention back to Lewis and Jenna. "And what brings you fine people to Las Vegas?" the guy said, an amiable smile stretching across his face.

Lewis didn't feel in the mood to make small talk, but Jenna rarely missed an opportunity to chat with strangers. It was a wonder she had never gone into politics.

"He had a business trip, but we decided to make a weekend out of it," she said, playfully leaning into him.

"You two ever been before?" he asked. "I'm Hank, by the way. My wife's Sandra."

"A couple of times. My name's Jenna, this is my boyfriend Desmond."

"Are you going to any Cirque du Soleil shows?" Sandra chimed in. She had a similar accent to her husband.

"Not this time," Jenna said. "But I'm trying to convince him to take me nightclubbing."

The bartender returned with the whiskey sours. Hank picked up his and took a sip as he nodded. "Vegas has *great* nightclubs. Sandra and I aren't into that as much anymore, but a couple of years ago we went to a fantastic club. It was unbelievable, felt like I'd stepped into another dimension, or outer space or something. The light show was incredible."

"Yeah, it was really fun," Sandra said, nodding in

agreement. "What was it called again?"

"I don't remember. I was probably too drunk that night," Hank said.

"We both must've been. Nine months later I had Jeremy."

They both burst out laughing, Hank's sounding like a drawn-out hiss and a horse neigh. He slapped the table. Lewis wanted to go.

"So what else are you two doing?" Sandra asked as Hank wiped a tear from his eye.

"We're going to this place called Arcadia tomorrow," Lewis said, speaking up for the first time. "It's kind of a virtual reality amusement park."

Hank nodded in recognition. "Yeah, yeah…oh, who was telling us about that?" He turned to his wife.

"Didn't Dale go to that? He was always really into video games. Wrote reviews about them for the paper and stuff."

"Oh yeah…shit." Hank took a big swig of his drink. "Dale…" He could tell Lewis and Jenna didn't follow. "My cousin. He went out to that place like a month ago or something, right before Christmas. Said it was really cool, like nothing he'd ever experienced. You two will have fun there."

"What happened to Dale?" Lewis said. "If you don't mind me asking…"

"What happened…?" Hank looked confused. "I didn't say he was dead, how did you…"

Neither did I. "Sorry, just seemed like you were talking about him in the past tense."

"He passed away a little while ago," Sandra said, placing a hand on her husband's shoulder.

"I'm so sorry," Jenna said.

"What was the cause?" Lewis said, his shoulders tensing up.

"Suicide," Hank said, nodding sadly. "Don't know why. Seemed like he had everything to live for. Everyone figured he must've secretly been battling depression. There was no note or anything."

"When was this?"

"Just a few weeks ago, actually," Hank said.

Lewis turned to Jenna. "We need to leave now."

They threw 50 bucks on the counter, said goodbye to Hank and Sandra, and left back into the din of the casino.

Lewis watched the bright lights of the city dance outside the window, lulled into a trance by the cars, the flashing words, the distant sounds of traffic. A horrible thought had occurred to him and now it wouldn't leave.

How many people had played *Rogue Horizon*? Did it do to all of them what it had done to Charlie? He recalled Ricky's words, spoken a lifetime ago last Sunday: "If you could make a game with psychoactive effects, it'd probably affect everybody differently." What if not all of its victims turned homicidal; what if the hallucinations and dreams drove some of them to take their own lives instead?

Investigators wouldn't be looking into those cases, nor would journalists looking to pin murders on video game violence. How many more people had died because of this thing that he had no idea about? How many had gone to Arcadia, returned to their corners of the U.S., and killed themselves? He was sure nobody else would see a connection in Hank's cousin's death to the other gamer-related fatalities recently; and even then, only he, Richter, Ricky, Special

Agent Gonzalez, and that *Atlantic* op-ed writer Fenster saw any semblance of a link between all of those.

If there even *was* a link.

But he didn't see any other explanation. They had to be connected. The only thing he didn't understand was how Arcadia fit into it.

Lewis felt a hand on his shoulder and lurched back, then relaxed once he realized it was Jenna. She looked concerned and took him by both of his shoulders.

"Hey, are you alright?"

"Yeah, yeah... Sorry, I don't think I'm down to fool around tonight."

She leaned over and gave him a slow kiss on the cheek, then leaned her head against his shoulder and gazed out the window. "No worries. We should probably get to sleep anyway." She walked back toward the bed and turned around. "We've gotta get up reasonably early tomorrow to trek off into the desert. Arcadia awaits!" She was trying to be cheerful, a big smile plastered on her face.

Lewis froze, feeling goosebumps all over his skin.

Jenna frowned. "What? Was it something I said?"

13

The two-lane highway curved north, taking them further out into an endless sprawl of sand, dust, and low shrubbery. The land rose and fell into hills and ditches. Mountains and higher land rises were visible miles away in each direction. Power lines running on the left crossed over the rented Corolla to the right side as US-93 gradually turned into a longitudinal straightaway.

Without another vehicle in sight, Lewis accelerated into the desert and kept his hands gripped tightly to the steering wheel. He could picture this place at night, dark and moonlit. The place where Jake Miller's life had come to an end.

Jenna sat beside him, navigating Google Maps on her phone. The stereo was tuned to a station currently playing Depeche Mode and Lewis hummed along to the lyrics.

The road gradually curved again as they smoothly slalomed through some rocky hills, then resumed a straight course. They passed by the Coyote Springs Golf Course on the right, then continued on into an interminable expanse of arid land for roughly twenty minutes.

Jenna said, "It'll be coming up on your right soon."

Lewis saw a turn emerge from the far distance and eventually reached the juncture, swerving the car onto an unmarked gravel road that took them into the rocky hills. Craggy rises rose above them now as the path twisted and turned through the land. Lewis saw they were headed northeast as it finally uncurled and became asphalt once more. The terrain got slightly smoother but was still much more uneven than it was along US-93.

It seemed the trail wore on for eternity. Lewis checked the gas tank indicator and was relieved to see it was still three-quarters full. If they got stuck this far from civilization, they'd be screwed. As if someone had read his mind, a gas station appeared over the hill. The sign read "Road Runner's Gas and Diesel" as they sped past it. A shiver shot down his spine. Miller had pulled a gun on a store clerk somewhere around here. With no other businesses in sight, he realized that must've been where the incident took place.

Lewis passed many tiny, dirt-path side roads. "Where's the next turn?"

"Not for another five minutes or so." She looked at him. "Jesus, this place is in the middle of nowhere."

"Not exactly a great business model," he noted.

Eventually, they came to the juncture for Old Highway 93. Lewis took a left and the road snaked to the northeast, then came around and settled in a northwestern direction. Jenna gently tapped her fingers on the window beside her and sighed, staring off into the desert. Even Lewis felt his mind phasing out as the minutes ticked by.

Then, on the horizon, a man-made structure rose up from the sand. He saw what looked like a giant black box, nearly three stories high, and as he got closer, a chain-link fence enclosing the area it encompassed. As they finally pulled up to the complex, he realized it was bigger than it had first seemed. To the left of the parking lot and the main building, the black, modernist warehouse-type structure he'd seen on the Andromeda Virtual Systems website, was a fenced-off construction site and behind that another, smaller warehouse of similar design. On the front of the main building was written in white, bolded letters: ARCADIA.

Lewis turned onto the entrance road, which seemed to go down the entire middle length of the compound and took a right again to pull into the parking lot. The Corolla slid into a spot right in front of the glass double doors to the main building. He and Jenna climbed out of the car. It was bright and sunny, but the temperature was barely 70 degrees. Lewis figured exiting an air-conditioned vehicle here in the summer would feel like stepping into a furnace.

A cool breeze whipped through the air and Jenna brushed her hair away from her face. Lewis squinted and looked around the parking lot. More than half the spaces were empty. He glanced at his watch: 9:04AM.

"Shall we?" Jenna said, gesturing to the doors.

Lewis joined her and they walked toward them together. Abruptly, the tinted glass panes slid open as the couple approached. As Lewis entered the building, he felt as if he were entering the jaws of a giant, rectangular beast.

The lobby was a vast, darkened space. To the right was a lounge area with plush, square-backed reclining chairs and an empty reception counter behind it. To the left stood several arcade machines and on the wall behind them was a giant timeline of VR technological development. Dead ahead was a dark corridor lined with neon blue LED strips running down the sides, looking like a passageway in some futuristic spacecraft. On either side of this hallway, along the back walls of the lobby, were a series of posters advertising the various games Lewis had seen on the website: *Aerial Adventure, Deep Dive*, *Everest Escapade,* as well as a few others such as *Retrowave Rampage, Lunar Latitudes,* and *Mayan Mayhem*. Like the corridor, the lobby was lit by neon blue LEDs, although all the posters and the timeline on the left wall were lit from below with white lights.

Nobody was here.

"Are we early or something?" Jenna thought out loud.

"Actually, you're five minutes late," came a voice. "But I'll forgive you."

The couple looked around them in all directions. No one was in sight.

Then a figure emerged from the hallway ahead of them and Lewis realized why they hadn't spotted him. He wore black from head to toe, his turtleneck matching his dark chinos and loafers. The only splash of color came from his silver belt buckle.

Lewis recognized him immediately from his website photo.

"I've never given a tour before," Victor Zhao said, his voice deep and mellifluous. "But this place is all about trying new things, so in that spirit, it is my pleasure to welcome you to Arcadia."

He walked up to Jenna and shook her hand first. "Ms. Bateman, it's a pleasure to meet you in person. I'm a big fan of e-sports, and I've seen many of your YouTube videos."

"Thank you, Mr.–"

"Call me Victor." He gave her a confident smile, then turned to her boyfriend. "And you must be Mr. Lewis. I'd like to thank you for taking the time to come all the way out here for your article. Word of mouth has been very strong, but a little free press never hurts."

"It's an interesting business strategy, having your place located so far from virtually any amenity. Took us over an hour and twenty minutes to get here. Why build so far from the Strip?"

Zhao shrugged. "Land is very cheap out here. We have water and sewage treatment through the closest town, Caliente, where the staff and myself live. But we try to recycle as many of our resources as we can, especially the water. Our electricity comes primarily from solar."

"Did it cost a lot to get this place hooked up to the grid?" Lewis asked, taking out a pen and his Moleskine notebook from his jacket. Jenna wandered over to the arcade machines.

Through his peripheral, Lewis saw Zhao's eyes watch her as she went. "A fair amount, but given how cheap the land is, it was worth it. And we're expanding the solar panels, so in the long run, we'll be self-sufficient."

"How was this placed financed?"

"The way all startup businesses are financed: private funding from investors, in this case from around the globe. People who are looking to get in on virtual reality before it goes mainstream. And it will go mainstream, Mr. Lewis. Without advertising, we've already secured full slots for the next six months. We were even able to raise prices."

"What's it cost now?"

"It was $100 a day, now it's $120."

"If you're sold out for the next six months, how come you're open and the parking lot is half empty?"

Zhao smirked. "Arcadia opens at 9AM, but we never book any appointments before 10. Visitors may arrive and enjoy the arcade machines and the lounge before beginning their experience. I had Katelyn slot you in at 9 because it would give me time to begin your tour before the first arrival."

"We'll be finished in an hour?" Lewis asked.

"Likely not. At first, I considered forcing you out with the first arrival, but it appears luck is on your side today, Mr. Lewis. Our 10 o'clock called to cancel yesterday."

Convenient, Lewis thought as he jotted down some notes. "So when did this place open, exactly?"

"July 13th of last year."

"And what's your average attendance per day?"

"Every day we have slots for up to 70 bookings."

"You have enough parking spaces for that?"

Zhao smirked. "They come at different times, no one stays the entire day."

"Seems a bit far to drive for a digital dine and dash."

"This place is more than a tourist center, Mr. Lewis," he scoffed. "It is the future of virtual reality."

"Bold statement. Enlighten me."

Zhao sighed. "Come this way." Jenna was currently playing a *Jurassic Park* arcade game, the most recent one from 2015. He could see her shooting at a *Spinosaurus.* "Jenna dear, would you care to join us?"

"Oh, sure," she said, slipping out of the seat. Lewis realized their host had dropped the formality of calling her "Ms. Bateman."

Zhao walked over to the timeline wall and turned to her as he spoke. "Virtual reality is all about deception, convincing the user that they are somewhere they are not, doing something they are not. For years, players of VR games would get dizzy wearing headsets and sitting in chairs while their in-game avatars dove for cover and leaped off buildings. The headset could lie to the user's eyes, but not their whole body. Here, we remedy motion sickness by giving you a physical space to walk around in, while haptic gloves and suits allow you to feel the digital world. But this created another problem: what happens when you run out of space? Simple: we use a technique called *redirected motion*."

He pointed to a diagram of a headset-wearing person walking in a circle labeled "actual motion" while another line labeled "perceived motion" continued straight ahead from their starting point. As he continued, it seemed to Lewis as if Zhao was addressing Jenna specifically rather than the pair of them. "You can think you're moving in a straight line, but really I'll have you traveling in circles all day. I call it the 'desert effect.'"

"Appropriate for a place in the Mojave," she piped up.

Zhao smiled smugly and said, "Indeed it is." He moved over to the next diagram. "What we have here at Arcadia, more so than at any other virtual reality attraction in the world, is an emphasis on changing sets."

Lewis saw an image of a darkened room with rising and falling walls, and objects that popped up out of the ground. "Our illusions are more convincing because we spin them out of reality. I can have any number of differently shaped items appear and your haptic gloves and headsets will feel and display them as anything I want them to. I can have you trapped in an ancient temple by four, real walls. Or those fences could be the sides of a city alleyway that disappear once you leave, a corridor on a lunar base, or just about anything. Haptic feedback only goes so far, but you can't push back against a physical barrier. We also have a number of fog, smoke, and smell machines, all perfectly safe, that contribute to the illusions we create. It's like a virtual set, and we can cast you as the star in any type of story. That's why we call them Studios. There are four of them in this building, that way." He gestured down the hallway he had entered from.

Then he pointed to a diagram of a headset on the wall. It looked bulkier than a Rift or a Vive, like something out of a 1980s sci-fi film. "This is Nebula, our in-house headset and haptic feedback rig. Once suited up, you'll be able to feel vibrations in response to a digital object or character touching anywhere on your legs, arms, or torso. The gloves enable you to hold items that don't exist in the real world or to augment ones that do. I can make you think a square foam block in your hand is the grip of a pistol or the handle of a sword."

The second half of the timeline was labeled *Future Developments*.

"These are our upcoming projects," Zhao explained. "In addition to working on more advanced haptic feedback hardware and higher-definition graphics for our headsets, we're creating a whole new type of Studio, one that's a much more efficient use of space."

The image showed a player wearing a full-body Nebula rig suspended from numerous cables, with fans and mist machines poised from every angle. Lewis noticed the headset looked sleeker and appeared to be actually part of the suit instead of a separate entity. Overall, everything seemed much more advanced.

"The player," Zhao went on, "will be able to rotate 360 degrees in every direction. Once combined with our next generation haptic feedback suit, the Nebula Mark III, we will have achieved the closest thing to a totally immersive simulation in history. And that extends beyond mere video gaming. We already have contracts with the military and NASA to develop realistic combat and space exploration sims. We have a stripped-down version here called *Lunar Latitudes* for the guests, but we're building a whole new structure – I'm sure you saw the construction site on the way in – for training simulators. NASA has paid us handsomely to deliver the most hyper-realistic Mars exploration VR sim in history. We're more than happy to deliver."

He strolled over to the very last diagram. It looked like the strangest of the bunch. The user lay on their back without any form of haptic gear, but a silver, metal band was fitted around the top of their head.

"This," Zhao said, "is our pipe dream. It's still ten years away at the very earliest, but when it arrives, it will change everything. We call it the Dream Machine, and it's exactly what it sounds like. A Brain-Computer Interface, or BCI, that the player controls with their brainwaves. However, after the user is placed in an unconscious state, the Dream Machine will enable us to send images directly into their mind and essentially influence their subconscious thoughts, creating personalized dreams that will feel like hyperreality."

"And you've begun development on this?" Lewis said, somewhat shocked.

Zhao turned to him. He looked surprised to remember that Lewis was still a part of this conversation. "I'm afraid only at the conceptual stage. Like I said, it's at least a decade away from being commercially viable. The Nebula Mark III has to take precedence, not to mention we're pretty busy balancing our daily visitors with construction and developing the simulations for our contracts."

"So what exactly do you have right now?" Lewis asked, growing impatient. Jenna looked mildly bored too.

Zhao gave a conceited smile. Lewis realized he had a very punchable face.

"Allow me to show you."

14

They made their way down the darkened corridor, passing doors for the other Studios. Lewis realized a fourth person had joined them, a short Latina woman with square-rimmed glasses. She held a heavy file folder as she walked a few paces behind them. He didn't see where she'd come from; it was as if she'd materialized out of thin air. Her unexpected appearance and the dim recesses of the hallway made him feel uneasy.

Zhao stopped before the back wall and turned to his left, where a heavy door was labeled STUDIO 3. Behind him, Lewis saw another door on the back wall of the corridor and made out the words "Rear Exit, PERSONNEL ONLY" in the low lighting.

"Given your skillset Jenna, I believe you'll find one of the experiences we offer in Studio 3 to be quite to your liking." He pushed the door open and all four of them walked inside. "This is Katelyn, by the way." He gestured to the woman who had joined them. "I believe you spoke with her on the phone, Mr. Lewis."

"Uh-huh, nice to meet you," Lewis said absentmindedly, his attention now focused on the area around him. It was a large space with several bright, white LED lamps hanging down from above. There were several thin, plastic walls erected around the room that went as high as nine feet tall, and he saw inch-wide slots in the floor where others could pop out. There were also different sized square trapdoors and he guessed this was where other objects could be deposited into the player's game. The air was heavily conditioned in here and he shivered, catching a chill.

Off to the right stood an area with several monitors on the wall and a desk where a bald technician in his mid-thirties sat in front of a keyboard and an additional monitor. A stern black man stood beside him wearing what looked to be a bulletproof vest. Lewis saw he had a pistol holstered to his right hip.

"Heavy security you got here," he said.

Zhao chuckled. "Our security guards have guns primarily for coyotes. Same reason why we have the fence. But we do own a lot of valuable equipment here and we're miles from the nearest police station, so I like to think of it as an insurance policy."

A rack of Nebula suits and headsets were hung up by the wall of monitors. Jenna walked over to them. "So I just put it on, or…?"

"Here, I'll show you," Zhao said, walking over to assist her. Lewis tried not to look annoyed as he pulled a suit off the wall and unzipped it for her. "There's a changing area at the back. Just pull the curtain across."

"Thanks," she said, taking it and slipping off her sneakers. Zhao retrieved a pair of what looked like black athletic boots from the ground beneath the other suits and placed them on the floor for when she returned.

"How long does each game typically last?" Lewis asked.

"Usually around 30 minutes," Katelyn said. He did recognize her voice from the phone.

"And it's all-day access?"

"All-day access, but the users can only play four games a day. It's still roughly 2 hours of playtime, and since each experience is entirely new for them, it feels like a very long two hours. Our exit surveys have all shown high levels of customer satisfaction," Katelyn said matter-of-factly.

Lewis just nodded.

Jenna strolled back toward them barefoot, now wearing her Nebula suit. He got a good look at it: it was gray with black patches around the elbows and knees, and he couldn't help but notice that it fit her figure nicely.

By the expression on his face, Zhao had noticed this too. "You look marvelous," he said.

"Thanks," she said awkwardly, putting the haptic shoes and gloves on.

"Only one thing left." He snapped his fingers. Katelyn retrieved a headset from the wall and returned, handing it to Zhao. He turned it over in the light, admiring his technological handiwork, then helped Jenna place it over her head. He was about to do the strap for her, but she brushed his hands away.

"I've got it," she said. "Don't worry, I've used a lot of VR gear before."

"Right," he said. "How foolish of me."

Jenna put on the haptic shoes and walked out into the center of the gaming area and slid the blocky visor down over her face. "I'm ready," she said.

Sitting at the desk, the technician punched in some

commands on his keyboard. The main LEDs dimmed, but a few spotlights shone on the area of play. A trapdoor opened a few feet away from Jenna and a platform rose with a gray, plastic object that looked like an assault rifle. It reminded Lewis of what the Colonial Marines used in the film *Aliens*. He glanced at the monitors along the side wall, the one in the center showing what Jenna saw through her VR headset.

There were two, semi-spherical views of the same thing: a landscape of purple-blue gridded lines stretching off to infinity. The only thing that occupied the cyberspace was a platform with a high-def render of an assault rifle. The other two monitors, on each side of that one, displayed a full-screen view of what her left or right eye was seeing. It made sense, Lewis figured, given that VR headsets gave their illusions by showing each eye a similar screen.

He decided to focus on the left screen since it had the same view as the right and was more comfortable to watch than the middle. Jenna strode forward through the neon grid toward the weapon. In the real world, she strolled across the gaming area and picked up the plastic prop. The platform immediately began lowering itself back into the floor.

"I'm digging the neon," Lewis admitted.

"I'm a big fan of retrowave," Zhao said. "I even named the game she's about to play after it."

Lewis nodded. Retrowave was a growing genre of music, video games, films, and other media that basked in synthesizers and 1980s retrofuturism. He looked back at the monitor. Jenna's view showed a logo of a bright orange sunset and palm trees behind the large, chromed words: RETROWAVE RAMPAGE, and below them: SHOOT ANYWHERE TO BEGIN.

Both the physical and virtual worlds began to change

around her. In the dark lighting of Studio 3, walls rose up at seemingly random places, while a darkened hexagonal corridor illuminated by orange neon lights constructed itself from the computerized void, stretching away from her until a door appeared at the very end. Jenna did a quick 360 and found another door behind her, but a red light glowed in the center, indicating it was locked.

She spun around and quickly trotted in a straight line toward the other door. Or, at least she thought she did. Lewis saw her walk in an increasingly tight circle while her vision never wavered on the screen. He had to admit he was quite impressed.

The door slid open automatically as she approached it, and she entered a loading bay full of metal crates with glowing green lights along the sides being loaded by armored men onto trucks with glowing red-rimmed tires. The sun was setting outside, bathing the virtual room in an orange hue. He saw storefronts outside across the street with bright neon signs for an arcade and a video store. A large building behind them towered upward and out of sight.

About fifteen feet in front of Jenna was a heavily armored non-player character sporting bulky headgear that looked almost like her VR headset but was clearly some kind of visor. A thin, neon yellow strip radiated from where his eyes would be.

"I want us out of here in five minutes tops. We don't know when the S.W.A.T. team will –" The NPC spotted Jenna's player character and gasped in shock. "Shit, they're here! Kill 'em!" He whipped out a blocky pistol and began firing at her. The other criminals, who had red visors instead of yellow, did the same. Jenna ran to the nearest chest-high crate and got down behind it.

Zhao leaned over to Lewis. "If she leans any part of her body against that crate, the suit will vibrate in that area to give her the illusion of touch. She's probably feeling it on her shoulder right now."

Bullets whizzed by over Jenna's head. Very smoothly, she leaned up over the protective barrier and fired her machine gun at the nearest henchman. The bullets shredded through his armor, blood sprouting from red holes in his chest as he fell back against a stack of crates. Jenna ducked a burst of incoming fire, then physically jumped out from her cover, did a ninja roll across the ground, and brought the gun up in a swift motion toward another criminal. She opened fire, the enemy's head exploding in a ludicrous amount of blood.

The next man was sprinting toward her, raising a shotgun to bash her across the head with it. He didn't stand a chance. Jenna's next round of gunfire blew his arm off at the shoulder and he collapsed to the ground and rolled around as a red geyser spurted from the horrific wound.

Lewis turned to Zhao. "A bit gory, isn't it?"

"It's a shooter game. Were you expecting puppies and unicorns?" he scoffed.

"Just seems a bit excessive, that's all."

Zhao shook his head, watching Jenna slaughter more NPCs on the screen. "I believe violence in video games is an underappreciated art form. It comments upon society's need to satiate bloodlust, yet also fulfills it at the same time."

Jenna swung her plastic prop, smashing the butt of her weapon across the man with the yellow visor's head. He stumbled back, dazed, as Jenna held the rifle at her hip and opened fire. The projectile hailstorm tore him to bloody bits at close range, and what was left fell to the floor in a gory mess. Judging by the entrails strewn about, these enemies were not cyborgs, merely men outfitted in heavy futuristic gear.

Lewis watched as his girlfriend grabbed something imaginary from the side of her waist and made the motion of jamming it into the bottom of her gun, sliding a fresh clip of ammunition home on the screen.

Having cleared the area of enemies, she jogged toward the street. Redirected motion once again tricked her into thinking she was moving straight, whereas in reality she nearly completed an ellipse around the gaming area.

She burst out onto the road and a police officer, dressed in similar attire to the enemies but with a visor that alternated between glowing blue and red, ran out in front of her. "Rookie, thank God you're here." He peered around behind her. "Damn, you made quick work of the Dragon Syndicate's men in the building. But the fight's not over yet. Come on, we're trying to fend 'em off up the street."

He took off running down the road to the left. Jenna took one look in the other direction, where a massive police barricade had been set up, then sprinted after him. There were a couple of DeLorean cop cars parked at different angles, and more S.W.A.T. officers taking cover behind them, occasionally ducking out to fire. Further up the street, the villains shot back from around the sides of ominous black vans with logos of neon orange dragons adorning their sides.

Jenna crouched down by the rear end of a DeLorean and looked up. Tall, black skyscrapers with neon blue and purple windows reached up toward a starry sky. She leaned out from her cover and fired at one of the Syndicate henchmen at the side of a van.

Lewis glanced at the others. Even in the dim light of the Studio, he could still see that Katelyn and the security guard had their attention on the monitors with an occasional glance at Jenna to see how her movements correlated with the virtual world.

Zhao, however, had his eyes fixed solely on Jenna.

After slaughtering countless henchmen on her way up the retrofuturistic street, Jenna's character was finally told by one of her cohorts that she was due for a promotion and a special medal from the mayor. Then everything froze, and the words MISSION SUCCESS appeared in front of her.

Placing the prop at her feet, she pulled the VR rig off and shook her head to straighten out her hair. She looked sweaty and tired but appeared to have enjoyed herself.

"Well done," Zhao said, clapping. "I've never seen someone move like that through this game. Your skill is unparalleled."

Lewis tried not to roll his eyes.

"Thanks," Jenna said in a professional tone, strolling toward them with the headset tucked under her arm. He realized she must've learned how to deal with this kind of attention from all her events, championships, and conventions. It was something she'd probably had to handle a lot given her looks and the predominantly male demographic of her profession.

Zhao turned to him. "Mr. Lewis, don't you think you should play the game yourself? You are writing an article on it, after all." An unpleasant tone had crept into his voice.

"Sure," Lewis said, looking at the Game Over screen on the monitor. "Although I'd prefer to play something a little less bloody."

He smirked. "I have the perfect one for you."

15

Lewis opened his eyes inside the Nebula headset. Legions of stars populated the sky above him, more than he had ever seen before. Slowly, he sat up and looked around. He was in the middle of a vast white, barren rocky landscape full of craters. Nothing else was in sight no matter which way he turned his head. An eerie track played softly in the background, emphasizing the oppressive loneliness of the setting.

Lewis got to his feet, trying not to panic. *It's just a game*, he told himself. He looked around again. There was no buggy or spacecraft to indicate how he had gotten here. It was as if he'd simply teleported to the middle of nowhere. Up in the sky, he could see the Earth far off across the frigid, empty void, and the sun shining its rays brightly down upon the moonscape.

He knew if this were real life, he'd have been blinded by looking at the star, but staring directly at it yielded no pain in his corneas. That was good, reminding himself that he was still on planet Earth, in a darkened room in the middle of the

Nevada desert, wearing a bulky headset that showed him a high-definition virtual environment.

Lewis breathed in and out, feeling calmer. Zhao hadn't told him anything about the game, just that there was no violence. He'd directed him to lie still on his back in the center of the gaming area in Studio 1 and to "use his instincts" once the game began. Unlike *Retrowave Rampage*, there hadn't even been a title screen. He supposed it was all for effect, throwing you out onto the Moon's surface with no explanation.

He turned around in a 360 spin. No, there really wasn't anything in sight. Only one thing to do then. Lewis picked a direction and started walking, one footstep after the other. On the real moon he would've felt lighter and been able to bound across the rocky terrain, but here it just felt like walking normally. Suspension of disbelief was evidently required.

After a while on the same track, he abruptly stopped. Studio 1 wasn't this big, he was clearly being tricked with redirected motion. Lewis walked forward again, paying careful attention to the path of his legs. When he really focused on it, he could tell he was moving in some kind of circle, but his vision showed only forward motion. Noticing the difference made him feel slightly motion sick, so he stopped and went back to pretending he was walking regularly.

It felt like minutes were passing by, but there was still nothing in sight. The creepy soundtrack snaked its way into his ears, making him shiver. "Alright Zhao," he said aloud. "What the hell am I supposed to do?"

No reply.

He knew they were all standing there, the fuckers, watching him stumble around in circles like an idiot. He imagined Zhao with that big, smug smirk on his face and Jenna standing beside him uncomfortably.

Lewis spun around, aggravated, then froze. Off to his right, he saw an American flag in the distance and some kind of vehicle parked beside it. He walked toward it as quickly as he could. As he came closer, he saw the moon buggy was much sleeker and more advanced than the original rovers back from the Apollo missions decades ago.

Just as he walked up to the vehicle, he felt a strange sensation. The same feeling he'd had as he entered the Mirage yesterday.

The feeling of being watched.

Lewis turned around. And then he blinked to make sure his eyes weren't deceiving him. Another astronaut was making their way across the Sea of Tranquility toward him. Its facemask glowed an otherworldly blue.

Frantically, he turned around and climbed into the buggy's driver seat. It somehow felt like he was actually sitting in a chair. Lewis guessed something had probably risen out of the trapdoors. He looked over the controls in a hurry. It seemed like a standard driving set up: steering wheel, accelerator and decelerator, etc. There was a holographic dashboard panel that displayed his current location, speed, and battery remaining. Right now, the charge was at 67%.

He floored the accelerator and felt his haptic suit push him back into the seat as the buggy gunned forward. Off to his left, he saw the astronaut-thing suddenly sprout clawed, reddish-black appendages out of its back and chest, and begin rapidly pursuing him at a frightening speed.

Lewis's hands began shaking, the haptic gloves vibrating to remind him of the digital steering wheel between them. The lunar rover didn't seem to be able to go faster than 30 miles per hour, and he'd already hit that speed.

He glanced behind him. The creature was gaining on him, crawling after him like some hideous spider. His eyes swept around the cockpit for any sign of a weapon, but there was none.

Shit.

The buggy approached a large crater, and as it flew over the outer edge and plunged down, Lewis actually felt for a moment as if he'd floated out of his seat. *How the hell did they do that?* The vehicle crashed back down and vibrations jolted through his suit. His heart pounded violently in his chest. What the hell was Zhao playing at? He'd said this wasn't a violent game. Had the douchebag put him in a psychological horror simulator instead?

As the rover shot over the edge at the opposite side of the massive crater, Lewis realized he'd made a horrible mistake in not looking at the GPS. His vehicle flew down into the mouth of a giant cavern and shuddered violently on impact as the wheels touched down again. Lewis winced, then opened his eyes and saw that the rover's headlights had come on, illuminating a dark tunnel that stretched off deep underground. The rover was currently speeding through it. He remembered reading about lunar lava tubes as a kid and how they'd created various cave systems across the Moon.

Lewis looked behind him again. The thing had followed him down into the tunnel, its blue light swinging chaotically through the dark as it scurried after him up the side and then onto the ceiling of the cave. *Christ, this has to be a nightmare.*

Up ahead, the cave forked off into two different directions. He swerved the rover to the left and held the steering wheel in a turn as he swerved out into a large cavern full of stalagmites and stalactites. The ceiling was open at the top of the cave, the sun casting a glow down into the center of the space. Evidently, the developers had gone for what looked coolest over accuracy since there was no way those spikes could have formed on the moon.

Lewis jerked the wheel to dodge a formation, while the creature jumped of off another rock behind him and scampered after the vehicle. He slalomed between two massive stalagmites, leaning into each turn, then threw his head over his shoulder. The spider-astronaut-thing leaped from one structure to the next, then back down to the ground, running about ten feet behind him.

He looked forward again–

As the front end of the buggy smashed into a large rock. Lewis tumbled sideways out of the car and fell to the ground. He didn't know how they'd created the effect, but it actually felt like he'd been in a minor car crash.

Grabbing a stalagmite beside him, he hauled himself back up. The creature was nowhere in sight. He looked back at the buggy. Its front was wrapped around the base of a thick rocky pillar; definitely out of commission. There was nothing left to do but run. He dashed for the center of the cavern, the area where the sunlight touched the ground.

He heard it above him, leaping from stalactite to stalactite to get the drop on its prey. Thinking quickly, Lewis slid behind the nearest rock formation and pressed his back against the structure. The haptic suit vibrated up and down his spine. He stayed for what felt like ages, just breathing in and out.

He didn't hear it climbing around anymore.

Cautiously, Lewis peered out and looked up and around. It was as if the thing had suddenly vanished. He spotted another tunnel about 200 feet to his left, which appeared to be his only option.

He walked across the cavern at a steady pace, guardedly glancing all around him to make sure the damn thing didn't jump scare him. Now the redirected motion got on his nerves; he knew he was running around a room and not taking a direct path. Nothing around him was real.

Then why are you letting it get to you so much?

Lewis stopped in his tracks and turned around. Zhao had promised him the game wouldn't be violent. Maybe this was all just a trick. Maybe the thing wasn't actually programmed to hurt him.

The creature suddenly jumped down in front of him and stood up, all six additional limbs reaching out in his direction. Two had sprouted from the chest, the other four out of its back. Lewis stood his ground and remained absolutely still, not even daring to breathe.

The astronaut tilted its head to one side, as if curious. Lewis didn't flinch. Then, slowly, using its two human arms, it grabbed its helmet and pulled it off. A blindingly bright blue light shot outward in all directions. Lewis raised a hand to shield his eyes and squinted, trying to get a glimpse of what lay within.

Then his blood ran cold.

Jake Miller's head stood there atop the creature's shoulders. His skin radiated cerulean bioluminescence although his eyes were entirely black orbs. His mouth hung open like a mouthbreather's, a dark substance trailing out of the corner of his lips. Then those lips curled into a cruel smile.

"You should have listened to me," he said, but it didn't sound like the normal Miller. It sounded like two voices in one as if he were possessed by an electronic demon. "I warned you…not to come here…"

The Miller-astronaut then flung itself at him, mouth snarling, arms and spider-like legs poised for attack. Lewis swiftly reached under his chin, unclipped the strap, and pulled the VR headset off in one fell swoop. The clunky piece of technology thudded to the ground.

Lewis fell to the floor breathing heavily, his arms shaking, his heart pumping like a locomotive. Three faces appeared above him: Jenna, Zhao, and the security guard. Jenna looked concerned, Zhao looked confused, and the guard bent down and asked in a voice that sounded very distant: "Are you okay?"

But he didn't answer. Instead, his eyes looked past them up at the ceiling, at the LED strip shining directly down on him, only registering the sound of his own breathing.

16

Jenna handed him a cup of water and rubbed his back, sitting on the edge of his chair. They were in the front lobby's lounge area with Zhao and Katelyn. Lewis brought the drink up to his lips with both hands and sipped it very carefully as if it were a lifeline.

"…really don't know what happened," Zhao was telling Jenna. "*Lunar Latitudes* is just a fun little exploration sim. I don't know what he saw that spooked him so much."

"It looked like he was fleeing from something," she said. "Are you sure there's nothing in the game, no sounds that follow you around or anything?"

"None at all," Zhao replied. "I mean, you watched the same footage from his feed that we did. There was nothing there."

"He's had a rough week. One of his friends died on Monday and then he got…attacked by a mugger the following day. It's why he didn't want to play anything violent here, he's normally fine with gory games."

"I'm terribly sorry to hear that, I really am."

"You son of a bitch."

Everyone looked at Lewis, whose eyes stared straight ahead.

"You know what you did. Maybe nobody else saw that thing, but I did," he continued.

"What thing?" Zhao asked. "The game was just an exploration simul–"

"The astronaut. The one with the glowing blue faceplate. From the video game you made, *Rogue Horizon*." Lewis finally looked up at him, just to gauge his reaction.

Zhao froze there, staring straight at him. Then he said, very calmly, "I'm afraid I don't know what you're talking about."

"How much did they pay you?" Lewis said, smirking. "To create something like that? Or did you do it for the thrill, after your little serial killer simulator got canned all those years ago?"

The CEO of Andromeda Virtual Systems clenched his fists into tight balls at his sides, but his face betrayed no change in emotion. "Mr. Lewis, I think you should take some time off and see about getting a psychiatric evaluation given the recent tragic occurrences you've experienced."

"You'd like that, wouldn't you? Write me off as crazy–"

"Des, please," Jenna snapped.

"There was nothing on that screen," Zhao said. "We all saw it, Jenna, Katelyn, the guard, the technician, and myself."

Katelyn nodded sternly beside him, still clutching her folder.

"When was the last time you had a journalist out here?" Lewis said.

"We've never had one before," Katelyn interjected.

"Really? Because my pal Jake Miller was here last weekend. And then he died not too far from here, in an accident on US-93."

"I've never met anyone by that name," Zhao said. "And I know nothing of any accident. I'm sorry for what happened to your friend, but I don't know what kind of connection you're trying to make by saying he came here. What, that I murdered him?" He laughed, clearly trying to relieve some of his tension.

Lewis didn't let up. "Miller was on to all of you. He came out here to investigate the connection with the game. And he found out something, something about what you do to people here that makes the players go crazy."

"This is all ludicrous," Zhao said to Jenna. "I will not tolerate accusations like this."

"People who've visited this place from all over the country have gone home and lost their minds. Some, like Dale from Texas, kill only themselves because they can't take the dreams and hallucinations anymore. But others, like Charlie Wong, completely lose their grip on reality and butcher the fucking FedEx guy when they knock on their door."

"Please, *stop*," Jenna pleaded.

He continued. "And I bet if I looked up the name of every gamer who snapped in that goddamn *Atlantic* article and cross-referenced them with your directory of previous visits, I'd find every single one of them."

"What are you…?" Zhao just looked confused now.

Jenna got up and started dragging Lewis toward the front entrance. "I am so sorry."

"Not at all," Zhao said calmly. "I'm just sad your first visit to Arcadia had to end like this. I hope before this incident, you both had a wonderful time here."

"We did, thank you," she said.

Then they were outside and into the brightness of the midday sun. It took a moment for Lewis's eyes to adjust. He glanced back at the automatic glass doors as they slid closed and looked back up at the giant text on the side of the building displaying the place's name.

"Well that could have gone better," she said beside him.

He turned to her. "There's something–"

"What the fuck do you think is happening here?!" Jenna blurted, exasperated. "You sound like a goddamn conspiracy theorist!" She walked over to the car door and threw it open.

"Jenna, please listen to me–"

"Get in the fucking car." She looked angry as hell.

Lewis obeyed and climbed into the passenger seat. Jenna got in, closed the door, and started the vehicle. "If you really thought this was some covert government research site, why the hell would you tell them that you're onto their master plan right to their face?"

"I wanted to gauge his reaction."

"So you're not sure yet."

"Well, I don't have any concrete evidence right now, but everything points–"

"Points to what?" she said, putting the car into reverse and backing out of the space. Lewis noticed that there didn't seem to be any more cars here than when they'd first arrived.

"Points to this being the epicenter of the gamer-related violence in the last six months."

"Those aren't connected and you know it."

"It was the only thing vaguely related to *Rogue Horizon* in the area." He had to admit, it was a pretty flimsy connection. "But as soon as I started looking into this place, I knew there was something fishy about it. Where are all the guests? What kind of venture capitalist funds a theme park in the middle of the desert, and then doesn't advertise it? This whole thing has to be a front for *something*."

"And if it really was, we'd be dead by now. They wouldn't have just let us walk out of there."

"No, I knew they wouldn't kill us. The gamers always get released back into the world so they can…go home…"

The realization just dawned on him. What if they'd already mucked around with his mind during the gameplay, placed subliminal images in it that only he could register because he'd played *Rogue Horizon*? Maybe that was the second half of the brainwashing. He glanced over at Jenna. Maybe she'd had it too and was just better at hiding it. What if they were both ticking time bombs, and Zhao had just sent them back out into the world, ready to sit back and watch the next results of his twisted experiment roll in on the news? If they didn't kill anybody until they got back to L.A., there might even be a new article in the *Atlantic* or some other journal criticizing the City of Angels' gaming scene for producing murderers the likes of Charlie, Jenna, and himself.

He shook his head. Maybe he really was just drawing conclusions from a pile of unrelated cards. Arcadia could be a front for something else, or it could just be a really poorly thought out business strategy. Heaven knew there were plenty of those in the world. And maybe *Rogue Horizon* was just a game that really got under some people's skin. Who knew what Charlie had been going through before he'd played it? He'd gone to Vegas, but that didn't mean he'd made the nearly hour-and-a-half trek out to this desolate patch of land off Old Hwy 93.

Still, Lewis couldn't help but feel that he was missing one definitive piece of proof that would tie it all together.

They were now turning back out onto the stretch of desert road. Jenna gunned the engine and they sped southwest, the Arcadia compound quickly diminishing in size in the rear-view mirror.

"Even if you are right," she said, "it'll just have to be one mystery we never know the answer to."

After watching the car disappear off into the distance, Victor Zhao stepped back inside through the automatic glass doors and brought his cell phone to his ear. It rang several times, then finally clicked as the person on the other end answered.

Zhao spoke first. "We have a problem."

17

"I think I'm becoming a paranoid lunatic," Lewis announced to no one in particular.

"Happens to the best of us," the bartender said, handing him his third margarita.

He sipped it and looked around. It was roughly 2PM and he'd made up his mind that he was going to get drunk. It was past 5 o'clock on the East Coast, and that was good enough for him. Jenna sat beside him, nursing her second G&T. They'd had some fun times getting wasted together. This would not be one of them.

Lewis glanced around the Dolphin Bar. It was located in the Mirage's pool area, surrounded by lush tropical foliage and the sounds of running water. This, combined with the alcohol and beautiful weather, was almost enough to make him feel better.

However, he couldn't get thoughts of Zhao out of his mind. He knew the accusations had been impulsive, but he'd really wanted to see if he could get a reaction out of him. And with the mention of *Rogue Horizon*, he was sure he had. As a journalist, Lewis could sense when people knew more than they were letting on. And Zhao seemed to know a lot more, restraining himself as best he could. The clenched fists had been a real giveaway. Anyone else would've simply had Lewis escorted out by security at that point. But Zhao let him talk and probably would've let him keep talking had Jenna not dragged him out.

He wanted to see how much I knew, Lewis thought. *The bastard was probing.* Then why had he been so angry? *Probably didn't like being reminded of what he's* really *doing, doesn't want to think of the ethical implications of his work.* He could imagine some CIA spook selling him on the project as a great research opportunity for both video gaming and neuroscience, laced with a little patriotism to remind him that he'd be somehow helping fight the good fight.

He sipped his margarita absent-mindedly. What purpose did Arcadia serve in all of this? Why lure everyone out from across the country to the same point? To anyone trying to piece the mystery of the murderous gamers together, the connection would be obvious. Getting people to believe it was the hard part, and Lewis bet Zhao and his associates were banking on that. But clearly, *Rogue Horizon* alone wasn't enough to drive people to commit violent acts. Something else was needed to set them off, a neurological switch that had to be flipped.

Granted, there was a lot of Arcadia they hadn't seen. It was entirely possible the main building was just a front to lend an air of legitimacy to the whole operation, but there'd been some kind of second building and more space behind the first. Not to mention that construction site. Lewis highly doubted they were really building a NASA training ground.

At this point though, he'd reached a dead end. There was nothing concrete he'd been able to draw from his visit earlier today and he couldn't go back there now. He wondered what Zhao would do. The lack of Google results indicated that he and his associates were trying to bury their front as far as possible. If that really was the case, they might try to interfere with him in some way before he left Vegas.

Lewis sighed and shook his head. He was losing his mind. Maybe it really was best just to let this all go. Drop the article, go back to his other story, to L.A., to some semblance of the life he'd had before this all started.

"You look deep in thought," Jenna said.

He snapped out of his reverie. "Sorry." He sipped his margarita again.

"Maybe we should do something fun tonight, take our minds off all the shit that's happened." She nudged his shoulder. "Maybe finally go to a nightclub?" She smiled and looked hopeful.

He shook his head. "I feel too tired today. Maybe tomorrow night, for our last night on the town. I'd honestly rather just chill back in the suite and watch a movie."

She sighed, understanding. "Okay."

He thought for a moment. "I think I'm gonna take a walk around the pool area. Just for five minutes or so. I'll be right back."

"Alright," Jenna said. She seemed emotionally deflated.

Lewis felt bad leaving her there, but he had to make this call. There was only one person who would still believe him. He strolled off to a secluded area of the pool, the only spot he could find that was devoid of sunbathers, and leaned against a tall palm tree.

Ricky picked up on the third ring. "Hey man, what's the

sitch with Arcadia?"

"Not great." He filled him in on the events of the day.

"Jesus," he said. Lewis could imagine him shaking his head with a hand to his forehead. "You shouldn't have gone off on Zhao like that. I know it's been a rough week, but you gotta keep it together, man."

"I'm not sure I can. I'm worried it may already be too late."

"For what?"

"I think that they shoved some subliminal imagery into my gameplay and that that's how they trigger the mental breakdowns, like what happened to Charlie and the others."

"Yeah, I'm not so sure about that," Ricky said. "That's not how subliminal messaging works. If it did, there'd be no reason to lure everyone out to Nevada, just playing *Rogue Horizon* by itself would induce the psychoactive effect. And you wouldn't be able to do anything that much different with the game they had you play, it was still a VR experience with a headset. I don't see how the haptic suit could have anything to do with brainwashing."

"So you think there's something else they do there. A whole process I haven't seen," Lewis stated.

"That's my best guess, but what that is I have no fucking idea." He paused. "Oh, my cousin in the Nevada State Police got back to me."

Lewis raised his eyebrows. "What'd he say?"

"Well, he had to call one of the Highway Patrol cops who work US-93. Most of the casework was handled by the Lincoln County Sheriff's Office, but the highway guys kept a close eye on that one, mainly because nothing ever really happens out there."

"And?"

"Turns out there was some debate over whether it was truly an accident. You see, the coroner believed the injuries Miller actually died of, a crushed ribcage and internal hemorrhaging, happened *after* the crash since he probably wouldn't have been able to crawl that far otherwise. Unless he was a really tough bastard."

"Yeah, Jake wasn't."

"And the toxicology report just came back today, so my cousin was able to snatch this detail: Miller was clean, no drugs."

"Figures. So why didn't they investigate further?"

"Pressure from the Sheriff. He wanted the case wrapped quickly and quietly."

"Why?"

"He didn't give a reason, just insisted it was an accident and that they were wasting their time because there was no indication the car had been rammed off the road. But I think you and I have seen enough movies to know the real reason."

Lewis massaged his temples. "Shit, no one else believes me about this."

"Say, you ever play the original *Deus Ex*?"

"Yeah," Lewis said. "Love that game."

"Remember how throughout the beginning, you hear all these conspiracy theories about various global events from different characters and as the plot progresses, *every single one of them turns out to be correct*? I'm starting to feel that way about the *Polybius* joke I made on Sunday. I'm starting to genuinely think I was on the money and didn't even know it at the time."

Lewis nodded. "Could be."

"The question is, now what?"

He gazed out at the pool. "I've got an idea. But it's a

really bad one…"

18

Lewis sat on the edge of the bed wearing a t-shirt and boxers, staring blankly at the nightly news. The hotel room's TV was the only source of illumination in the room, save for the light that curled under the bathroom door. He could hear Jenna just finishing up her shower. She'd probably be out soon, so he needed to think quickly.

The registry was the key to everything and it was probably sitting there in Arcadia's main lobby, or on the receptionist's computer. If he could just get on there, he was sure he'd find the name of every person listed in that *Atlantic* article, plus Jake Miller and Charlie Wong. If he could send that to FBI Agent Gonzalez, it would be the crucial evidence she needed to get a warrant for Arcadia.

Unless of course, she was in on it. But in that case, he'd have to write up an article for the *Technologist* and tell Richter that if anything happened to him, she should go ahead and publish it along with the document.

Arcadia should be closed by now. Surely, he could scale

the fence and find some way in. And even if he couldn't, he'd at least be able to get a better look around the place.

Lewis shook his head, snapping out of it. It was all bullshit. There was no way he'd be able to get in there and hack the computer. Who the hell did he think he was, Jason Bourne?

The bathroom door opened and Jenna stepped out in her pajamas, still drying her hair with a towel. "Hey," she said. "Wanna watch a movie?"

"Honestly, I think I'm too tired. Sorry, we'll do more fun stuff tomorrow, I promise."

"No worries. Are you feeling better?"

He nodded. "Yeah… Much better."

"I'm just glad we can finally put this whole Arcadia thing behind us," she said, climbing into bed.

He gazed blankly at the TV, lost in a trance. "Me too."

Lewis grabbed the remote and turned the screen off, then came around to the other side of the bed, turned on the lamp, and climbed in. He gave Jenna a peck on the cheek, but as he pulled away she drew him in again and their lips met for a long kiss.

After, he said, "Hey, I just really want to thank you for coming out here and going all the way to the middle of the desert. It means a lot to me."

"It was nothing, really. It was actually pretty cool to go to a place like that."

"I'm sorry the owner was such a creep."

Jenna gave a dismissive wave of the hand. "I've dealt with worse. Let's not think about it anymore."

She kissed him and the next thing he knew she was straddling him and everything moved in a blur. Her shirt came off, then his, then the rest of their clothing, and for the first time all week, *Rogue Horizon* receded into the depths of his mind.

He stumbled out of the forest again, back onto that same road, falling onto his hands and knees as he did so. Cursing, he got back up and looked toward the wreck of the SUV lying in the middle of the asphalt.

The mother was still there with her son, still looking to the stars, still uttering those same damn words over and over: "Everything's gonna be alright." The astronaut-thing stood watching them with its back to him. Slowly, it turned around, shining the blue glow toward him.

"You're not going to forget me too, are you Desmond?" came Miller's demonic, synthesized voice from within its helmet. "You're so good at letting things go."

There were tears in Lewis's eyes now. "No, I'm not. You know I'm not. It took forever…"

"You know it's been there all this time," the thing said, stepping closer. "It never left. You pushed it into the dark recesses of your mind, locked it up, and threw away the key."

"What the hell do you want?"

The astronaut walked over and began circling around him, moving past his shoulder. "I want to help remind you whose fault all this was."

The little boy was crying, looking up past his mother to the twinkling night sky, doing anything to prevent looking back at the wreck he'd just survived.

"You did this, Desmond," the voice continued from behind him. "You nearly killed them both. Do you remember?"

Softly, he said, "Yes."

"And to think," the creature said, coming up beside him, "it was all because you wanted to be an astronaut."

Lewis could feel the tears rolling down his cheeks, but the rest of his body remained perfectly still. "Yes," he said again. "Yes, it was all my fault."

"You run away from everything. But do you really think you can run away from this without knowing the answer?"

Suddenly, the little boy turned toward Lewis and said, "*Arcadia awaits.*"

His eyes flashed open. The digital clock on the nightstand read 10:45PM. He'd been asleep for about half an hour. Very carefully, he looked over his shoulder toward the other side of the bed. Jenna lay naked on her back, breathing in and out in a deep sleep.

Lewis got out of the bed as quietly as he could. Using his phone's screen as a light source, he rummaged around in his suitcase for some underwear and a pair of black jeans and a black shirt to go with his jacket. He needed the clothing to be as dark as possible. Once dressed, he grabbed a USB flashdrive out of the suitcase's inside pouch and slipped it into his pocket.

Taking the rental car keys and being careful to make sure his girlfriend was still asleep, he slid out the door and closed it gently behind him. Then he walked down the hallway to the elevator, pressed the button, and patiently waited for the lift to arrive.

This is crazy, he thought. But he knew he had to go. He could feel an unseen force, pulling him, willing him back out into the desert.

Arcadia awaits.

The image of the kid was seared into his mind. He'd stared straight into Lewis's eyes with a blank look, the words spilling from his lips. That's what had really gotten him. He wanted more than anything in the world to forget that terrible night long ago, to forget about Arcadia and the game, and to just climb back into bed with Jenna.

The doors in front of him parted and an empty elevator waited for him. He hesitated for a moment, placing his foot in front of the sensor to keep the door open.

"What are you waiting for?" came the astronaut's voice again. Lewis didn't dare look behind him.

I don't think I can really do this.

"You're afraid of what you'll find."

No, it's just the whole thing is stupid. What if I get caught breaking and entering?

"If these people wanted you dead, you'd be dead already. You said so yourself."

Lewis stepped into the elevator and pressed the button for the lobby. The doors closed and he felt the carriage begin its descent. "Good," the voice echoed. "Maybe you'll actually resolve something for once in your life."

His eyes slowly swept around the elevator. He was alone.

The doors opened and he stepped out into the lobby, walking past couples and groups of friends in expensive suits and fancy dresses. He felt underdressed even walking to the parking lot. Strolling beneath the glass dome amidst the botanical garden, everything around him felt like a trance. He scarcely believed he was really going through with it but was powerless to stop.

They hadn't valeted that afternoon. Lewis finally reached

where they'd left the rental car, slowly opening the door and climbing in. He took out his phone once he'd turned the vehicle on and put the address for Arcadia into Google Maps. At this time of night, it would take him an hour and seven minutes.

He drove the car out of the garage, turned onto the Strip, and headed north. Bright lights of all colors swept across his windshield as he passed by the last few casinos before the signs and excitement began to peter out. Lewis turned left onto Sahara before he got to the Stratosphere and took it over to the northbound entrance for the Las Vegas Freeway.

"Remember what you're doing this for," the astronaut said as the lights of the city receded behind him.

"Refresh my memory," Lewis said. At this point, he was genuinely lost.

There was a pause, and he thought he heard the voice cackle softly, but only for a brief moment. Then it spoke again.

"Closure."

19

A pair of headlights streaked by him going the opposite direction, then his view returned to the empty dark road before him. His car's own lights revealed stretch after stretch of asphalt taking him further away from the city into the desolate Mojave. Behind the wheel, Lewis felt fatigued but didn't lose his focus. The Corolla never swayed in its lane.

Several times over the past hour he had told himself that he was in control, that he could go back to the hotel at any time now, that he didn't have to do this.

The astronaut hadn't spoken to him for a while, and that made him feel relieved. The voice made him think of Miller beneath the helmet, with black eyes and bioluminescent skin, his speech distorted into an electronic menace.

He finally reached the unnamed road and hung a right, the tires crunching over the gravel just as they had done that morning. Lewis realized he hadn't looked at Google Maps once this entire ride; the memory of the route was carved into his brain. The car turned left onto Old Hwy 93, and he knew this was the final stretch, the last chance to turn back.

Despite this knowledge, he didn't alter his course. It didn't even feel like he was guiding the steering wheel anymore. Several minutes later he saw the compound approaching up on his right, several lights still on at the front of the main building. That seemed odd for this time of night; the place should've closed up hours ago. As he got closer, he swerved the car off the road and barreled over the uneven desert terrain.

Lewis stopped, turned off the vehicle, pulled out the keys, and grabbed the door handle beside him. He took a deep breath. There was no going back now.

He opened the door and swiftly shut it behind him. The car's interior lights were still on, but they'd soon shut off. Keeping low, he began jogging toward the complex. The moon looked to be full in the sky, so it wasn't too difficult to see now that his eyes had adjusted.

Lewis was still about 200 feet from the fence when he heard the sound of vehicles approaching from the road behind him. He spun around and crouched down. Two pairs of headlights were traveling up Old Hwy 93. The rental car's lights had mercifully shut themselves off by now. As they passed, he could make out a black Chevy Suburban and a Malibu of the same color right behind it. They turned right at the entrance to Arcadia and swung around into the parking lot.

He moved briskly toward the fence, then got on his hands and knees to crawl closer.

People were getting out of the cars, dressed in security attire or suits. He recognized the guard from earlier, helping a figure with a bag over their head and their arms tied behind their back climb out of the rear of the Suburban.

Jesus, Lewis thought. Had they kidnapped somebody?

There wasn't enough light for him to make out anybody's face. The suited figures remained in the shadows, although it appeared there were five people plus the hostage. Then they disappeared through the front glass doors.

He scurried back into a darker area of the fence, away from the lighting at the front of the building. Holy shit, he hadn't expected anybody to be here, and he certainly didn't expect to witness a crime taking place right in front of him. He should've filmed it. Forget the registry, if he could get footage of Arcadia employees committing a federal felony, he'd have more than enough to take to Gonzalez or Richter.

Lewis looked up. The fence was about eight feet high. He jumped up and grabbed the highest handhold he could reach with his right hand, then a slightly lower one with his left. He shoved the front of his right sneaker into a gap about three feet off the ground and pushed himself upward, grabbing two higher handholds and then bringing his left leg up. Eventually, he reached the top and carefully slid his right leg over, then his left, all the while clutching the metal bar tightly. He lowered himself about half of the way down, then dropped the last four feet or so, bending his knees to absorb the impact.

He now stood in a roughly ten-foot gap between the side of the main building and the fence. It ran the length of the building and opened out into the parking lot ahead of him; there was an open space at the back of the lot in the opposite direction. Trying to get in through the front door probably wouldn't be the best idea. Also, he hadn't seen much of the property's rear and wanted to get a better picture of the place.

By keeping directly beside the building, he was entirely in shadow. Lewis moved this way until he reached the back corner of the warehouse-like structure, and carefully peered out. Behind the main building sat several rows of large solar panels. Zhao hadn't been lying about Arcadia's self-sufficiency. Though he couldn't see them, he knew there would be several more rows atop the edifice he was currently hiding behind.

The fence continued around the back of the solar equipment, and Lewis saw the other building he'd only caught a glimpse of this morning when he and Jenna pulled in. Like the main one, it was ostensibly a black cube-shaped structure, and like the main building, it had several front lights on. He looked up and along each of the two sides of the structure beside him that were currently visible. Seeing no cameras, he darted forward into the rows of solar panels and took cover behind one of them. Then he continued moving forward, using the energy equipment as cover.

He heard a door opening and looked out from behind a panel to see three people walk out with the hostage. Once they came out into the light a little more, he made out the faces of the guard, Katelyn, and the technician from earlier. The door had swung wide open on their way out and it was closing slowly.

Lewis saw his chance.

He ran as quietly as possible, trying to keep his heels off the ground, managing to grab the door handle with an inch to spare before the door closed. Neither the guard, the technician, nor Katelyn noticed him, seemingly engaged in conversation with each other about thirty feet away.

Pulling the door open slightly more, he stuck his head inside. The corridor was even darker than it had been during the day, but there was still enough illumination from the neon blue LED strips running down the side of each wall for him to judge that the coast was clear. Swiftly, Lewis slipped inside, the door clicking shut behind him.

His heart pounded very, very quickly.

Lewis listened carefully for any sounds, but none came. He inched down the hall toward the main lobby. As he came out into the open space, he decided it had a far more sinister ambiance that it had in the morning. The three arcade machines stood across the way to his right, just beside the entrance. Their screens were all turned on, blank white and occasionally flickering.

His gaze swept around the room. He appeared to be alone.

Lewis walked over to the reception desk and climbed over, keeping low as he took out his phone and turned on the flashlight feature. He waved it over the reception desk, looking for a binder or logbook of any kind, but the surface was bare save for a landline telephone, computer monitor, mouse, and keyboard.

Lewis moved over to the keyboard and tapped the spacebar a couple times. He could hear the desktop whirring to life below the desk, and a second later the screen flashed on, displaying a standard Windows 10 log-in screen. The user was called "ArcadiaReception."

He tried "roguehorizon", "arcadiaawaits", and "blueastronaut", along with a couple variations in capitalization but none worked. Lewis sat on the ground and gazed up at the monitor, feeling defeated. There was just no way he was going to hack this thing.

Wait. There was something there, attached to the desktop just above the glow of its power button. A post-it note. *No fucking way*, he thought, illuminating it with his phone. Sure enough, it read "Retr0w@veBl00dlust".

Retrowave Bloodlust. Zhao's favorite music genre and

the name of his serial killer simulator. Over the past few years, people writing down their complicated passwords on post-it notes and leaving them on office desks had become a real security risk. Whoever had put this here, probably either Zhao or Katelyn, had assumed that by keeping it on the actual computer beneath the desk, it would've been safer.

Happy to prove them wrong, Lewis punched in the 18-character code and a galactic desktop background appeared. There didn't seem to be much on here, just some promotional material files and the icons for the internet browsers Chrome, Edge, and Firefox. He opened up the file explorer and went to the Documents folder. There he found what he was looking for: "guestregistry.xlsx."

He clicked it open.

A spreadsheet containing the name and date of everyone who had visited Arcadia since July 13, 2018, along with the time of their appointment, appeared before him. He didn't bother scrolling. Instead, he opened the search-bar and began entering specific names. His pulse quickened with every row that it highlighted.

Lola Hayworth, who'd shot her YouTube gamer boyfriend Shane Dempsey, had visited on August 16, 2018. Trevor Mann, who'd strangled a friend before pitching himself off his high-rise balcony, came by on October 20th. Dan Folsom, the college student at UC Santa Barbara who'd gone home for Thanksgiving to butcher his mother and hospitalize his sister, went to Arcadia on the 10th of November. There were two people on the list with the name Dale, one Callahan and one McGregor, but he'd bet one of them was the cousin of the man he and Jenna had met at that bar in the Mirage.

And then there was Charlie Wong, with his name entered

for last Saturday: January 19th, 2019.

Jake Miller didn't make an appearance, but aside from that nothing about this document surprised Lewis. It frightened him to finally have proof and he feared the implications of being correct, but here it was it. It didn't even shock him that only about thirty people had visited the VR attraction since its opening. He didn't know what funding was keeping them afloat, but he could guess.

The only thing left now was to get the file out of here. Lewis pulled out the flashdrive he'd stashed in his pocket earlier and slotted it into one of the desktop's USB ports with the help of his phone's illumination, his hand trembling as he did so.

Quickly, Lewis opened an additional file folder window and copied the spreadsheet onto his device. As soon as he did so, he heard a noise, and his head whipped to the right. Someone was approaching from down the corridor. Abruptly, Lewis yanked his USB stick out and turned off the monitor. He slid underneath the desk and hid next to the computer.

Lewis listened very carefully, but at first all he could hear was the soft humming of the device's internal fans beside him. Then he heard the footsteps again. Louder, closer.

The person had entered the main lobby.

Lewis tried to keep his breathing as quiet as possible. He just needed to wait here until the guard left, then sneak back out the way he came – no, maybe that was too risky now. There seemed to be more activity at the rear of the compound than at the front. Okay, so he'd slip out through the front doors, scale the fence, get back to his car, and then get the hell out of here. But he had to be careful to not let them spot his headlights. Miller had probably been killed on the run, speeding away from this place, just as Lewis was about to attempt to do.

Suddenly, a beam of light swept over the desk and along the back wall, then moved out of sight. Shit, they were searching the area. Something had set them off. The flashlight moved back in his direction and stayed there, swaying gently back and forth across the desk. Lewis heard the footsteps getting louder as the person drew closer.

Thoughts raced through his mind. How well could he throw a punch? If he took the person by surprise and found a gun on them, maybe he'd have a fighting chance. There didn't seem to be many people here, he could shoot his way out if he really had to. Not that he'd ever fired a gun before, but he'd watched enough TV, played enough games. It was time to put the theory that video games trained you to use weapons to the test, although he feared his PlayStation controller may have inadequately prepared him for how to pull a trigger.

The flashlight clicked off. He heard several loud footsteps receding, followed by some softer ones. Then nothing. Lewis started to breathe easier. He waited a few more seconds, then slowly began to crawl out from under the reception desk. Grabbing the edge, he pulled himself up and looked out at the lobby.

He didn't realize that the opaque spot just off to his right was a person until they swung a heavy object – probably the flashlight – at him, a dark blur flying toward him out of the blackness. Lewis ducked and the instrument passed over his head by less than an inch. Thinking quickly, he jumped over the desk, past the guard, and began running for the door.

The entrance slid open in response to his approach and a gunshot went off somewhere behind him, a bullet whizzing by his head. Lewis dashed out into the chilly night air, turned on a dime, and began pumping his legs toward the fence off to the left. He tried not to think of how unlikely it was that he'd make it back to the car without being shot. Even if he made it around the corner of the building before the guard could get a good shot at him, he'd undoubtedly catch up by the time Lewis made it over the fence.

Then, just as he rounded the bend, a figure leaped out of the shadows in front of him. He saw a fist sail through the air toward him at a frightening speed. Then it connected with his forehead.

There was a sudden burst of pain, then blackness.

20

Lewis bolted upright, gasping. He lay in the hotel bed unclothed, Jenna still sound asleep beside him. A stream of daylight shone in from between the closed curtains. He put a hand to his head. It still hurt but didn't feel like it was bruised. Throwing the sheets off, he leaped out of bed, pulled his boxers on from off the floor, and began frantically searching through his suitcase.

His clothes from last night were there, neatly folded as if he hadn't worn them. He reached into both of the jeans' pockets. The flashdrive was gone. *Shit*. He looked all around the room. Nothing seemed to have changed from when they went to bed last night. The car keys were even precisely where he left them.

Jenna stirred in the bed and rubbed her eyes. "Morning," she said, stretching her arms. She pulled the sheets closer to cover her bare chest as she sat up. "Sleep well?"

He didn't answer, merely staring at her with a curious look.

She tilted her head slightly to one side. "Des, what's wrong?"

"Do you remember me leaving the room last night?"

She looked confused. "You left? No, I didn't notice anything. I think yesterday really tired me out, especially that game. I slept like a rock."

Lewis put a hand to his head. Did he remember anything after the second guard had hit him? It seemed like there was something there, but he wasn't sure if it had been a dream while he was unconscious. As for how they got him back here, it wouldn't have been that hard. If people really had been watching him and Jenna as they entered the Mirage, they'd have known this was where they were staying. Lewis had had his room keycard in his pocket. One of the guards could have just pretended they were one of his friends, helping him back to his place because he'd gotten blackout drunk during a night on the town. They could have walked up to the counter and asked which room the card belonged to.

Then they would've brought him back up, stripped him, placed him in bed, and folded his clothes to put them away and give the illusion that he'd never left. The thought made him shiver. He didn't know how they'd put the car keys in the right place. Maybe just a lucky guess.

Or maybe they had cameras in the room.

He began walking around, looking all over the walls. Jenna laughed. "What the hell are you doing? Where did you go last night?"

Lewis kneeled down beside the bed and put her hand in his. "I need you to believe me."

She started to look concerned. "Okay..."

"I went back to Arcadia last night. I climbed the fence and snuck in. The shit I saw was crazy. There were still people there, even though it was almost midnight. And these black cars pulled in, and they got out with a hostage, someone with a bag over their head. They took the person to one of the other buildings. I didn't see what they did with them, but I managed to get back into the main lobby and access the computer."

"What? How?"

"Some dipshit left their password on a post-it note attached to the computer, underneath the desk. I got into the registry of everyone who'd visited Arcadia since it opened. And guess what? Barely anyone has. There are many days when they have no visitors at all. But that's not the strangest part. I looked up the names of everyone listed in that *Atlantic* article, the gamers who went nuts and killed people. Every single one of them had gone there about a week before they died. Even Charlie's name was there."

She put a hand to her head. "Oh my god."

"I know it sounds–"

"Ridiculous? Because it is, Des. You had a fucking dream!"

He gave a sharp exhalation of breath and lowered his head. Of course she wasn't going to believe him, he sounded batshit insane. And without the flashdrive, he had no proof. That's why they hadn't killed him, they knew nobody would believe him. And the fewer people who died related to Arcadia, the less suspicious it seemed.

Lewis looked back up at her. Jenna's facial expression was a mixture of sadness, disappointment, and distress. "I think you need help."

"What I need is someone who'll believe me about this."

"No, you need a fucking therapist."

"Jenna, please…"

"There's nothing wrong with therapy. I've done it for

many years, and it really helped me get in control of my borderline. You're probably developing some form of PTSD from Charlie trying to kill you, which is perfectly understandable."

Lewis looked off at the window. The stream of light from in-between the curtains illuminated tiny specks of dust drifting through the air. He tried hard to think about that vague image in his mind, which slowly became clearer.

Lab coat. He'd seen someone with a lab coat, the technician. Was that a memory or just a dream? There had been other people there too, looking down at him. Were they checking if they'd given him a concussion before taking him back to the hotel?

"Jenna, it wasn't a dream. I really, really wish it had been. But that's just what they want you to think."

She rolled her eyes. "Jesus Christ, you sound like Agent Mulder from the *X-Files*."

"And he always wound up being right, didn't he?"

"No, sometimes Scully was correct. Mulder would come up with some outlandish theory, she'd offer a more logical explanation, and then the truth would often be somewhere in between."

"But in all the episodes dealing with the main conspiracy, Mulder was on the money."

"Des, it was just a TV show. Entertainment is not the same thing as reality."

"No, but the truth can be stranger than fiction."

Jenna nodded. "It can be, but that doesn't mean that a virtual reality theme park is the front organization for a government test project. I mean, do you not recognize how ludicrous that sounds?"

He did admit it sounded crazy. "But I was there last

night. If it was a legitimate place, I'd be in a Lincoln County jail cell for breaking and entering. But if they'd done that, I would have told the police about the kidnapping. So they had two choices: kill me, or bring me back here and leave everything the way it was so that you or anyone else would just think I'd had a bad dream. Hell, they might've even wanted *me* to think that."

"And why didn't they kill you?"

"Too many deaths, too soon. Looks suspicious, draws too much attention to them. They must know the Feds are onto them."

"Oh, so now the FBI is part of this whole thing?"

"An FBI agent asked me questions while I was at the Pasadena station. She said all the recent gamer deaths were suspicious and shared similar details, but she couldn't go into specifics. And no, that was not a dream. See, I have her card here." He walked over to his wallet on the nightstand, withdrew it, and handed it to Jenna.

She looked it over and sighed, then handed it back to him. "Alright, is there any way you can *prove* to me what you saw last night wasn't in your head?"

He thought for a moment. "I just might."

After they'd gotten dressed, he led her to the parking garage. When they reached the space where they'd left the car yesterday after getting back from their morning trip to Arcadia, Lewis was surprised to see the rented Toyota Corolla sitting there.

"Okay, so what's the deal here?"

"I don't get it," he said. "This is exactly where we parked it."

Jenna sighed. "What's suspicious about that?"

"Well, it means they must've been surveilling us pretty closely if they knew the exact spot where we'd put the car."

"Or it means it hasn't left the spot since I put it there yesterday."

Lewis walked around the whole car. Something was off about it, something he couldn't quite put his finger on. It was as if the parking job was too perfect, too symmetrical. He was certain Jenna hadn't parked it exactly that way yesterday.

"Look," she said, putting a hand to her head. "It was a dream. And that's a good thing! It means there was no murder, no kidnapping, no conspiracy. You know what? Let's go get some drinks at the bar, or just hang out around the hotel. It's our last day in Vegas, we can just have a nice relaxing day and then maybe do something fun in the evening if you feel up to it. Okay?"

Still staring at the tires, he nodded. "Okay."

They sat by the pool on lounge chairs, soaking up the sun. Neither of them had wanted to go swimming, but it was a beautiful day outside so they'd agreed to sit here for a little while, and then decide what they wanted to do. Lewis adjusted his sunglasses and rubbed his forehead, which still felt sore. Of course, there was no point mentioning that. There was no visible bruising or swelling so it wouldn't support his case.

He'd found himself in one of the few circumstances where the rational explanation couldn't be the correct one, and no one would believe him unless he found concrete evidence to support that fact.

Not that there was anything he could do about that at this point. They'd played him well, Zhao and the others. They still had secrets, but he'd have to be content knowing that at least he'd been right about the link between Arcadia and the gamers. Maybe he could tip off the FBI about that, set them on the right trail. The registry wouldn't be proof of anything, but he knew investigators rarely believed in coincidence.

Jenna sat up. "Hey, I left my phone in the room. I'll be right back, but can you order us some drinks?"

"Yeah, sure," he said. He watched her get up and go, then as soon as she was out of earshot, he pulled out his own phone and dialed Ricky.

"Hey," his friend said, answering. "So, how's the big plan going, detective?"

"Not well," Lewis replied. He filled him in on recent events.

Ricky paused for a moment. "And you're *sure* it wasn't a dream?"

"I'd bet my life on it."

He sighed. "I don't know what to tell you, man. I really don't. This shit's crazy."

"They've kidnapped someone, Ricky. They're holding a person hostage."

"Then go to the police."

"I would if I still had the list, but they took the damn flashdrive," Lewis said.

"Look, barely anything interesting happens in Lincoln County, Nevada. If you tell them a VR theme park has taken a hostage, they'll probably be curious enough to swing by and check it out."

Lewis shook his head. "They'd never believe me. Besides, the Sheriff might be on their payroll, remember? He didn't want people investigating Jake Miller's death."

"Then I don't know what to tell you." He sounded

concerned. "Look, Des, maybe it *was* just a dream. The whole thing sounds very unlikely. It's not that I don't believe you, it's just... Look, if there actually is a conspiracy, and this place is the epicenter of it, and you snuck in there after dark and nearly made off with an important file... Then you, my friend, are very fucking lucky to be alive. Walk away while you still can."

21

Lewis walked up to the Dolphin Bar's counter. "I need two pina coladas. And a shot of rum."

The bartender smiled. "Luck run out at the tables?"

He looked off at the pool. "Yeah, you could say that."

"It's about to change again."

The voice sounded familiar. Lewis turned around and was surprised to see Special Agent Sara Gonzalez standing to his left, wearing much more casual clothing than she'd been in on Tuesday. She looked like any other tourist with her L.A. Kings t-shirt, leather jacket, and jeans.

"Taking a vacation?" he said.

"Officially, yes. Unofficially, I believe I'm here for the same reason as you. Let's get a seat over there once you get your drinks." She turned to the man behind the counter. "I'll have a margarita, please."

They waited there in silence for a few moments, watching the bartender make the two pina coladas and then pour some Bacardi Black into a shot glass. While they waited,

Lewis's mind ran through the implications of what she had just said. Gonzalez was investigating this by herself, which meant her superiors probably didn't believe her. Or, maybe they were in on it.

He downed the shot, waited for her to get her margarita, and carried the two pina coladas over to a table by the edge of the bar area, as far away from other people's conversations as they could get.

Gonzalez immediately got straight to business. "After our last conversation, I looked into *Rogue Horizon*. I'd originally told you the name hadn't come up before in the other investigations, but I realized that wasn't true. No copies of any game by that name were found on the perpetrators' computers, but in two separate cases, some friends of the killers mentioned that they'd been playing a strange horror game set in space that had, and I quote, 'really disturbed them.' One of these witnesses said the game had the word 'rogue' in the title but couldn't remember exactly what it was called."

Lewis nodded. "I knew it. Installing the game must give the people behind it a backdoor into the computers, one that allows them to delete the game if anything goes wrong."

"I thought the same thing," Gonzalez said. "But my boss said the theory was nuts. Then I noticed that in all of the cases, the perp had visited Las Vegas about a week before their incidents. In some cases, they mentioned visiting a place called Arcadia to their friends. Once I found there was a virtual reality theme park with that name in the desert about an hour north of here, I started connecting the dots. Especially when I heard about the mysterious death of a tech journalist named Jake Miller, about twenty minutes from where Arcadia is located. Then I looked into the *Technologist* and found you listed as a staff writer on their website. Small world, huh?"

"How'd you find me here?"

"I called your boss, Valerie Richter, to ask her some questions about Miller. She didn't want to go into details, but when I said I was taking the case into my own hands because I didn't trust the higher-ups, her lips got a little looser. Mentioned you were heading out here, staying at the Mirage. Looking into this Arcadia place. I decided we needed to have another chat. So let's have one."

He gave her an abridged version of everything that had happened since coming to Vegas. The strange emptiness of the VR park, the creepy behavior of Victor Zhao toward his girlfriend, and finally the late-night trip back there that may or may not have happened.

Gonzalez sat back, letting her eyes drift around the bar while the gears in her mind turned. "And everything was the way you had left it?"

"Exactly the same."

She nodded. "Highly trained operatives could definitely pull that off. As for how they got your same parking space, I'm sure they've had people watching you since the moment you landed at McCarran Airport. I wouldn't be surprised if they had to move someone else's car in the middle of the night just to put yours back in the same space and maintain the illusion."

"How would they do that?"

"Towing. Or maybe hacking, since it's a little more discrete. There were documents from WikiLeaks a few years ago about how the CIA has been hacking cars, sometimes to kill targets by making them look like untraceable accidents. The 21st century is a scary fucking place."

Lewis took several big sips from his pina colada. He

wished he'd ordered a double. Maybe even a triple.

"There's just one thing I need to know," she continued, leaning across the table. "Did you play *Rogue Horizon*?"

He sighed. "Yes."

She slouched back in her seat again. "That would have been helpful to know when we first talked at the police station."

"I wasn't sure if I could trust you, then."

Gonzalez sipped her margarita. "That's fair. You figured this had government written all over it. I flashed you an FBI badge, but you had no idea if I really worked for that agency. Who knows, I could've been a CIA spook."

"Or NSA. Hell, any of the three-letter agencies could be behind this."

She nodded. "My money's on the CIA for now, though. The NSA is mainly just a bunch of pervs who like to spy on people's phone calls. When it comes to brainwashing conspiracies like this, they'd be a little out of their league."

"That would explain why there was so little security at Arcadia," he said.

"Maybe they're underfunded. Or they don't want to have too many guards to arouse suspicion in the few normal visitors they get there." Her face grew stern again. "We're getting off-topic. Has the game affected you?"

"What, do you think I'm gonna go postal like Charlie?"

"I don't know, but if these people wanted you dead, you'd be dead. But if you've been brainwashed and are ready to lose your shit in a couple of days like some uncontrollable Manchurian Candidate…"

He shook his head. "I didn't play the game nearly as much as Charlie did."

"And your girlfriend, Jenna, how much did she play?"

"I'm honestly not sure. She always skirts around the question."

"That's suspicious."

"Everything seems suspicious to me these days."

"And you both played games at Arcadia?"

"Yes."

"Is it possible that could have been where a second round of subliminal psychoactive imagery was implemented?"

"It's possible, but I don't see how they would've done it. We were still playing games in headsets, just like *Rogue Horizon*. Anything they had the chance to do to us yesterday, they should've been able to do with the game alone. I still don't get why they need to lure all the gamers out there." He told her about the dreams, about how *Arcadia awaits* must've been burned into his subconscious by *Rogue Horizon*, and how those two words were the final ones Charlie spoke.

"Well, that's concerning." She took another sip. "Has Jenna displayed any of these symptoms?"

"Not that I can tell. She won't talk to me about it."

Gonzalez looked around. "Speaking of which, where is she?"

"She said she was just going to get her phone from the room."

"And when was that?"

He thought for a moment, glancing at his watch. "Nearly twenty minutes ago."

Gonzalez stood up. "Where is your room?"

"The 19th floor."

"She should be back by now. Call her."

Lewis whipped out his S9 and dialed her number. The phone rang many times, then her voicemail began: "Hi, you've reached Jenna Bateman. Please leave a message–"

"Shit," he said, tapping the End Call icon.

"We need to get moving." Gonzalez stood up.

"You don't think…?"

"You're the paranoid one, you tell me."

Lewis swore under his breath, leaving his pina colada next to Jenna's untouched one as both of them headed into the hotel at a brisk pace. Inside was roughly the same temperature as the outside.

They reached the elevator and wound up sharing the lift with a heavyset man in a Golden Knights jersey. With Gonzalez in her Kings tee, he realized he was the only one in the elevator not wearing a hockey shirt.

The Golden Knights fan got off on the 12th floor. The lift resumed its ascent. He felt more nervous with each number that ticked upward. *It'll be fine*, he told himself. *She's fine.* Gonzalez said nothing beside him. A tense mood hung in the air.

Finally, the doors to the 19th floor opened.

The hallway was dark.

"Shit," Gonzalez said. She pulled out a pistol she had concealed underneath her leather jacket.

The only illumination in the corridor came from the soft red glow of the emergency exit signs. Gonzalez looked left and right with her weapon at the ready, then turned back to Lewis.

Keeping her voice low, she said, "Alright, the coast seems clear. Stay close."

Together, they inched down the hallway. There was no sign of movement. Carefully, Lewis led her to the door to his room. He took out his keycard, slid it into the slot, and retracted it when the light glowed green. There was a click as it unlocked.

He grabbed the handle and turned to her. Gonzalez nodded, gun at the ready.

Lewis threw the door open and she darted forward, checking the bathroom with her weapon out in front of her, then moved into the main area where the bed and the TV were. The lights flickered on and off. Gonzalez looked at something on the ground, then up along one of the walls. From where he stood by the entrance, Lewis couldn't see what she was examining. He looked left and right back down the hallway, making sure no one else had appeared.

"Lewis," she said, very serious now. "You need to look at this."

He dreaded what he was about to see but tried to contain his fear as he entered the room and turned the corner. Jenna was nowhere to be found, but a nightstand was turned over and the suitcases looked ransacked. A bullet hole had been made in the wall. One of the bedside lamps lay on the floor.

Part of its white base was stained red with blood.

22

Lewis covered his mouth. "Jesus Christ."

"It's not necessarily hers," Gonzalez said, putting up a hand as she bent down to pick the object up. "She may have fought back against her attacker and bashed them over the head with this in self-defense."

"Did someone kidnap her?"

"I don't know. It looks like it."

"Shit." He turned around and leaned his forearm and head against the wall, angrily kicking the baseboard.

"This happened in the last twenty minutes. Probably less. We need to move."

Gonzalez led him back out into the darkened hallway, and they started making their way back to the elevator. Lewis abruptly stopped. "Wait, do you hear that?"

The FBI agent turned around and listened carefully.

Now they both recognized it. It sounded like a person sobbing.

Gonzalez and Lewis headed back past his room and

further down the hall, where the weeping noise came from a supply closet. Gonzalez threw the door open, keeping the gun at the ready. A Filipino woman in a maid's uniform sat on the ground, tears streaming from her eyes. She shrieked back when she saw them.

"No worry, ma'am," Gonzalez said, withdrawing her badge from a pocket inside her jacket. "I'm with the FBI. What's going on here?"

"Two people, a man and a woman, came up here and…" She sniffed and wiped her nose with her finger. "I saw them break into a room. I heard a struggle, then a gunshot. But a muffled one, like one with a silencer…"

"How'd you hear a silenced gunshot?" Lewis asked. "Were you right outside the door?"

"Near it," the woman said with a nod.

"Those things aren't perfect," Gonzalez said. "That's why we refer to them as sound *suppressors*."

He nodded. It would've been loud enough for someone listening carefully in the hall, but not loud enough to send everyone on this floor into a panic. Although, he wondered why more people weren't freaking out about the power outage.

The maid continued her story. "Someone got hurt, I could hear them cry in pain. Then a girl, she ran out of the room and went down the stairs. I hid in the closet, but I heard the two people go after her."

"The attackers, what did they look like?" Gonzalez asked, leaning down.

"They wore suits. Both the man and the woman wore black suits."

The FBI agent nodded. "Thank you. Call the police. We're going after them."

She and Lewis began running down the hall toward the elevator.

"Jenna could've gotten away," Lewis said.

"It's possible, but it's also possible that they caught up with her on another floor." She slammed the down arrow button.

"Where do we look?"

"We go to security, which should be somewhere on the first floor. With my badge, we should be able to get in and review CCTV footage to see where they went."

"What if she's still hiding in the building?"

"Then the people who came for her are still here too."

The doors opened. Both of them got in and Lewis quickly hit the button for the ground floor. The lift descended several levels, then stopped at the 14th floor to let in a family of four.

"Shit," Gonzalez muttered, slipping her gun back into the holster before the new arrivals could see it. The elevator became pretty crowded with all six of them.

As they continued going down, Lewis realized one of the kids was looking at him strangely. He glanced down and saw his hands were shaking. Abruptly, he clasped them together behind his back and looked up at the ceiling.

They reached the 8th floor when suddenly the elevator slowed to a halt. *Christ, not again*, he thought. But when the doors opened there was no one there. At first, he thought the two attackers had somehow gained access to the maintenance system, but then he saw the family's little girl was pressing a bunch of the buttons.

"Oh, sorry," the mother said. "She does that sometimes. Judith, *stop it*."

This can't be happening, Lewis thought. The entire situation felt surreal.

His reverie came to a halt as Gonzalez grabbed him by the hand and pulled him out of the elevator doors before they could close. "Come on," she said, leading him to the stairs.

Eight flights. *Damn.*

The pair took the steps two by two, Lewis remaining as close to the railing as possible for fear of wiping out. Gonzalez had clearly had more training in this regard and sailed down flight after flight effortlessly, getting almost a whole floor ahead of him.

"Hey, wait up!" he panted. Shit, he really needed to do more cardio.

"Come on!" she called back up to him, then kept running, ducking down out of sight.

By the time Lewis reached the bottom he was exhausted. He burst out of the staircase door and took several deep breaths as his eyes swept the surrounding space. He was in an area behind the casino, near the elevators to the upper floors.

Gonzalez was nowhere in sight.

"Ah, shit," he panted, taking off toward the lobby. That's where the reception was, she must've gone there to ask for the location of the security office.

After winding his way through the casino tables, Lewis came out into the atrium and walked along the path that cut through its planted jungle. As he did so, a man dressed in a dark trench-coat and black suit suddenly stepped right in front of him. He sported a fedora and wore dark sunglasses.

"Don't move." His voice was quiet but filled with menace.

Lewis glanced down and saw the man was aiming something at him, holding his coat out with the other hand to prevent anyone else from seeing it.

A silenced pistol.

23

Lewis froze. The man swiftly slid around behind him and pressed the gun against his back. "You say a word to anyone, you try to alert anyone, you try and run, I will fucking pump you full of lead, you got that?"

The man's voice sounded vaguely familiar, but he couldn't quite place it. He looked almost as if Lewis had seen him somewhere before, too. Carefully, he nodded.

"Good. Now walk forward." Lewis began moving, the man in black close in step right behind him. "Keep it steady. Where's your FBI friend?"

"I don't know," he said.

"Better tell me now, before I have access to interrogation tools."

"I don't know, I swear," Lewis reiterated. "She beat me down the stairs and when I got out onto the first floor, I couldn't find her. I don't know where she went."

They were out from under the atrium now. Lewis saw he was being steered toward the front entrance. Crowds of people passed all around them, none of them realizing they were witnessing a kidnapping. A businessman nearly walked right into them, texting on his phone.

"Oh, sorry," he said, sliding out of the way.

Lewis began mouthing the words "Help me," but the businessman didn't see it. His eyes swept left and right, hoping to see Gonzalez anywhere, someone to help him. But the man in black nudged him forward, out the sliding doors, and into the cool evening air. Taxis and guests were arriving and leaving, a buzz of energy all around.

Beyond the roof of the porte-cochère the sky had become a red-orange canvas diffusing into the darkening blue. He couldn't believe it was evening already, the day having gone by so fast. Then again, it was winter and the sun set pretty early this time of year. His kidnapper pushed him forward through throngs of people as he led Lewis across the lanes to the area reserved for valet parking and dropping off guests.

A black 2015 Chevy Malibu sedan with tinted windows waited with its engine purring on the other side of the tropical flora-laced divider. The man opened the rear right door and forced him inside, then climbed in after. He grabbed Lewis by the shoulder and turned him around, sticking the silenced barrel of the pistol in his face.

"The doors are locked. Don't try anything stupid and I won't put a bullet in your head."

Lewis nodded, his body incredibly tense. He tried to keep a clear head as he looked around the car. A woman with cappuccino-colored skin sat behind the wheel, wearing a black suit and sunglasses just like her partner.

"Where's Jackson?" the man asked.

"He's coming. He went after the girl but lost her on the Strip."

"We've got him for bait now, I'm just worried about how we're going to contact her."

"She didn't leave her phone in the room. I did a thorough sweep."

Silence followed. Lewis looked between the two of them, but they kept their faces staring straight ahead. It was unsettling.

"So," he said. "When you two do *Men in Black* roleplay, which one of you is Will Smith?"

His kidnapper turned and hit him across the head with the butt of his pistol. Lewis fell back against the door. "Shut up," the man said, looking out the window.

Clutching where he'd been hit, Lewis slowly rotated his head upward. He saw the door's lock, just within reach. A plan began to formulate in his mind. If he could wait for just the right moment, he could pull the lock up with one hand and open the door with the other. He'd have to be swift. If he got out of the car, he'd have a chance. They wouldn't shoot him in front of all these people, no way. They'd have to pursue him on foot, and if he could just get to a police officer, he'd be safe.

Lewis slowly craned his neck around to look at the others, still clutching his head. His two captors glanced elsewhere, although at what exactly it was hard to discern with their sunglasses.

Very carefully, without taking his gaze off of either of them, he began to slide his left arm up toward the lock. Several agonizing moments of anticipation finally yielded the touch of plastic against his fingers.

Neither the man nor the woman had noticed.

Lewis slowly began moving his right hand from the side of his head to the door handle.

Abruptly, another person threw open the passenger door and climbed in. This must've been Jackson. Lewis's hands retreated to where they'd been. The new arrival, a tall African-American man with a goatee and an attire similar to the other two, shut the door and stared at the woman. Lewis saw blood dripping from a nasty gash on the side of his head. It was easy to guess which of these three had been the one struck with the lamp.

"No luck."

"She got away?"

"For now." He glanced back toward Lewis, staring at him through his polarized lenses. "I see Blackwell grabbed her S.O."

"He'll make a good bargaining chip."

Jackson scoffed. "Assuming she actually cares about him." He turned his attention forward. Lewis realized he also looked vaguely familiar, and so did the woman.

She shifted the transmission and began driving, sliding past the valets and guests' cars out into the fading daylight. The white man, Blackwell, turned toward Lewis and leveled his gun at him again.

"Remember," he said. "Don't try anything stupid."

"Where are we going?" Lewis asked.

"You're on a need to know basis," the man replied, shifting his fedora. He realized that beneath the hat the man was bald.

The car pulled up to the intersection, coming to a rest just beneath the large archway that displayed the casino's name. Scores of people walked up and down the sidewalks and the traffic on Las Vegas Boulevard was packed. Vehicles honked at each other as they inched forward in the twilight's glow.

It would've been the perfect time to escape if Blackwell

hadn't kept his gun trained on him. The man never looked away from him. Lewis tilted his head and narrowed his eyes. "You know, those sunglasses don't really fit your face."

Blackwell's face contorted in anger and he lunged forward and pistol-whipped him again. It was just as hard as the previous instance, but this time Lewis pretended to be unconscious as he fell back against the door.

The Chevy began moving forward again. He could feel it turning through the intersection and then reducing speed as it caught up with the rest of the traffic. Lewis carefully began sliding his hand up to the lock again.

"Where did you lose her?" the woman asked.

"She was headed in this direction," Jackson said. "Disappeared into the crowd."

"She nearly split your skull open."

"Please, it wasn't that strong of a hit." Lewis could imagine Jackson's face, seeing him get all defensive. His fingers reached the lock again. Now he began moving his right hand toward the handle.

"You should be more careful," the woman said.

"No shit, Caruso. I'll try to get whacked in the head next time too."

"Both of you, can it. This operation has been a failure so far and will be until we bring the girl to Zhao."

"Would've saved us some hassle if we'd just kept this fucker in the backseat last night instead of having to chase his ass down again – wait, what the hell is he doing?"

Shit. He'd wanted to wait for the next red light, but there was no choice now. Lewis pulled the lock open as he grabbed the door handle and pulled it. His eyes opened to see the asphalt moving beneath the vehicle as his exit grew wider. He willed himself forward, preparing himself for the impact on the road, but a hand roughly grabbed his shoulder.

Blackwell. So much for shooting first.

Lewis jammed his elbow backward as violently as he could. It caught the man in black under his chin, plowing into his trachea. He clutched his throat and reeled back. There was no time to hesitate now.

He threw himself out of the moving vehicle.

24

Lewis hit the ground and tumbled, keeping his arms tucked to his chest. An SUV abruptly swerved into another lane to avoid barreling over him. A Mercedes sedan right behind it slammed on its brakes, causing a jam and several loud horns behind it. Lewis hurt all over, but there was no time to see if he was seriously injured.

He hauled himself to his feet and began stumbling for the divider in the center of the Strip. His legs felt okay, he could definitely do this.

A bullet whizzed by his ear. Lewis threw his head over his shoulder to see that the black Malibu was stopped in the middle of the street up ahead. Jackson had gotten out of the passenger door and was firing at him over the roof of the car with a silenced pistol.

Lewis dove onto the divider, which was about five feet across. Planted palm trees were surrounded by various shrubs around their bases. He landed in a patch of green plants and quickly scrambled to get back up, running out into the oncoming traffic of the northbound lanes.

A taxi slammed on its brakes and nearly hit him, his hands slapping down on the hood of the car as if that would've helped stop it. The driver honked and began screaming obscenities, which were muted by the windows.

"Sorry," he said, looking at the next lane. A Ford Escape sped by and he leaped forward after it passed, sprinting for the sidewalk. Voices shouted behind him as he touched the pavement and looked over his shoulder to see both Blackwell and Jackson running out into the northbound lanes after him. Lewis didn't look if Jackson still had his gun out. He pushed his way through the gathering crowd, the commotion on the street having attracted a large audience. They apparently hadn't seen Jackson firing at him; if he hadn't used a suppressor, there would've been pandemonium right now.

"Excuse me, sorry," he said, snaking his way through the throng of people.

"Fucking move!" Blackwell screamed somewhere behind him. Lewis could hear him aggressively shoving people aside.

Up ahead, the crowd parted and he saw open sidewalk beyond. He slid past the last of the clustered bystanders and broke into a full sprint across the pavement, dodging stray pedestrians. The pathway curved around some tropical foliage, swerving him away from the street. Glimpses of orange rays of sunset broke through the palm fronds beside him as he dashed past stores and shops on his left. The footfalls of Jackson and Blackwell were not far behind him.

Then the row of foliage ended and Lewis found himself sprinting toward the intersection of Las Vegas Blvd and Flamingo Road. An elevated pathway stood in place of a crosswalk at each corner of the juncture, each with its own elevators and escalators to get pedestrians up to the bridge.

His lungs burned and it hurt to breathe. Pain and exhaustion racked his entire frame, like his body just wanted to collapse in the middle of the pavement. Clenching his teeth, Lewis pumped his legs faster and raced for the intersection.

The three men running drew attention from a cop standing by the wall of a building. "Hey, slow down!" he began, but Lewis barely heard him. The escalators and staircase faced south and he was coming from the north, so he had to swing around to jump onto the moving metal steps.

"Watch it!" a woman with several boutique shopping bags said as he pushed past her.

"Sorry," Lewis said, gasping for breath. He knew he must've looked like a mess to everyone around him, drenched in sweat and frantically fleeing for his life.

Blackwell and Jackson had taken the stairs, which would give him a slight lead so long as all these damn people didn't slow him down. Shoving a man talking on a Bluetooth headset aside, Lewis scrambled up onto the top of the bridge and took off toward the other side of the street, unable to admire the breathtaking auburn sky above him and the way the city began to light up in the fading sun.

Not far behind, the two men in black reached the top of the stairs and continued after him. He heard a man say "Oh my God!" and there was a muffled *pfft* sound, followed by a searing pain in the side of his right leg. Lewis stumbled, glancing down to see a gash in his jeans next to his shin and red blood spilling freely from it.

He turned and grabbed the railing as he fell, his right hand going to the wound. Someone screamed. Jackson held his pistol out and Blackwell stood right beside him, turning to the ten or so people around them.

"It's alright," he said. "This man is a criminal. We're investigators here to arrest him."

"He's lying," Lewis spat. It was just a flesh wound, he realized. They were trying to immobilize him, not kill him. But Jackson wasn't as good of a shot as he thought he was. If he'd aimed properly, Lewis wouldn't be able to walk right now. "Show them your badges!" he shouted.

The men in black didn't move.

"Come on," he said, trying to think of his best avenue of escape. No, the bullet hadn't really got him that deep at all. It felt pretty shallow, just stung a lot. He could run on that. He was going to have to. "Show us all who you work for."

Jackson came closer. "Put your hands up and turn around."

"DROP THE GUN!"

Jackson and Blackwell spun around. The police officer from the street corner stood there, his sidearm aimed at Jackson. "Put down the weapon, asshole."

"We're investigators," Blackwell said. "This is a federal case."

"Show me your badges."

"I'm afraid that's classified."

"Bullshit."

Lewis began tepidly retreating as the men argued.

"Show me your goddamn badges," the cop said. "Several witnesses say you shot this man."

"He was trying to get away," Jackson said.

"Show. Me. Your. Badge."

Neither of them moved. Keeping the gun aimed with one hand, the cop moved his other to a radio clipped to his shoulder and pulled it closer to his mouth. "This is Lasky, I'm on the northern bridge at Vegas and Flamingo. Requesting backup–"

Blackwell rushed forward and grabbed the officer's gun-wielding hand, forcing it skyward. The weapon discharged. The remaining observers screamed and fled. They struggled for a moment, then Blackwell whipped the cop's arm downward and Lewis heard it break. The officer screamed, then the man in black pulled him to the railing and aggressively threw him over the barrier.

Lewis watched the man sail down through the air, arms flailing, and crash headfirst through the windshield of an oncoming SUV. It passed under the bridge and there was a squeal of tires as it careened out into the intersection. Seconds later, Lewis heard the screeching metal and shattering glass of a multi-vehicle pile-up.

He didn't turn to the other side of the bridge to look. Instead, he turned and ran like hell. He realized that Blackwell knew exactly what he was doing: creating a distraction for all the cops in the area. The focus would be off the two of them – for the moment. The officer was dead before he'd been able to radio their description.

A set of escalators and steps stood to his left, but Lewis kept sprinting straight down another, wider staircase ahead that led toward a towering casino complex. A giant globe sat atop the dark, modernist, glass-paned building with a space shuttle swinging on a set track around it. The words "The Orbital Hotel & Casino" were emblazoned on the side in glowing blue letters.

Without thinking and gasping for breath, he staggered toward it as he came off the base of the steps.

A blast of cold air hit him as he burst through the front

revolving doors. The entire area was lit with blue and magenta lighting from the floors, the ceiling, the walls, everywhere. Even the chairs and tables of the casino, a massive sprawling area that stretched off to his right, were lined with lights. Some softer fluorescent bulbs shone down from the ceiling.

Directly ahead lead out into a large atrium, and off to the left was a row of shops with big screen advertisements along the walls and windows like something out of *Blade Runner*. All in all, the place felt like he had just stepped onto the set of a sci-fi movie.

Mustering the last of his strength, Lewis bolted for the casino just as Blackwell and Jackson came through the revolving doors. He barely registered the pain in his leg as he began weaving through the network of tables. People from all over the world in clothing from business to casual sat playing blackjack, craps, roulette, and various forms of poker. Their contemporary attire almost seemed out of place in the futuristic setting.

His running, panicked expression, and bleeding leg drew many glances as he made his way toward the rows of slot machines and other automated games. He looked back and was surprised to not see the two men in black right behind him.

Then he realized why. Blackwell and Jackson were keeping to the edges of the casino area, one on each side of it. They walked with brisk, determined paces.

The claws of fatigue finally dug into him enough that he was forced to slow, a slight limp in his step. The vast sea of card tables finally gave way to the slot machines; he ducked into the nearest row and took a seat, keeping his head down.

Lewis brought his fingers to his temples. He needed to think, but he didn't have much time. The only hope for escape was to hide somewhere. Jenna had managed to get away from Jackson in a crowd, but at this point, he didn't have enough energy to keep running. He needed to trick them.

All the people around him were engrossed in their gambling, not even bothering to look as he slid off the chair and crawled along the black, carpeted floor to the end of the row. He peered out and couldn't see Blackwell or Jackson in either direction. That meant they'd continued around the edges to try and find him in the maze of the machine games. He couldn't risk darting back through the card tables. One of them might look back and spot him, and even with his head start he didn't think he'd be able to outrun them.

Carefully, Lewis crept around the side of the slot machine to his right at the end of the row. He stood up and peered over the top, his eyes scanning for his two pursuers. He spotted Blackwell by some solitaire machines but didn't see Jackson anywhere during his quick glance.

He crouched back down again and took a deep breath. Time to make a move.

Lewis got up and began walking at a normal pace, trying not to draw attention to himself. Past the other machines stood a large opening out into the hotel's central atrium. He could see a large, dark pillar in the center that appeared to be surrounded with holographic imagery of stars and planets. Several people stood by the metal railing, looking up.

His eyes flicked to the right. Blackwell still hadn't noticed him and was moving deeper into the maze of vice. Jackson had yet to make a re-appearance. It wasn't until Lewis reached the atrium that he saw him angrily pushing people aside along the back wall of the casino. He was a charging bull, his face contorted in rage.

And he was headed straight for him.

Lewis walked faster as he entered the atrium and strode straight for the railing, taking in his surroundings. The hall was large, extending upward at least ten stories, and descending one floor to a lower level beneath. Directly below him was some kind of vending cart, it's roof no more than a ten-foot drop.

Jackson came tearing out of the casino, making a beeline right for him. "Stop!" he screamed.

No time to hesitate. To the horror of the onlookers beside him, Lewis slid his legs over the metal railing and plunged down, his arms windmilling wildly as the top of the vending stand came up to meet him. He bent his knees on impact but it was rougher than he expected and he toppled over the edge. Most of his body slid off, but he managed to grab enough of a hold to prevent himself from falling.

The surrounding crowd emitted gasps as he dropped to the ground of his own accord and brushed himself off. He looked back up and saw Jackson dart away from the railing, trying to find the nearest staircase.

Lewis turned and pushed through the onlookers, heading away from the atrium. This direction appeared to lead to more shops, but he saw a darkly lit corridor coming up on his right. He slipped down it and tried all the doors. One labeled "Maintenance Storage" was mercifully unlocked, and he tore it open, slipped inside, and slammed it behind him.

Immediately everything went pitch black, and he stood there catching his breath in the blackness for several moments, his head resting against the door. It had all happened so quickly. He'd gone from finding out Jenna was missing, to being kidnapped, to running for his life, to witnessing a policeman get murdered before his eyes, to jumping over a railing in the middle of a casino atrium to make his getaway. And now he was here, holed up in some closet in the basement of a place he'd never been before, two armed killers scouring the building to find him.

He never should've come here. He should've just accepted the explanation that Miller had tried drugs and that it went very badly for him. He should never have continued playing that game. And he never should've gone to Arcadia. The truth wasn't worth dying over.

Lewis turned around and opened his eyes.

Then froze.

He was standing in the middle of a dark forest road, a starry sky high above him.

25

Lewis blinked multiple times, but he was still there. An overturned SUV lay in the middle of the asphalt. A cool breeze sifted through the leaves of the tall trees above. There was no sign of the woman or her crying son. He turned back to the door, but it was gone. Somehow, he was really here.

That's bullshit, he told himself. *You've passed out in a storage closet. This is some kind of dream, wake up.*

And it did feel as if he could snap back to reality at any moment, but something nudged him to stay. Slowly, he began walking toward the vehicle. The other car, the red Chevy Trailblazer, was just up the road with its trunk against the tree, a single high beam blazing out of the gloom. He didn't want to look inside it; he already knew the evil that awaited within.

"Lewis..."

It was the Miller-astronaut's synthesized voice again, sounding like a breathy whisper. He spun around. It seemed like it had come from all around him.

"For Christ's sake, what do you want?" he asked.

No answer.

"This place is in the past, there's nothing left here." There was a nervous edge to Lewis's voice.

"We both know that's not true."

"I won't let you hold this over me, it was too long ago."

"Was it really? My, time does fly…" The voice gave something akin to a chuckle, then sighed. "I want you to remember how it all went down."

"No."

"You see Lewis, you may have locked these memories up and tossed away the key, but I've found that key. And you know what? It really wasn't that hard to discover. I just had to push the right buttons."

"I can leave any time I like."

"Sure, go ahead and try."

Lewis stood there, staring at the wreck and clenching his fists. Tears started forming in his eyes, his breath coming in ragged gasps.

"That's what I thought," the voice said. "You don't have the will to leave. This is what happens when you don't dwell on the past."

He forced a laugh. "That's terrible advice."

"I want you to immerse yourself in this night, remind yourself how it went wrong. Remember the pain you felt. Know that you don't deserve anything better than to feel this pain every waking second of your life."

"Fuck you, I don't need to hear this." He turned and began walking up the road, which lead into pitch blackness.

"Everything's gonna be alright."

Lewis stopped. He slowly looked back over his shoulder. The woman and her boy had appeared in their usual space, still trapped in the same loop. He walked back toward them, tears streaming down his face now. It all felt so surreal.

He crouched down beside them. The boy didn't notice him, but his mother gradually twisted her neck in his direction. Lewis jumped back in horror. Her eyes were completely black and glowing blue veins ran across her face.

"This is all your fault."

Desmond Lewis screamed.

A violent shudder convulsed through him and he opened his eyes, suddenly very awake. He stared into complete darkness and a cold, hard surface pressed against his back. He shot to his feet and threw open the door, stumbling back out into the hallway of the Orbital's lower level, gasping for breath.

Lewis looked back at the darkened closet. He'd have to find somewhere else to hide. No way he was going back in there.

After closing the door, he began walking toward the main concourse. The cut on his leg where the bullet had grazed him barely bothered him anymore. Once he reached the corner, he looked both ways for any sign of the men in black, and, seeing none, continued off to the right toward the shops.

Where high-fashion boutique stores reigned on the upper floors, here he saw window displays full of science fiction themed clothes and accessories. Video game franchise names from *Halo* to *Dead Space* to *Half-Life* to *Deus Ex* were featured prominently. As he moved on, he saw the focus shift to movie titles including *Star Wars* and *Alien*.

Tourists ambled in both directions, some entering and exiting the shops. Lewis spotted the sign for a public restroom up ahead and slipped into the men's. Nobody else was in here.

It was pristinely white and lit by snowy fluorescents running the perimeter of the large mirror wall mounted above all the sinks.

He went into the biggest stall, locked it, and placed his hands on the edge of the sink inside. There was another mirror in here, a vertical rectangle unlike the horizontal one outside. It too had white fluorescent light emanating from each side. Lewis stared at his own reflection. He looked haggard and on edge.

Sighing, he turned on the faucet and splashed some water on his face. He had no idea how he was going to find Jenna and Gonzalez with the people from Arcadia scouring the city for them. He considered calling them, but realized they'd probably have access to his phone calls. That also meant they could track him on GPS.

Shit. Frantically, he fumbled for his phone and turned the location setting off. He realized he should've done that before he came in here. If any of their people had hacked into any of the casino's surveillance equipment, he'd be a dead man. There was an ungodly number of cameras all over Las Vegas so it wouldn't take long for them to locate Gonzalez or Jenna either.

He slammed his fist against the wall and swore.

Maybe a payphone would work. He had Jenna's number on his phone and had kept Gonzalez's card in his wallet. Of course, Jenna might've ditched her phone for the same reason he wasn't going to use his, but he should be able to contact Gonzalez. If he couldn't reach either of them, he was fucked.

The door to the bathroom opened. The new arrival didn't make straight for a stall or a urinal. Instead, there was silence for several moments, then one carefully placed footfall after the other. One stall door creaked as it was pushed open, then another.

Lewis froze. There was no point in trying to climb up on the toilet seat. He'd locked the door, they'd know someone was in here. And even if he left it unlocked they'd still look inside. He was cornered.

Maybe he could take them. He could use the element of surprise, grab their weapon. Of course, these people were highly trained professionals. There was no telling what–

His entire body tensed up.

A blue glow swept across the floor. Slow, deep breaths through a muffled respirator reached his ears. Very slowly, he looked down and saw white futuristic boots approaching along the tile.

No way, no fucking way.

The figure drew nearer. He heard it opening the stall right beside him.

It's not possible. You're seeing things again.

A shape moved in front of the door, blue light shining in through the tiny gap between the door and the stall's outer wall. Lewis's entire body became immobile; he could barely breathe. Then an acute pain exploded in his head, burning from a single point inside his skull.

The latch slid open and the astronaut entered, it's breathing now deafening in his ears. He collapsed onto the pristine white floor, panting, his vision blurring. The migraine was unbearable now. He could pinpoint the source, he could feel it. He just wanted someone to slice open his head and cut it out.

Lewis's mouth contorted into a silent scream, tears dripping to the floor that was just inches from his face. He heard Charlie's voice off in the distance. "Make it stop!" he screamed. "Make it stop!"

Now he knew how he had felt.

Grabbing the edge of the sink, he hauled himself back up and looked in the mirror. His eyes were red from the tears and blood trailed from both nostrils. *Jesus, when did that start?*

He turned on the water and washed it off, sniffling. Then he washed his hands thoroughly and put his face in both palms. The migraine was receding, but very slowly. Muffled voices called to him off in the distance, staticky as if they came from a radio. He couldn't even understand what they were saying, but in the mirror he saw that the stall door had remained closed and there was no sign of the astronaut. At least that was something.

After another minute standing at the sink, Lewis stumbled out of the stall and tried to get his bearings. The lights around him now glowed blue instead of white. He had to get out of here. He stumbled back out the door and into the concourse.

Off to his right stood a large map and directory of the casino on a large screen. He ran over to it, accidentally shoving a passerby aside. "Sorry," he said, his eyes frantically taking in the image before him.

He was on the lower level's southern concourse, which began with shops and led into an interactive exhibit on space exploration. On the main floor, one above him, was the casino, more expensive shops, spas, restaurants, and exits to the pool deck at the rear. There also appeared to be a nightclub called Solaria adjacent to the shopping area. It took up a sizable chunk of the first level. The upper floors were mostly conference and hotel rooms, and the first floor and subterranean level were definitely the largest.

Lewis moved on, not wanting to stay in one place for too long. Despite the pain in his head, he made his best effort to walk normally and to act as inconspicuous as possible as he headed toward the space exploration exhibit. He needed to find a payphone; most people thought they'd gone extinct, but he frequently noticed them all around cities. Especially in hotels. He figured he'd just walk around this level until he found one. If not, move one floor up. There had to be at least one nearby.

Up ahead, the concourse ended with the entranceway to a dark corridor with the sign "Spaceflight: The Exhibition" glowing white at the top. He followed a crowd of tourists in and began taking a look around. Projections of stars lined the ceiling above while timelines ran along both walls. The wide corridor curved to the right and downward. Ambient darkwave music played in the background, contributing to a sense of eeriness and wonder – much like outer space itself.

The timeline jumped back and forth between the walls, beginning with the launch of *Sputnik* in 1957. Tiny replicas of the satellite and America's *Explorer 1* were displayed in small glass cases on the left. Up ahead he saw a full-sized moon buggy from *Apollo 11* surrounded by red rope off to the right. There appeared to be a space shuttle replica suspended from the ceiling up ahead, but the corridor curved out of sight for him to see the rest of it from where he was standing.

Lewis looked around at the crowd milling about. There were a number of parents here with their children, some wearing NASA shirts and holding toy shuttles. It reminded him of a cross-country trip his family once took to Florida just before he turned five, when they'd visited the Kennedy Space Center to witness one of *Discovery*'s launches. He'd always been obsessed with space, but it was that moment at 10:41 AM on August 7, 1997, as the shuttle rocketed off into the atmosphere, that he decided he wanted to be an astronaut.

Years later, he'd discovered he would've been too tall, but by then his interests had moved on.

However, that day he'd dragged his parents to go to the gift shop. And there, he'd found a plush space shuttle and decided he wanted it more than anything else in the world. It took a lot of begging to his mother and father, but eventually it was his dad who caved and bought him the toy. His mother was worried it wouldn't fit in the luggage, but Lewis wound up keeping it in his backpack or in his hands. He never let it get far away from him.

Then one day he threw it away. It had become too painful to look at.

26

Lewis snapped out of his reverie. He was standing in the middle of the exhibit and people were saying "Excuse me" and trying to get around him. Putting a hand to his forehead, he continued deeper into the hall.

The corridor completed a semi-circle and ended in an area with elevators that opened into the stores on the level above. A short hallway jutted off to the left with restrooms, water fountains, and at the very back, an old payphone.

Making sure Blackwell, Jackson, or Caruso were nowhere in sight, he strode down the corridor and picked up the receiver. He should've known Jenna's number by heart, but he'd always just called her from his Galaxy S9's contacts. Lewis slid the device out of his pocket, found her information, and dialed it into the payphone. Then he retrieved two quarters from his wallet and inserted them into the slot.

He took several deep breaths while it rang. He wasn't even sure she'd pick up, but calling was the only way he had of reaching her.

She answered on the fourth ring.

"Holy shit, Des! You were right! You were so fucking right, oh my God…"

Lewis normally liked being vindicated, but this time the gratification evaded him. "They came for Gonzalez and me too."

"Gonzalez?"

"The FBI agent who talked to me on Tuesday. Turns out she's in town investigating this too. We went to the room to try and find you when you didn't come back, but you were already gone."

"Jesus, who are these people Des?!" Her voice sounded understandably frantic. From the background noise, it seemed like she was in a crowded area.

"I don't know exactly, they seem to be feds. But they mentioned Zhao, they're definitely from Arcadia."

"Fuck!" She paused for a moment, breathing heavily. "Where are you?"

"The Orbital Casino."

"How the hell did you end up there?"

"They kidnapped me. I managed to get away and hid here. At least two of them are in the building, looking for me."

"There's some big accident at Vegas and Flamingo," she said.

"Yeah, they caused that."

"They killed a cop?"

"Right in front of me and about a dozen other people."

"Holy shit, I thought conspiracies were supposed to be subtle."

Lewis glanced behind him. "Clearly, they've become desperate. And they probably have the means to wipe themselves out of any camera footage. I wouldn't be surprised if they'd gotten their fingerprints removed."

"I still can't believe this is happening. I've been hiding out at Caesar's Palace for the last twenty minutes. They chased me out of the Mirage, but I managed to get away and came here. This place is a fucking labyrinth, so good luck to them finding me."

"Don't tempt them. We need to meet up with Gonzalez and strategize. She's the only one who can help us."

"Can you reach her?"

"Yeah," he said. "I've got her business card. We need to pick a place to meet, but somewhere very public." He thought for a moment. "There's a nightclub here called Solaria. It's dark and full of people. If we can find each other in there, we should be able to slip out through the crowd undetected."

"Okay, I'll start heading to it. And Des?"

"Yeah?"

She paused. "I'm sorry I didn't believe you."

He chuckled bitterly. "I don't blame you. I probably wouldn't have, either."

"Stay safe. I love you."

"Love you too. I'll see you soon."

He hung up, took out Gonzalez's business card and another two quarters, and input the number and the money. The FBI agent answered quickly.

"Jesus Lewis, it's dangerous to call–"

"Don't worry, I'm at a payphone."

"They can still tap those, you know." She lowered her voice. "I need you to listen very carefully."

"Okay."

"I saw them take you. I couldn't stop it, but I took a photo of their rear license. Lewis…it was a G14 plate. Government."

That didn't surprise him. He remembered watching a documentary about alien conspiracies on the History Channel as a kid where they mentioned some mysterious men in black driving a Cadillac with a G14 license plate. When the investigators looked up the number, they'd found it registered to a Parks & Rec Jeep Wrangler in Texas.

"We can't confirm it's the CIA though," he pointed out.

"CIA, NSA, EPA, I don't really give a shit at this point," she said. "The point is we are in over our goddamn heads." She paused. "How did you escape?"

"Jumped from a moving vehicle in the middle of Vegas Blvd. They followed me on foot, threw a cop off a bridge, and chased me into the Orbital Casino."

Gonzalez sighed. "Okay, okay... Man, this has turned into a real clusterfuck. Our only way out is to get concrete evidence of what they're doing at Arcadia and show it to the world."

"What exactly *do* they do at Arcadia?" he asked.

"Whatever it is, it's evidently worth tearing up Las Vegas to keep it from getting out."

His shoulders suddenly tensed, the migraine in his head returning. He breathed deeply in and out as his vision became blurry again. The phone slipped from his fingers. He turned around and fell back against the wall as his normal sight returned. The astronaut stood in front of the elevators, evil blue radiance shining out of its helmet. Nobody else seemed to notice it.

"Lewis...Lewis?" her distant voice came from the handset, dangling by its cord.

The creature began aggressively stomping toward him. Never taking his eyes off of it, he reached down for the phone and picked it up. "Gonzalez, it's here. It's here with me."

"What? The Arcadia agents or–?"

"No, the thing from the game. The astronaut, it's here!"

People nearby started looking at him. A mother began pulling her daughter away back into the exhibit. One person even said: "What are you looking at?"

The thing was only five feet away now.

"Lewis, listen to me. It's not real. They're fucking with your mind. There's no monster. It can't hurt you if you don't let it."

It stopped right in front of him, breathing heavily. Its gloved hands rose to the sides of the helmet and began pulling it off.

"Lewis…"

The bright blue light spilled out in all directions. He brought his right hand up to shield his eyes. His left was still pressing the receiver to his ear.

"Lewis," Gonzalez said sternly. "It's the brainwashing. Nothing is there."

The helmet fell to the floor. This time, it was the little boy's face that stared back at him. His eyes were black as coal and large veins ran all over his glowing blue head. He smiled, revealing sharp teeth. "*Desmond…*" the thing coaxed, in a voice way too deep. The little cranium was far too small for the hulking body of the suit.

"It's standing right in front of me," Lewis said slowly. Sweat dripped from his forehead. "It's talking to me. It's been following me through the entire casino."

"No, it hasn't. Only those men have. It's not there. You're going to draw attention to yourself and the *real* monsters will find you if you don't–"

The abomination grabbed him by the throat, pinning him back against the wall. He began choking, the phone still clenched in his hand.

"Jesus," a man said. "Somebody get security, this guy's going nuts!"

Snap out of it, Lewis told himself.

The astronaut tightened its grip, the little boy's face grinning evilly. "How could you ever forget about *me*?"

"Fuck you," he gasped. In a swift motion, he smashed the receiver into the creature's head as hard as he could. It roared and fell back, collapsing to the floor. Lewis turned around and spoke rapidly into the phone. "Meet me and Jenna at the Solaria nightclub!"

Then he hung up and ran, past the astronaut as it climbed back to its feet, past the shocked onlookers, and straight around the corner into the nearest elevator, just as the doors closed. The people inside shrunk back against the walls, clearly disturbed by his appearance. He knew he must look like he was hopped up on drugs. He now understood why that gas station clerk had assumed that about Miller.

"Sorry," Lewis said as the doors opened to the main floor. He dashed out and took a right, finding himself running down the cyberpunk-style boutique corridor with its neon-lit LEDs and giant digital ads paneling the glass walls. The nightclub had to be this way.

He turned a corner and saw the entrance. A giant logo stood over it displaying a model of the solar system with the sun in the center. The letters S-O-L-A-R-I-A were spaced out and glowing orange. Beyond the mouth of the venue, he saw darkness and flashing lights.

Lewis's joy was cut short the moment he stepped forward. Blackwell and Caruso walked out from an adjacent concourse which led back to the atrium. They looked surprised to see him but said nothing.

All three parties froze.

Then Lewis dashed for the entrance. The two government agents lunged forward, racing to block him. Too late. He barely slipped past Blackwell's outstretched hand as the blackness of Solaria engulfed him.

27

As his eyes began to adjust, he saw a tall, buff man materialize before him with his palm out in a stop symbol. He had to speak very loudly so Lewis would hear him over the blaring techno music.

"I need to see some ID, bud. Those are the rules."

Lewis glanced over his shoulder. The silhouettes of Blackwell and Caruso stormed toward him.

"Hey, buddy! Show me that ID and you're good to go." He had his arms crossed now and appeared to be chewing gum.

"Yeah, yeah, sure," Lewis said, fumbling to get out his wallet. He flashed the man his California driver's license, but the bouncer grabbed it to look at it more thoroughly. Lewis tapped his foot impatiently. *Come on man, I don't have time for this bullshit right now.*

A heavy hand smacked down on his shoulder. He turned to see the two agents right behind him. "You're coming with us," Blackwell said. "Or your girlfriend dies."

"Bullshit," Lewis told him. There was no way they had her.

"Yo buddy," the bouncer said. "You're clear. Have a nice night."

He took the card, discretely flipped the bird to Blackwell and Caruso, turned, and entered the nightclub.

Solaria was a large venue with two levels. Directly ahead of him was a free-standing metal staircase that led down onto a dance floor with alternating blue, fuchsia, and white tiles. A large bar called the Lagrange Point ran the length of the back wall, a crimson light strip radiating along the front of it. Directly above the bar was the DJ's booth, a glass and metal structure that looked the like the bridge cockpit of a sci-fi starship. He could see a twenty-something guy wearing sunglasses and working a glowing blue mix table.

The upper level, where he currently was, featured two balconies overlooking the dance floor that stretched to the back of the venue, the left balcony leading to a women's restroom and the right leading to a men's. Square, black tables jutted off the railings and walls here, each with opposite-facing swivel chairs that were attached to the banister or walls by sturdy metal bars. To his immediate right and left were some standing tables where patrons chatted to their friends or dates while sipping beers and cocktails. A small square bar was situated past them in each corner.

But the most striking feature of the whole club was the array of holographic planets floating above the dance floor in front of the DJ's booth. He saw the entire solar system orbiting around the sun, complete with moons and the asteroid belt. They'd even included Pluto. A rig rotating strobes on the bottom of the booth flashed multicolored light in all directions, casting the planets in different hues.

Despite being the early evening, the place was already packed. Nearly every table on the upper level was occupied and scores of people were bopping on the dance floor. Quickly, he made his way down the steps and joined them.

Ever since his university days, Lewis had never particularly liked nightclubs. He'd often found them sketchy, full of shady characters and strange vibes, and it took a lot of alcohol to make him feel comfortable dancing in front of other people. However, having his life on the line had a similar effect. He did his best to blend in, trying to keep his shoulders and hips swaying somewhat in-tune to the beat. It felt clumsy, but everyone seemed to be too drunk or interested in grinding on their partner to care.

He looked back at the stairs. There was no sign of Blackwell, Caruso, or Jackson yet, but he spotted a dimly lit area with more standing tables back beneath the area where he'd first walked in. Lewis decided it would be harder to find him on the dance floor and resumed his attempt at dancing.

He continued that way for several minutes, his eyes constantly scanning the crowd. There was no sign of the men in black, or Jenna, or Gonzalez. He started to get worried. How long would it take the others to get here? Would the agents try and snatch them before they even got in? No, that was unlikely. It was too open out there.

With a chill, he realized that a nightclub would actually be the perfect place to kill someone. It was dark and most people were intoxicated or preoccupied. You could stab someone, inject them with poison, or probably even shoot them with a silenced pistol on the dance floor and no one would notice. You could then carry the body over your shoulder to one of the tables, and set them down, seeming like a concerned friend, then exit the venue and be long gone before anyone realized the person slumped in their seat was deceased.

The one thing he took comfort in was that they definitely wanted to kidnap Jenna. Pulling a kicking and screaming person out of a public space would make their jobs very difficult. However, he realized that if they injected her with a sedative and carried her unconscious out of the club, they could probably pass off as her friends taking her back to her room.

There, on the stairs. Jackson, now minus his shades, scanned the crowd as he stepped onto the dance floor. With his extremely stern expression and aversion to any form of dancing, he stuck out like a sore thumb.

Lewis ducked his head down as Jackson entered the throng of partiers, his pulse racing. He thought about trying to head for the stairs but realized that must be what they wanted. They'd sent one down to flush him out while the other two waited above to pounce. One was probably patrolling the top floor, while the other waited just outside the venue in case he slipped by. His best bet was to try and stay undetected until Jenna and Gonzalez arrived.

Jackson pushed through the crowd, still scouring the mass of dancing figures. Lewis hadn't been spotted yet. He awkwardly jived his way to the edge of the dance floor and walked into the hangout behind the stairs. As he passed by the steps, a hand suddenly reached out and grabbed his arm.

He reared back and spun around.

Jenna put a finger to her lips and motioned for him to join her under the stairway. As soon as he did, she pulled him into a tight embrace and fervently kissed him.

He smiled. "Missed you too. When'd you get here?"

"About 30 seconds ago. I saw one of them out there and

immediately ducked under here."

Together, they peered out through the steps at the multitude of clubbers. At first, Lewis didn't see Jackson, then Jenna pointed him out by the right side of the bar. He stuck to the edge of the crowd, trying to get a better view of everyone.

"The other two must be somewhere upstairs."

"There's just the three of them?" she asked.

"That I know of."

Jenna nodded, still staring out at the mob as strobe lights cast alternating blue, green, and pink glows across her face. Then she turned toward him again. "It's dark and crowded enough in here that we could probably slip back out and nobody would notice us leaving."

He nodded. "True, but I told Gonzalez we'd meet her here."

"You trust her?"

"If she was working with them, she had ample opportunity to turn me over to them directly. Or to knock me out when we investigated the hotel room." Jenna looked hesitant. He shrugged. "She's the only help we've got."

"Where was she when you called her?"

"I don't know. I got…interrupted." He rubbed his neck. Of course, the astronaut hadn't been there. How had he let himself think that? But the way it grabbed his throat…it had felt like something was *actually* choking him. "I just told her to meet us here."

"This isn't *that* big of a place. They *will* find us eventually."

"Then we have to keep moving."

Lewis looked out at the dance floor. Jackson was now leaning against the bar sipping a drink, evidently having decided to put in some effort toward blending in. Caruso and

Blackwell must've still been upstairs. He scanned the seats lining each balcony and finally spotted the two agents sitting across from each other toward the rear of the left wing. They had removed their sunglasses and looked like they were having a casual conversation over some drinks, but Lewis saw them each take long looks around the venue and down at the dance floor.

"I see them," he said, pointing.

She nodded. "Good spot for a lookout."

"If we can get to one of the corner bars up there, it might be dark enough that they can't really make us out. And we'll have a good view of the door to see when Gonzalez comes in."

"Unless she's already here. Can you call her?"

Lewis whipped out his phone and took the business card from his wallet, glad that Jackson hadn't checked out this area yet; he knew it was only a matter of time. He dialed Gonzalez's number. It rang several times, but she didn't pick up. "Damn." He slid the phone back into his pocket.

"Guess we'll just have to go," Jenna said, grabbing him by the hand.

She pulled him out from behind the staircase, and then they moved around and up the steps at a normal pace, just two patrons heading back to the main floor. Lewis didn't dare look back until they had reached the upper landing, where he stole a quick glance toward Blackwell and Caruso's table.

Both of them were gone.

"*Shit*," he hissed.

Hearing him, Jenna pulled him to their left and toward the bar tucked away in the corner. There were a few stools surrounding it, but only one was not taken.

"Have a seat, I'll grab some drinks."

Without looking at him, she said, "They might not have noticed me yet, but you're the one they followed in here."

"Yes, but you're their main target."

Now she threw him a curious glance, an eyebrow raised. "What?"

"I'm expendable. They were only holding me to get you to cooperate."

"But…"

"Think about it. *Who did they send the game to?*"

They arrived at the bar. Her face had gone pale. "I thought they were trying to kill us because you were onto something."

"No, they're trying to kill *me* because I was onto something. But you were their next target anyway. You play a lot of violent video games. Plenty of people would probably believe that's what drove you crazy if you were to ever snap and stab somebody. Hell, your parents would believe it wholeheartedly! They'd probably do interviews for the next big thinkpiece op-ed about video game violence. These people couldn't have picked a better scapegoat."

"But *why*? What does all of this serve?"

He glanced around. Still no sign of the men in black. Or Gonzalez.

"My guess," he postulated, "is that it's testing brainwashing for assassinations. It's the only logical explanation. If some gamer shoots a politician, and it's blamed on games, nobody suspects a conspiracy. It would be too ludicrous. So everything in the past six months has been all the foundation work. They're creating a culture that fears violent video games so that when important, influential people start dying it's chalked up to the same thing."

"Jesus," she said, thinking of the implications. "You

could have them commit domestic terrorist attacks and use them to justify more public surveillance. You could orchestrate mass shootings and use them to argue for tougher gun control."

Lewis nearly said something, then restrained himself. Guns were a political area where they disagreed, but he respected her opinion on it. He focused his attention on sweeping the area for any sign of their pursuers.

"But I still don't get what the game has to do with Arcadia," she continued.

"The game lures their victims out there."

"Why?"

"Fuck if I know. They must do something there to complete the brainwashing. And that's what we're going to find out."

"I think not," a voice spoke, off to his left. He turned and found Blackwell standing there, once again pointing a gun at his chest. The man with the fedora turned to Jenna and said, "Come with me, or he dies."

Nobody around them noticed this situation. Lewis spotted an empty beer glass that a bar patron had left unattended as he chatted with a red-haired woman beside him. His eyes flicked from it to Jenna's and then back again multiple times. She spotted it too.

He turned back to Blackwell. "You're not going to shoot me here in front of all these people."

"Forget what I did earlier?"

"No, and I bet the Las Vegas PD haven't either."

"I'm afraid they have a shorter memory than you do, Mr. Lewis. If you check the street cameras, you'll see no sign of an altercation. Truly tragic what happened to that officer." He smirked.

Lewis wondered how long he needed to stall him. Evidently, it was long enough because a split-second later Jenna's arm sailed into his view and smashed the glass against Blackwell's head. It brought a smile to his lips for a brief instant as the man stumbled in reverse, one hand clutching his face.

Then he saw the other, gun-wielding hand rise into view and pull the trigger.

28

A searing pain shot through Lewis's left shoulder and he fell back, colliding with the wall just as Blackwell smashed into a pub table, knocking it over, and collapsed to the ground. The couple that had been at it reared back in shock. Grimacing, Lewis grasped the wound and took a glance at it. The bullet had entered just below the collarbone, missing any organs but still hurting like a bitch. Red blood looked black in this light as it trailed down the front of his jacket.

A hand touched his other shoulder. He looked up to see Jenna's expression of extreme concern, her other hand covering her mouth as she looked at his shoulder. "I'll live," he said, staggering forward. She put one arm under his right arm and helped him walk toward the entrance. Instead, he pointed down the stairs where two red signs stating EXIT were located at each end of the Lagrange Point bar.

"Alleyway," he grunted, not wanting to revisit the labyrinth of the Orbital Hotel & Casino.

Together, they stumbled down the steps as two bouncers

ran over to where Blackwell had fallen. Lewis clenched his teeth and tried to spot Jackson and Caruso in the crowd. The former no longer stood by the bar and the latter was still nowhere to be seen.

"Come on," Jenna said, pulling him off the last stair onto the dance floor.

People around them barely took notice as she helped her injured boyfriend across the tiles flashing from blue to magenta to white. As the alternating colors of the strobes danced across the clubbers' upper bodies, Lewis spotted a tall, dark figure cutting a swath through the masses toward them. In the next flash of bright light, he saw it was Caruso. Her face was stern and angry. She must've seen them coming down the stairs.

"Ten o'clock," he shouted over the roar of the music. The DJ was now playing a techno version of the Rolling Stone's "Paint it Black." Jenna turned her head, her eyes widening as she spotted the agent. She jerked Lewis's arm and tugged him in another direction, spinning him through the crowd.

Lewis lost his sense of direction. The music blared and the people around them whirled in an indistinguishable mass of sweat, alcohol, and poor decisions. Suddenly, he felt her hands on his right shoulder and left hip. She pulled him closer and he did his best to keep her rhythm as they subtly glided through the horde.

"Do you see her?" he asked, leaning closer to her ear.

"No," she breathed. "Try to keep low. Don't look around too much. It draws attention."

He focused on his peripheral. Most people around them were just dancing badly, but in the very corner of his view, he could see Jackson on patrol. Lewis was about to warn Jenna when a sudden look of surprise came across her face and she pulled him against her very tightly, pretending to nuzzle the side of his neck.

"The woman's right there, five feet behind you."

"Does she see us?" he said, making a show of caressing her shoulder as he lowered his head.

Jenna glanced up briefly, then back down again. "I'm not sure. She's not walking this way anymore."

"I see another one back there behind you. They must be circling the floor, trying to narrow us into the center before they close in."

"And what about the one that shot you?"

"I haven't seen him for a while. He must be dealing with the bouncers still. Or maybe he's down here and we just haven't seen him yet. He must be bleeding from the head, so he should be fairly easy to spot."

"Where's the nearest exit?" she asked.

Lewis raised his head and looked left and right. "We're near the right side of the bar. The exit's still about thirty feet away." He saw Jackson moving toward that area and realized that if Caruso blocked the other door, and Blackwell stayed up near the entrance, all three exits would be barricaded. It would just be a waiting game.

He was confident that was going to be their strategy until Jenna suddenly wrenched backward out of his grasp, Jackson dragging her in a half nelson. The two of them disappeared into the throng. Lewis prepared to spring himself after them when someone grabbed his right shoulder, spun him around, and gave him a strong right hook across the jaw. He briefly registered Caruso's furious snarl before his vision momentarily blacked out and he stumbled back into a group of college kids dancing.

One of them, who was pasty, slightly overweight, and

wore a baseball cap backward, aggressively pushed him off while shouting, "Watch it, asshole!"

He staggered and managed to turn around just as the woman in black leaped for him and swung again. Lewis barely managed to dodge her flying fist, but she delivered a roundhouse kick to the side of his abdomen and he crumpled to the floor, landing on his hands and knees.

The crowd finally took notice of the altercation and began scattering back, a circle forming around Lewis and Caruso to watch the violence. Ignoring the pain in his left shoulder, Lewis got back on his feet and began pushing his way through the crowd to find Jackson and Jenna.

It was then that a gunshot erupted behind him, and the crowd began stampeding toward the exit. He spun around. Caruso was grappling with another figure for her pistol, the weapon discharging into the air multiple times. A burst of neon green strobe lights flashed across her attacker and Lewis saw the determined face of Sara Gonzalez.

As he watched, she slammed the heel of her shoe down on top of Caruso's foot, and the black-suited woman slackened her grip on the handgun just long enough for Gonzalez to pry it out of her fingers, twirl around while swinging the pistol in a wide arc, and smash it into the side of her head. Caruso went down hard onto the glowing tiles as bystanders continued to rush for the stairs.

It all happened quite quickly. He spun around to locate his girlfriend and her captor and saw Jackson attempting to haul her away from the top of the stairs, away from the rush of fleeing visitors. She was putting up quite a fight and Jackson had difficulty restraining her.

Lewis went up the stairs behind the others. He glanced up at the struggling figures. Jenna bit down on Jackson's hand. The man let go of her in an instant and she ran toward the charging crowd. She almost made it. Blackwell, blood from the forehead wound running down the side of his face, appeared seemingly out of nowhere and grabbed her roughly by the arm.

Another gunshot rang out behind him. Halfway up the stairs, Lewis turned back. Gonzalez was firing at the two men in black with Caruso's pistol. Both ducked, enabling Jenna to break free and slip into the crowd. By now most of the throng was gone, the bouncers motioning them out into the concourse just past the main entrance. Lewis guessed the cops had been called and the staff were trying to contain the situation until they arrived.

He almost made it to the top of the stairs with the last few stragglers when he saw Blackwell turn toward him with his pistol in hand and pull the trigger. The bullet sailed right past his head and Lewis spun around to the grab the railing, everything a blazing blur in the strobe lights. He had no cover. The next shot would take him.

Thinking quickly, he flipped himself over the railing and somehow managed to land on his feet. The impact drove the breath out of him, but it was a smoother landing than when he'd jumped in the atrium. He took cover underneath the stairs and looked out between the metal slats at the gunfight unfolding.

Gonzalez had taken refuge on the other side of the bar counter and occasionally popped up to shoot another round or two. Caruso's body lay unconscious on the empty dance floor. Jackson and Blackwell, unseen, returned gunfire from above. Lewis backed away from the stairs, his pulse racing. He hoped Jenna had managed to slip out with the crowd.

A figure began running down the stairs, illuminated by

the strobe lights in quick bursts. More gunshots fired above. One of the men in black was advancing while the other provided covering fire. Lewis seized the opportunity. He ran forward as fast as he could and reached both of his hands through the stairs just as the agent's foot touched down, wrapping his fingers tightly around the boot.

It almost seemed to happen in slow motion. The figure tripped and flew headlong toward the dance floor, barely having enough time to put out their hands before they smashed onto the illuminated tiles. The next burst of neon light showed him Jackson scrambling to get back up, raising up onto his knees and swinging the handgun toward the bar, an enraged scream tearing from his lips as Gonzalez leaned out from cover.

He wasn't fast enough.

The FBI agent squeezed the trigger before Jackson could get an aim, her bullet tearing through his forehead and out the back of his skull. Blood splattered across the floor and stairs and Lewis wheeled back, trying to brush the crimson drops off his face.

He tripped over a drinking glass someone had left on the ground and fell over backward. Grimacing, Lewis did his best to ignore the pain in his shoulder and crawled back away from the underside of the stairs.

After a few moments, he realized no more shots had been fired. The club was quiet save for the music. From here, it appeared the DJ had vacated the booth but left his equipment playing. Lewis slowly got back up and waited, listening carefully.

When he heard nothing, he cautiously inched forward out into the open, away from the staircase, and looked back up to the second level. Blackwell was gone.

"Lewis!"

He turned. Gonzalez slid over the counter and began jogging toward him, her gun still at the ready. "Don't worry, I saw him duck out once I iced his friend."

"Nice shot," he said, glancing back where the dead man lay.

"Good thinking tripping him through the stairs. I would've been toast without that. Thank you." She tucked her gun back into her holster and pulled out her FBI badge. "We're probably gonna need this in about thirty seconds."

"We've gotta move," Lewis said. "Blackwell must've left to chase Jenna. She's who they really want."

They sprinted up the stairs, but as they reached the top, something caught Lewis's eye. Jenna was climbing out from behind one of the upper floor's corner bars, looking suitably shaken and rubbing one arm with her other hand. He grabbed Gonzalez's shoulder and stopped them both, pointing.

"When you started firing," Jenna said to her, "the two of them were distracted. I figured hiding would be better than slipping out like they'd expect I would."

Gonzalez nodded. "Smart." She looked around. "Well, we finally have the group all together."

"Fucking FREEZE!"

The trio turned in unison as numerous S.W.A.T. officers rushed in through the front entrance wielding assault rifles. "Hands where I can see them, on your knees, now!"

They did as they were told, but Gonzalez turned her badge toward them. "Sara Gonzalez, FBI. These two are with me."

The lead officer took her badge, looked it over, and handed it back to her. "Thank you. So what the hell happened here?"

All three of them got back to their feet. "These two are witnesses in a political corruption case. Three hitmen have been trying to kill them all evening. Two are downstairs, one dead and the other unconscious, but the third one got away."

A cop leaned over the railing and looked out across the dance floor. "I only see one body," he shouted over the music.

Everyone froze for a moment, then walked to the top of the stairs. Lewis had to peer over someone's shoulder just to get a good look. In the light of the flashing strobes, he could see Jackson on his back with his brains scattered across the floor, but where Caruso had fallen, there was nothing but glowing pink and blue tiles.

29

Camera bulbs flashed all around the interior of the nightclub. The music had been shut off with the strobes, and now the main lights glared overhead as the police worked to turn Solaria into a crime scene. Jackson had been placed in a body bag and taken out minutes ago, but the blood remained next to a yellow A-frame marking tent labeled "2."

Lewis stared blankly at it. One of the officers had given him a wet washcloth to get the blood off his face, but she'd said he wouldn't be permitted to go back to his hotel and change for a while. They'd wanted to take him to the hospital to get the bullet removed, but Gonzalez forbade them to let him leave, so they had a well-trained EMT do it at one of the tables upstairs. He was now all patched up, and both he and Jenna had already been thoroughly questioned.

Gonzalez told the cops that, due to the nature of the "corruption" case, neither he nor Jenna were permitted to discuss why exactly the "hitmen" had been after them, citing national security concerns. Lewis did, however, tell them everything that had happened over the past few hours, including the murder of the policeman on the bridge. He also told the officers that Blackwell had bragged about the footage being edited or even deleted, which given the hushed frantic conversations of the detectives in charge, appeared to have some validity to it.

Once they became concerned with a mole in the police department, the investigators quickly lost interest in Lewis and he was left without instruction. He'd been aimlessly wandering around the dance floor since.

Jenna sat on a bar stool some distance away, still being questioned. Gonzalez finished talking with one of the detectives, then approached him.

"How are you feeling?" she asked.

He shrugged. "I've had better days."

"Some vacation, huh?"

"Technically, it was a business trip."

Gonzalez looked around Solaria. "Seemed like a nice club. Shame we had to tear it up."

"I'm just glad nobody innocent got hurt."

"But they already have," she said, growing more serious. "This Arcadia business has been going on for months. We need to put an end to it ASAP."

"Blackwell and Caruso are planning their next moves as we speak. Once the S.W.A.T. team leaves, they'll find a way back. They've invested too much in this to let either of us go."

"We're going to be out of here soon. I've requested an unmarked car from the Vegas PD. The three of us are going to Arcadia. Tonight."

"Tonight? Still?" He glanced at his watch. It was barely 9PM, but he felt exhausted.

"You said they weren't well guarded. We should be able

to sneak in and get to the other building. Whatever agency is behind this is never going to let us get a warrant; they'll find a way of interfering with due process. The only way to get hard evidence is to sneak in there and take it, like you tried to do. Although this time, you'll have backup."

"That's crazy. Jenna and I aren't trained at all."

"I know, but you're alternative is staying here like sitting ducks. If a government agency wants you dead, not even the police will be able to protect you. I'm surprised they haven't altered your and Jenna's criminal records and forged warrants for your arrests yet. I'd rather not wait around for that to happen."

"I have no clue if what we find there will be any use."

"We know that Arcadia has to be where the final brainwashing occurs. Clearly, the game by itself is not enough to induce homicidal psychosis. So they must do *something* else to the gamers there. Not to mention they kidnapped a person last night. Remember?"

He nodded. He hated to think what they might be doing to the poor person.

"They have access to the security cameras all over Vegas," Lewis pointed out. "I wouldn't be surprised if they had a special drone flying overhead. They'll know we're on our way."

"Not necessarily. In movies, they always make it seem like the conspiracy is much larger than it actually is. Whoever is funding this Zhao guy, it's probably a rogue element of an existing agency that is funneling money from other projects toward this side venture. Think about it, they could have framed you for murder and had the Vegas PD come after you by now, but they haven't yet. It doesn't mean they're not trying to get access to those sort of things, it means they don't have *easy* access to begin with. They sent some of their own people after you two as a quick op, and then those people fucked up.

"There were three of them. Two were probably surveilling you at the pool. They followed Jenna up to her room and were supposed to grab her there while one waited in the car, keeping the engine running. It was supposed to be in and out. But she got away, and then you got mixed up, and then one of them killed a cop, and then the whole incident here happened, and now one of them is dead. Zhao is probably freaking out right now. He ran a low profile in the desert for six months, but now his people have become a liability. I wouldn't be surprised if his bosses decide to torch everything and terminate the project – and him along with it."

"If they killed everyone involved, that would be convenient for us."

Gonzalez shook her head. "Probably not. If they bring in real professionals – I'm talking top-level black ops teams who you won't be able to outrun – then we're *all* dead. Zhao's employers will want to wipe the slate completely clean, and they'll leave nothing behind."

"How long do we have before that happens?"

"Probably not long. I would say tonight is our last chance to get in there before the clean-up crew scrubs it off the face of the Earth."

Lewis nodded and sighed. He hated the thought of going back there, but those two words sifted through his memory like the whispers of a distant dream.

"*Arcadia awaits.*"

He could see Jenna standing there, drenched in blood, her eyes turning black and her lips curling into a sinister smile.

Lewis shook his head and turned back to Gonzalez.

"When do we leave?"

"Soon," she said.

One of the detectives, a lean Japanese man in his late 40s, walked up to them. "Agent Gonzalez, Officer Rogers just informed me that the car you requested is here."

"Excellent. Thank you." She turned to Lewis. "Get Jenna. We're out of here."

30

A cool breeze greeted Lewis as he climbed out of the passenger seat and looked around the gas station. It was a quiet night out here along this lone section of desert highway. US-93 stretched off to the horizon in each direction beneath the stars. A full moon shone down from the heavens. A large sign just off the road displayed a giant, glowing white letter G against a gray background. Theirs was the only vehicle here.

Gonzalez shut the driver's side door of the unmarked white Nissan. "Can't believe they didn't give us a car without a full tank."

"Guess they didn't think we'd be driving so far," Jenna said, getting out of the back and stretching. It was over 70 miles from downtown Las Vegas to Arcadia, and then another 70 back.

"We're still about a half-hour away," the FBI agent noted, glancing back the way they came. They hadn't seen another car in ages.

"Can we grab some snacks or something quickly? I haven't eaten in ages," Jenna said, putting a hand on her stomach.

"Sure, be quick," Gonzalez said, moving to the pump.

"Come on, Des." There seemed to be something off about her tone. She led him to the convenience mart entrance and they went in. The air conditioning gave the store an unnecessary chill and the clerk behind the counter looked pale and bored reading a weathered paperback novel. His eyes flicked up from the page as they walked in, then returned down again.

The store had three aisles and a bunch of drinks along the back wall. Chips were in the second aisle and Jenna led him over to it. She sighed and put a hand to her forehead.

"You alright?" he asked.

"Hey, you're the one that got shot."

He shrugged. "Shit happens."

She laughed. "I just never figured someone would want to target e-sports champions as part of a government plot."

"To be honest, it does seem a bit far-fetched."

Jenna narrowed her eyes and looked back out the window. "Listen…this whole thing has me worried. I don't know what Gonzalez is thinking! We're not trained at all, why is she bringing us along without backup?"

"She doesn't want anyone else to get involved in this. And we've both actually been to Arcadia before, she hasn't. We're more familiar with the layout."

"Or…" Jenna glanced out the window, then leaned closer. "She's taking us *straight to them*."

Lewis blinked, confused. "What? She can't be working for them, she shot one of them in the face! She's been helping us both this whole time."

"Des, what did she say to you just before we got into the car?"

"She said a lot of things."

"The *clean-up crew*. The agency that employed Zhao and all his people at Arcadia is probably going to terminate everyone involved if they think there's a risk of them getting exposed. First, your buddy Jake dies while doing a story on them, but they manage to pass that off as him doing drugs – which is improbable to anyone who knew him, but whatever. Then Charlie, their next target, is scheduled to go nuts in L.A. this past week. So they send in one of their operatives, Gonzalez, and have her pose as an FBI agent to make sure the investigation doesn't turn up anything. Hell, *she's* probably the one who deleted *Rogue Horizon* off Charlie's computer!

"She realizes you know more than you're letting on, and through surveillance or whatever finds out you're going to Vegas. Actually no, she doesn't even need surveillance. You called Arcadia and booked a tour for you and me. Her superiors would've told her. How else did she magically know to run into you here? That would've been an incredible coincidence if she was here on her own, wouldn't it?"

"No way. My boss told her I'd be here."

"Did you confirm that with Valerie Richter?"

Lewis was horrified. He stared at the floor and listened as she continued.

"So, let's say her superiors, the people who even Zhao works for, are concerned with his performance as of late. Maybe there's a whole bunch of other fuck-ups we don't know about that they've sent her to Nevada to look in on too. Point is, she's in Vegas, meets up with you, and sees the total mess that Zhao's people cause here. They murder a cop in public, they shoot up a nightclub, they get recorded all over street cameras and CCTV. She plays it slick though. She's gonna befriend you and me and trick us into spying on Arcadia with her. Meanwhile, she's captured us without ever having to use handcuffs or putting bags over our heads. When she sees the mess that Blackwell, Caruso, and Jackson have caused she decides they're liabilities who need to be killed and written off as random hitmen. So now she's going to turn us over to Zhao and then wait for orders from her superiors to see if she needs to torch the whole place with us inside or not."

He shook his head. "It's just…it's too…"

"I thought you were just being paranoid earlier, and see where that got us? I need you to trust me here, Des. Think about it: why did she suddenly disappear on you back at the Mirage? She *hid*. She knew Blackwell was about to capture you. And how did the men in black know you were headed to Solaria? *Because you had just told her!* Once the fight broke out and they failed to do their job properly, she decided the best way to salvage the situation was to kill them and save us so that we'd drive all the way out here with her. Sara Gonzalez probably isn't even her real fucking *name!*"

Just then, the door chimed and swung open. Lewis and Jenna both looked up over the aisles to see the face of the woman who had driven them here taking in her surroundings. She glanced back at them.

"Come on," she said, looking almost angry. "It's time to go."

Lewis became perfectly still, a thousand different thoughts racing through his mind. Everything his girlfriend had just said made sense of the past several hours. And in truth, he had been skeptical of Gonzalez – if that was her actual name –

from the moment he'd met her. One of the lead investigators in a national FBI case just happened to be in L.A. in time for the next incident to happen? It was possible, but unlikely.

The probability of her just finding him like that at the Mirage's poolside was even more unlikely still.

The real question was: what did they do now? Gonzalez had the car and would've told Zhao that she was inbound with the two of them. Arcadia would be expecting them. There was no way they could sneak in now. Flight was the only option. Even if they managed to somehow subdue her and drive into the compound pretending to be her, Zhao would have people waiting as soon as they opened the doors.

"What are you waiting for?" Gonzalez said. "Buy something or don't. We've gotta get a move on."

He could practically see the gears turning in her brain, the thoughts streaming through her mind: *They've finally started to figure it out. They're onto me and they're very bad at hiding it.*

Jenna looked at him, hesitating. "Actually, I don't think I'm gonna get anything."

"I thought you were hungry," she said.

Jenna scratched her shoulder. "I guess I'm not anymore," she said, forcing a smile.

"Okay," Gonzalez said.

It happened very quickly. In a flash, her pistol was drawn and aimed toward the counter as her finger curled around the trigger. The clerk looked up and opened his mouth to scream, but the bullet tore through his face before he could emit a sound. Cranial matter exploded all over the rack of lottery tickets behind him, and his body was thrown back like a ragdoll before sliding down out of sight.

Lewis and Jenna hit the floor.

Gonzalez sighed loudly. "Alright, the jig is up. Let's not make this any more difficult than it has to be."

Lewis tried to keep his breathing quiet. His heart beat rapidly and his pulse pounded in his ears. This was a small store. There was nowhere to hide or run and with two well-placed shots, Gonzalez would have them both incapacitated. At this point, he realized she'd probably kill him and deal with Jenna by herself. She couldn't hurt her too much because she had to be released back into the world with her completed programming.

Unless she really was planning on killing everyone at Arcadia. Then it wouldn't make a difference if she shot them here or not.

He heard her footsteps walking around the other end of the aisles. He and Jenna quickly scurried to the end of their row and hid around the back. Somewhere at the other side of the store, Gonzalez stopped. "I know where you are. Hiding is pointless," she said.

Lewis turned to Jenna. "Run for it?" she said.

He shook his head. "No, she's too good a shot."

Gonzalez began advancing up the middle aisle. "A pity it has to end this way…"

Tires squealed outside as headlights splashed across the store's inventory. A car door slammed, then another. The entrance chimed as it opened.

"You traitorous bitch!" He recognized Caruso's voice.

Now he leaned out around the corner just in time to see Gonzalez swing her arm toward the entrance and pull the trigger. Gunfire erupted in the store and glass shattered. Gonzalez crouched down, then moved around the corner and headed toward the door. More shots came from outside. He turned to his girlfriend.

"Run," she said.

They got up and bolted. There was an exit to the rear with a piece of paper taped to it that read RESTROOMS LOCATED OUTSIDE. They burst through the door and into the night.

A red Jeep Wrangler with a soft top was parked there. "That must be the clerk's car," his girlfriend said. "We've got to get the keys."

"I'll find them," he said, diving back into the store.

Keeping low, he took cover behind the back row and cautiously peered around the corner. From this vantage point, he could see Gonzalez standing outside and firing at somebody off to the left. The front door seemed to be stuck open and its glass had been shattered by bullets. Jagged shards jutted around the metal frame.

Lewis didn't hesitate. He ran behind the counter to where the dead clerk lay and began frisking him as if he were a corpse to loot for supplies in *Rogue Horizon*. He found the car keys in the left pocket, took them, and ran, briefly catching sight of what blocked the door. Caruso lay on her back, half inside, half out, her white shirt stained dark with bloody bullet holes.

He dashed back through the rear door, climbed into the Jeep, and slid the key into the ignition. "Caruso's dead," he said as the engine roared to life. "Blackwell and Gonzalez are having a little shootout in the parking lot."

"Then let's get the hell out of here."

Buckling his seat belt, he floored the accelerator and the Jeep barreled out into the desert. He swung the wheel to the left, aiming them back at the road. As they pulled onto US-93, Lewis glanced in the rear-view mirror to see a black sedan swerving out of the gas station, a pair of headlights racing after them through the dark.

31

"Shit!" Jenna swore as she looked back. She turned to him. "Does this thing go any faster?"

"Working on it," he said, pushing the pedal all the way.

The Jeep revved forward, its speed ticking past 100 miles per hour. Even the slightest twitch of the wheel caused the vehicle to sway wildly in the lane. The car behind them continued to gain ground, closing the gap between them.

Lewis looked ahead. There was nothing but empty road in front of them and bumpy, open desert on either side of the lanes. Nowhere to turn, nowhere to hide. The car went as fast as it could; it felt like he was steering a rocket with wheels. Air violently battered the front window, wind whipping around the sides of the Wrangler.

The black sedan got closer in the mirror every time he glanced at it, gliding forward at a frightening pace like a vehicular angel of death. Soon it was right behind him, and he saw a gun-wielding hand reach out of the front window and begin firing. The rear window cracked. He and Jenna ducked as shots sailed over their heads and made bullet holes through the front windshield.

Lewis felt the vehicle swaying wildly side to side, and looked back up to get it under control. In the side mirror, he saw the driver of the car behind them leaning their full upper torso out the window to get better aim, their other hand remaining on the steering wheel inside. More shots rang out in the night.

Past the glare of the pursuing vehicle's headlights, Lewis could make out the snarling face of Blackwell. He'd ditched the fedora and exposed his bald head to the roaring air, and in that instant Lewis *knew* he'd seen him somewhere before. He just couldn't place—

"Des!"

He whipped around. Jenna stared back at him, looking both sad and dreadfully scared. One of her palms was red with blood. Hers. A stray shot had gone through the back of her seat and come out toward the side of her abdomen.

Lewis opened his mouth but never got the chance to speak.

The rear left tire burst in that second, a well-placed round by Blackwell having found its mark. The Jeep swerved wildly, fishtailing like a beast from the sea. He tried to wrangle it, tried to keep the front aimed straight, slammed on the brakes, but it was little use. He lost all control and the car veered off the road, the wheels useless to direction, and the whole world spun on the other side of the windshield. He closed his eyes, his worst nightmare come true, and felt his entire body restrained against the terrifying force of the crash as the car tumbled and rolled and glass and steel and bones cracked all around him. Something heavy collided against his chest, cracking a rib, as long strands of hair brushed across his face. Finally, the Jeep came to a halt on its roof. He kept his eyes squeezed shut, ignoring the pain all over his body, pushing the dark memories deep back down the well.

And then, in that awful instant, he realized he never saw Jenna put on her seatbelt.

Lewis's eyes flashed open. Everything was upside-down; all the blood rushed to his head. Dazed, he looked up – down, really – toward the ceiling and at that moment a terror he had not felt in years gripped his body.

Jenna lay face down among the glass shards at an awkward angle, her head turned to the side. Her eyes were open and devoid of life.

"No," he said, unable to fight back the tears. "No, no, no, no, no, no."

Lewis desperately fumbled for his seatbelt and finally found the release. With a *click*, he was free and falling toward her. He just managed to put his hands out to land to reduce the impact, but it still hurt. At that moment, he didn't even register his broken rib.

"No, no, no…" He turned her over but her dead eyes stared up past him, a saddened but ultimately peaceful expression cemented on her face. He stared at her for several long moments, unable to comprehend the sight before him. But ultimately, deep down, he recognized that she was gone.

Lewis squeezed his eyes shut, tried to hold back the deluge of tears welling up in his eyes. It was no use; the dam burst. Memories flooded his mind. He saw himself on that Friday evening five months ago, when Ricky had introduced him to some of his gamer friends as they went bar hopping through Santa Monica. Jenna had been there, and it wasn't just how pretty she was that made him fall for her. She had had a certain energy about her, a vivacious spirit in her eyes that complemented her broad smiles and infectious laughter.

He'd been so worried about making a good first impression that he'd accidentally spilled his drink on her while turning around at the bar. A couple months later, Jenna told him that she'd found it endearing. In the moment, she'd laughed it off and they wound up have a long conversation while the others were back at the table. They'd traded numbers before they each departed for the night and made plans to meet again, just the two of them.

And now here she was, lying broken inside an overturned car.

Not again.

The astronaut laughed maniacally somewhere off in the distance. The tears streamed down Lewis's face now, just as they had that night so long ago. The night his mother held him tightly by the side of a lonely forest road, directing his attention away from the twisted wreck of her car toward the stars above.

The night he caused the death of his baby brother.

PART THREE
GAME OVER

32

If he held it up against the window just right, it almost looked like it was flying through the stars. He could imagine himself at the helm of a real space shuttle, the whole *three, two, one* takeoff, the blue sky fading into blackness, and then the lights of distant galaxies and supernovas all around him.

That was going to be him someday.

Desmond Lewis, Astronaut.

At age seven, it was all very certain. He could see his whole life ahead of him. First, he was going to graduate high school as a Valedictorian and then go to Stanford, where he would double major in Astrophysics and Engineering. He was going to get an internship at NASA and then go right into their astronaut program right out of college. He would move to Cape Canaveral, that beautiful place he and Mommy and Daddy and Georgie had visited two years ago, the place with all the palm trees and the beach, the place that was only an hour's drive to Disney World, the place where he'd convinced them to buy the plush space shuttle.

The space shuttle was his favorite thing in the whole wide world. He took it everywhere, except school. The kids there were mean and might try to steal it or throw it in the garbage because they knew he loved it so much. He wore NASA t-shirts and talked endlessly of space and *Star Wars* and sci-fi. Some of his other friends were into that stuff too, but the other kids made fun of him for it. It didn't matter. One day he was gonna blast out of this world and leave them all behind.

And when he did come back from his adventures colonizing the Moon and Mars, and establishing space stations at Lagrange points so that they stayed in the same spot relative to Earth, everyone was going to think he was *so* cool. His science teacher said she was impressed he even knew what a Lagrange point was at his age.

He was going to marry his friend Virginia who once kissed him on the cheek and said she loved him. They were going to have a big house on the beach with lots of palm trees and have kids and a dog and a wonderful life. And at Christmas, Mom and Dad and Georgie would all come to his place because it would be the nicest house out of all of theirs.

Lowering his plush space shuttle from the window, Desmond looked around the car. He was sitting in the rear left seat of his mother's Ford Explorer. Georgie sat to the right of him, staring out the other window. His mother was up front behind the wheel, one elbow propped against the door beside her. The Rolling Stones' "Paint it Black" played at a low volume on the radio.

Desmond looked over at his brother. George Lewis was three years younger than him and 100 percent more annoying. He hated how Georgie always came into his room and trashed his stuff, then ran out laughing. He was such a little jerk. One time, he'd grabbed one of Desmond's favorite action figures and flushed it down the toilet. That's why he now kept his most sacred toys and stuffed animals up high on a shelf in his closet. Georgie wouldn't be able to reach that high for years. He dreaded the thought of his little brother trying to shove the space shuttle into the toilet.

Right now, Georgie was playing with his seatbelt. He always liked doing that even though their parents always told him not to. Georgie was so stupid sometimes. And annoying. Sometimes he wished Georgie had been given up for adoption. After Georgie flushed the action figure down the drain, Desmond had screamed "I hate you!" and spent an entire night wishing Georgie had never been born, that his parents had never had another child. Or if they had, that they would've given him a sister. She would've recognized he had cooties and kept her toys separate from his. She would be too busy playing with Barbie dolls to try and steal his action figures and toss them down a whirlpool to a watery grave.

"Mommy, how long until we get home?" he asked impatiently. They'd spent the weekend at her sister's place, and she lived off in the middle of nowhere, which was why they were driving through a dimly lit forest road late at night, instead of on the highway like ordinary people.

"Another hour or so, baby," she replied, sighing. It had been a long day. She'd argued with her sister a lot. Desmond didn't understand why she kept hanging out with her relatives if she didn't like them that much. He didn't want to hang out with Georgie when he got older. Georgie was such a drag. Desmond was going to move to Florida and become an astronaut, and Georgie could go flush his own toys down the toilet then.

The weekend hadn't been that fun. He and his brother

had sat around and watched old VHS movies from the 80s, but he'd already seen them before. Aunt Nicole hadn't given them much to do and was either very patronizing or rude to them. Desmond guessed it was why she never got married and had kids. Their dad was lucky; he'd spent the whole weekend at home with the dog.

Desmond looked back outside. Beyond the road's edge, the forest stretched off into the black. It gave him the chills just thinking what could be lurking in there: mosquitoes, bears, maybe even an axe-wielding lunatic. He liked space because it was open and the stars lit up the dark no matter which direction you looked. And, like the horizon, it went off to infinity. You could never reach the end of it. There was always something new to explore.

Suddenly, he felt the space shuttle wrenched from his hands. He turned to see Georgie, triumphant, holding it up like he'd won a prize.

"GIVE IT BACK!" Desmond screamed.

"Des," his mother said, glancing in the rear-view mirror. "Stay calm."

"Make him give it back!" he cried.

"Georgie, you know that's not yours. Give it back to your brother."

"No!" Georgie cried, hugging it tightly. "It's mine!"

"Give it back!" Desmond reiterated. His hands were shaking now, watching the space shuttle carefully.

"George Lewis, give that back to your brother this instant!"

Georgie giggled and leaned farther away. "Never!"

Desmond turned forward. "Mom, make him stop it!"

She gave an exasperated sigh. "Look Des, I'm driving. I can't deal with it now. Georgie, just give it back." And then she continued in a lower voice, thinking her children couldn't hear her, "I don't have the energy for this shit right now."

Georgie kept laughing and Desmond's blood began to boil. He watched anxiously as his brother carelessly swung the plush shuttle around and bashed it against his knees, the window, and the back of the seat in front of him.

"Stop it!" he hissed.

Georgie turned toward him and, with a taunting laugh and an evil gleam in his eye, dug his fingernails into the plush and began pulling, trying to tear it open.

Desmond flipped. "STOP IT STOP IT STOP IT STOP IT!" He leaned over and grabbed the toy spacecraft, and tried to pull it out of his brother's hands, but George tugged back.

At this point, Desmond did the only thing he could think of: he screamed at the highest pitch he could. Then Georgie started screaming the same way, too.

Their mother whipped around to face both of them in the backseat. "For the love of Christ, would the two of you shut the fu–"

Had she still been looking at the road then, maybe she would've seen the Chevy Trailblazer that had accidentally drifted into their lane and was now heading for a direct collision. Lewis saw the headlights grow brighter and brighter as the other car tried to course correct by swerving off the road at the very last second. His own mother turned around, her hands flying to the wheel, but about a third of the fronts of each car still collided with each other.

Desmond closed his eyes as he felt the vehicle spin around and then the wheels lost touch with the ground, the entire steel body of the SUV started rolling over and over–

He blacked out.

When he came to he was dangling upside-down, blood trickling across his forehead. Slowly, he tilted his head down at the ceiling. Georgie lay unnervingly still on his back, his eyes wide open. The space shuttle lay overturned beside him about a foot away.

It took Lewis a while to fully process that his brother was dead. When he finally did, he began to cry, quietly, alone there suspended in his seat. He cried for what felt like eons before a figure, sobbing loudly, opened the door beside him and unbuckled his seat belt. After making sure he was safely on the ground, she crawled over to Georgie and wept over his body for some time.

Desmond crawled out onto the asphalt and began crying louder. His mother came up behind him and, taking his hand, led him away from the wreck. He saw she was limping heavily as she pulled him to an empty patch of asphalt by the side of the lane. Then she sat down and hugged him tightly.

Desmond looked back to the car and continued crying, but she tapped him on the shoulder. "No, no, no. Look, look up there." She pointed and he shifted his eyes to the heavens.

The sky was beautiful that night, but despite his years of stargazing, it had suddenly lost its luster. He no longer pictured his toy spaceship sailing through it; instead, he looked up and saw only blackness and a scattering of bright points.

His mother gazed up there too, trying to stop her tears to poor effect. "Don't worry, baby. Everything's gonna be alright. Everything's gonna be alright." She sobbed and heaved but never took her eyes off the stars as she kept saying those words, over and over again. "Everything's gonna be alright."

It wasn't until another car passed by that someone actually called 9-1-1. Of the two teenagers in the Chevy Trailblazer, one was dead and the other was in a coma. She'd been texting and driving and accidentally swerved into their lane. Her boyfriend, who had sat in the passenger seat, died instantly on impact. She would later wake up and send an apology letter to the Lewis family. Desmond's mother read it once and violently ripped it up.

Things were tense in the household for a long while. His parents fought more and more. Desmond went to therapy for years. He sat there sobbing on a sofa, saying it was all his fault. He should have let Georgie rip up the stupid space shuttle. His brother died and it was all because of him. Over time, the therapist helped him accept that Georgie was only a child, so was he, and that sometimes children do childish things. Georgie was also the one who'd undone his own seatbelt while playing with it, and the driver of the other car shouldn't have been texting behind the wheel. Neither of those things had anything to do with Desmond.

In his teens, he was diagnosed with a form of post-traumatic stress disorder. By the time he was in his twenties, he'd found a way of moving past the memory. Ultimately, it was simple.

He never thought about Georgie.

It was as if he never existed. He locked him up in a box and shut him away in the dark recesses of his mind. He accepted that nothing would ever change what happened and decided to shut the past out completely. He quickly lost interest in space beyond the occasional sci-fi movie. After that, he went to undergrad at UCLA for journalism, stayed in the city, and set up a new life there without ever looking back.

Until now.

33

Headlights burst through the overturned Jeep's windows as Lewis heard the black sedan roll to a halt at the edge of the road. A door opened and closed somewhere outside. The killer's footsteps grew louder as they approached the wreck.

Slowly, Lewis sat up as grief turned to rage. He frantically searched the car for anything he could use as a weapon, but he was out of luck. He ducked down and glanced out of the broken window at the dark figure approaching. It was Blackwell, silhouetted by the glare of the headlights behind him. Lewis could just make out his angry expression and a bandage across his forehead.

The man in black raised his hand. Lewis saw the gun's muzzle flash just before a bullet narrowly missed him, embedding itself in the metal of the door.

He scrambled back, took one last look at Jenna's motionless figure, then fumbled with the passenger door handle and managed to push it open. Grunting, he pulled himself out into the desert and clenched his teeth to ignore the pain from his broken rib and his wounded shoulder. Agony wracked his body, but he pushed past it as he took cover and breathed deeply.

"I know you're alive, Mr. Lewis!" Blackwell's voice called. "There's nowhere left to run."

He clenched his fists. *Think, think, think.* Somehow, he had to get to Blackwell's car. If the agent didn't know he had exited the Jeep, he might be able to sneak past him and make a break for it while he inspected the wreck. It was very risky, but at this point, he was out of good options.

Then he looked to his right and found a better one.

It was a rock, small enough to fit in his hand, but it looked weighty enough to do some damage. Cautiously, he reached forward to grab it, then retreated to the side of the Jeep. It was quite heavy after all, perfect for what he needed. He heard Blackwell getting near to the left side of the wreck.

Lewis started slowly around the rear of the flipped vehicle, keeping his breathing measured and quiet. The cold air stung his lungs.

Blackwell stopped. He could hear him crouching down. Any second now he was going to see that Jenna was dead – that would slow him down for a moment, she'd been the main mission after all – but then he'd look past her corpse and see the other door open and Lewis gone and–

He made his move.

Lewis sailed around the side of the car, the rock raised high. Sure enough, Blackwell was crouching down and peering in, a look of horror washing over his face as he realized he had made a terrible error. Then he turned and dismay turned to shock. The man in black's quick reflexes took over as he swiftly sprung to his feet and whipped his pistol toward Lewis.

He grabbed Blackwell's arm and barely managed to sidestep the gun just before it went off, bringing his other hand around to slam the rock as hard as he could into the other man's chest. There was a sharp *crack* and Blackwell gasped, the pistol slipping from his fingers as he careened back and fell into the dirt beneath the pale moonlight.

Lewis turned and dove for the pistol; he hit the ground and his fingers curled around the grip. He turned over onto his back to aim, when an enraged Blackwell launched himself on top of him, the two men falling onto their sides as they struggled for the weapon.

He violently lashed out with his foot and hit Blackwell's shin. The man hissed through gritted teeth and jerked back slightly, but it was all Lewis needed. He pulled the gun to the left, swinging the end of the barrel toward his opponent's abdomen, and squeezed the trigger.

Dark blood spurted from the wound and the man in black finally let go, enabling Lewis to scurry back while keeping his aim trained on him. Slowly, he got to his feet as Blackwell clutched his side and pulled himself back against the wreck.

Lewis stayed where he was, the gun shaking in his grip. He held onto it with both hands.

Blackwell threw his head back and began laughing.

"What?" Lewis shouted. "What's so fucking funny?"

The man in black pretended to wipe a tear off his eye. "Alright Mr. Lewis, you did it. You killed me. Are you happy now?"

Lewis stood there, seething with rage. "You killed her! You people killed all of them, every fucking one of them!"

He laughed again. "I did you a favor. She was going to die anyway once we finished the brainwashing and sent her back home. She was going to butcher her friends, probably you too, and then kill herself just like the rest. Inadvertently, I just saved her legacy."

"I suppose that's one way of putting it," Lewis said. He wanted to pull the trigger right now, to blow this asshole's brains all over the side of the car. But other ideas floated through his head. *Punch him, beat the living shit out of him, break every one of his fingers, smash his fucking skull in with the rock.*

"Come on, Lewis. Kill me. Kill me and go to Arcadia and kill all the others. You have to now. The woman you love is dead. Isn't that a wonderful cliché? Now you can go avenge her, but deep down you'll always know it was you who killed her. Just like you killed your little brother."

"Shut up!" he barked. His hands shook again.

"You brought her to Vegas. Turns out she hadn't been playing that much *Rogue Horizon* after all. You were the one who got brainwashed by accident. You answered the call and brought her right to us. She was the one we'd wanted all along. You're a nobody Lewis, but her...she was really somebody, wasn't she? A gaming celebrity, while you're just a middling tech journalist."

"I said shut the fuck up!"

"You wanted to be an astronaut. You wanted to explore the stars. But instead, you wound up living in the shadow of your rich, famous girlfriend. Tell me, were you ever stupid enough to think that *you* were important enough for us to target?"

"No," he said. "It was never like that."

"Then why did you pursue all this?"

"I just wanted to know." His voice was softer now. "I wanted the truth."

"Ah, truth." Blackwell sighed. "Well, truth hurts Lewis."

He laughed again, but the pain was evident. He raised his head slowly, the evil smirk on his face illuminated by the full moon.

Lewis tilted his head to the side, suddenly realizing where he'd seen the man in black's face before. And then in that instant, it all became perfectly, painfully clear to him.

He knew why the day had been so strange, why some things had been so familiar, why other things so illogical, and why it all kept going to shit. The realization hit him hard and he stumbled back, putting his hand to his head and suddenly laughing uncontrollably. It had been right in front of him the whole time. They'd played him well.

Blackwell looked confused. "What's so funny? I don't understand."

"No," Lewis said, calming down. "But I do. I can't go back to Arcadia anymore."

He frowned. "Why not?"

To the other man's surprise, Lewis brought the pistol to the side of his head. "Because I never left."

He pulled the trigger.

For a second, a brief jolt coursed through his entire body and everything went black.

It stayed that way for one very long moment.

Then two words in bright blue, computerized text flashed before him.

SIMULATION ENDED.

34

Lewis blinked multiple times and suddenly the blackness was gone; instead, a harsh glare shone down on him from above. It took him a few seconds for his eyes to adjust as everything around him came into focus. He lay floating on his back in a dimly-lit high-ceilinged room, with a bright white LED lamp shining straight at him. Directly in the center of his field of vision stood a large robotic arm contraption that aimed something down at his face. He'd never seen anything like it before.

He tried to sit up but found himself restrained at his wrists and ankles by waterproof Velcro straps that kept him spread-eagled like a Vitruvian man. Lewis managed to sit up enough to look down; he was dressed in some kind of silvery haptic wetsuit and, although he couldn't see it, some form of silicone cap covered his head. The water tank he found himself in was the size of a small swimming pool.

"Congratulations," came a familiar voice. "In the six months I've been doing this, you're the first to wake up."

Lewis turned his head to the side and saw Blackwell striding toward him. Gone were the black suit, fedora, and sunglasses that had constituted his ensemble before. Instead, he sported the same white lab-coat and khakis he had while he served as the technician for his and Jenna's tour of Arcadia.

"Jesus Christ," Lewis said, looking around the room. He couldn't believe all this was happening. But he knew it was; dreams could seem shockingly vivid when you experienced them, but there was something different about the way the world looked and felt after you woke up that signified the change back to reality. As strange as his current predicament was, it actually made everything enormously clear.

"So this is what you do here. The game wasn't enough to brainwash them, so you put them in a sensory deprivation tank to fuck with their minds using experimental neurotech."

"Very good," Blackwell said, pulling over a rolling chair from the nearby desk. Lewis saw a number of thin, advanced monitors placed before it on the wall. One displayed the Orbital Hotel & Casino, another the gas station at the side of US-93, and another featuring the astronaut watching him and his mother cry by the side of the forest road.

"What the hell is this thing?" Lewis said, gesturing up to the robotic arm with a flick of his eyes.

"This," he replied, gesturing from the computer monitors to the deprivation tank and assorted equipment, "is the Dream Machine. Or, at least, a very early prototype of it. It's nowhere near as seamless as the concept Zhao showed you in the office today." He glanced at his watch. "Or yesterday now, I guess."

"What time is it?"

"4:24 AM, Saturday, January 26th. We nabbed you just before midnight, and you've been in the simulation for just under four hours now."

"How the hell did you do it? I mean, was that all...a *game*?"

"No, no. First, we place you in a stable, unconscious state using sedatives. When you were trying to escape with the flashdrive earlier tonight, you got hit pretty hard by Jackson –"

"Wait, Jackson?"

"Yeah, the security guard. You imagined him, Katelyn Caruso, and myself as men in black in the dream world. But I'll get to that in a moment." He was excited, clearly ecstatic to be telling one of his victims this after months of keeping it under wraps. "You almost woke up, but we stuck a needle in your neck, and you went back under pretty quickly. Then we changed you into the haptic suit, placed you in the pool here, and fitted the electrode cap over your head. It enables us to see what you're thinking. We've had the ability to turn brainwaves into images for a while, this is simply the next step. And that thing above your head projects a beam onto your retinas, allowing us to bypass sight and send images directly into your mind. I'm able to keep your eyes open by sending certain signals into that part of your brain through the electrode cap. This tech has all come a long way in the past few years, and we're not the only ones developing it. But the stuff we have here is better than anywhere else."

"I don't understand," he said. "How did you create a fully working prototype with today's technology? This level of VR only exists in science fiction."

Blackwell shrugged. "As my favorite author William Gibson once said, 'The future is already here. It's just not evenly distributed yet.'"

Lewis nodded. He was aware of developments in brain-computer interfaces and had considered writing an article on them at some point in the future, but had wanted to wait for them to get a little more advanced so the article would be more interesting to the average reader. Companies such as Neurable and Elon Musk's Neuralink were currently working to take human-computer connectivity to the next level, and many more were beginning to follow suit. He'd been aware of efforts to create direct-to-brain VR long before Zhao had gloated about his future endeavors to try and impress Jenna. But just like many in the tech world, Lewis hadn't believed this kind of tech would work until the late 2020s or even into the 2030s. Evidently, he'd been very, very wrong.

"Once you were knocked out, we decided to let you start dreaming. I began influencing your brainwaves and activating specific areas of your brain through the electrodes. I played up your paranoia and fear of not being believed, so when you began, you 'woke up' in your hotel room thinking it was Saturday, and that we'd brought you back and made it all seem as it was. You were so worried that everything would be exactly the way you found it that the simulation built that for you. Your girlfriend reacted exactly the way you thought she would in that situation. You began questioning if the car was too perfectly parked and other paranoid details.

"While the main dream was occurring, other memories and thoughts were drifting around your mind at different levels of brain activity. From this, I was able to pick up on part of your investigation, including the meeting with the FBI agent back in Pasadena. Part of you distrusted her, so I added her into your narrative to advance the plot forward. You began thinking it was a strange coincidence that she found you. It seemed so unrealistic – but part of your mind began wondering if she was a spy for us, so I introduced the words Jenna said to you into your mind about Gonzalez being in on it. From there your brain took it and ran with it – boom, Gonzalez is now a villain in the story."

"So it operates mainly via the power of suggestion?" Lewis pulled his right hand below the water and began fiddling with the Velcro straps wrapped around his wrist, doing his best to make sure Blackwell couldn't see what he was doing.

"Pretty much, but I can also introduce direct images into your brain and see where you take them. Like the Orbital Casino, that was one of our inventions, both inside and out. But you added the nightclub and extrapolated the space theme onto it."

"Jenna really wanted to go to a nightclub."

"That was probably it."

"So what normally happens?" Lewis asked. "They don't wake up and you keep messing with them until they snap?"

"Not exactly. With you, I kept re-introducing the image of the astronaut and you really didn't like that. I mean, most people we bring here all have some phobia of it. It's probably the most striking image from *Rogue Horizon* and I always find it drifting somewhere through everyone's subconscious when we put them in the Dream Machine. But it had a really strong effect on you, probably because you were so obsessed with NASA and space as a kid. Maybe that's why you kept seeing it in your dreams by the wreck of your mother's car. You associated that night with astronauts because your brother nearly ripped up your favorite toy, and you think that you trying to get it back caused the accident that killed him. In that case, it makes sense that your brain would associate the subliminal images of the monster we placed near the beginning of the game with that incident.

"Anyway, it's a different amount of time in the tank for

everyone. Some people can take up to ten hours, other's it's less than two. Everyone's brain is different, and that's shaped by the experiences they have. Those with weak mental fortitude crack the earliest. And that's not limited to those suffering from some form of mental illness or health concern; some people are just easily influenced and allow their emotions to control them too much. I believe you were so resilient *because* you mostly overcame the grief caused by your brother's death. I had to work very hard to resurrect your old guilt, and it probably would have worked eventually had you not been already suspicious of this place when you came here.

"But anyway, once I see that my...*patients* have been completely broken down – their reality in the simulation has become completely devoid of any logic and it's just violence, anger, and fear – I determine that the procedure is complete. I call in some assistance, we top up the sedative and you enter a dreamless sleep, then we get you out and back into your normal clothes, take you back to your hotel – we've hacked into your records and know exactly where you're staying – and you go back home feeling fine for a few days. But not really, because the damage to your subconscious has already been done.

"The dreams and hallucinations keep getting worse and worse. You start to lose your grip on reality, and finally, you lash out. You think the enemies from *Rogue Horizon*, mixed with your past trauma, are everywhere, and that the only way out is with blood. Voices in your head become unbearable and suicide seems like your only relief. Otherwise, you'll just keep killing and killing. It's beautiful, really."

He sat there with his hands in his lap as if they were chatting about sports or movies. It was unbelievable. Here was the man who had been culpable for the deaths and suffering of many innocent people, and he dared to take pride in his work as if it were some twisted science fair project.

The Velcro strap was being difficult, but Lewis finally managed to bend his wrist enough to begin pulling it off with his fingers. The last part was still tricky.

Blackwell sighed. "You know, this is the first time we've ever had to use both tanks. There's another in one in a second room, on the other side of that wall. We've always had a back-up and sometimes we use this one, sometimes the other one, just to keep it fresh. But tonight, we had both you and our other special guest."

Lewis suddenly remembered the kidnapping victim, the one he had seen being taken out of the SUV with a bag over their head.

"I was initially disappointed they gave you to me instead of Katelyn. You're not as much of a gamer as most people we get here, but I was pleasantly surprised. Your whole sci-fi conspiracy thriller dream was great! I love that kind of stuff, much more interesting than the other narratives I've seen people spin in the Dream Machine. Your pal Charlie, he was here last week, and it was just all depressing bullying shit from high school. The astronaut took the voice of one of his 11th grade tormentors and chased him into a bathroom. He'd once gotten beaten up in there or something – anyway it was really pedestrian and lame. But *you*. That nightclub shootout had me at the edge of my seat. I couldn't stop laughing when Jenna smashed the bottle in my character's face. It was just like a movie! Actually, the whole nightclub scene really gave me major *Deus Ex* vibes – classic game, you must've played it. There's that whole nightclub scene in Hong Kong where Majestic-12's black ops unit begins a shootout on the dance floor and there's techno music blaring and neon everywhere and, oh man..." He smiled nostalgically, his mind lost in a reminiscent trance.

"And let me guess, you cribbed the gas station in the middle of the desert from the game too?" Lewis said.

Blackwell nodded. "Yeah, I even took the same "G" logo on the sign. It was my little director's Easter egg. Katelyn, she's a big *Half-Life 2* fan – we both love those early 2000s FPSs, and she always tries to throw in a little thing or two from there when she's at the controls. Keeps the job interesting. But wow, after that I really have to thank you. You made this night way more fun than I thought it would be. Getting to explain it all to you has been the height of my career here."

"Well," Lewis said bitterly, "I'm so glad you enjoyed it."

"Oh yeah, no worries," he said, giving a dismissive wave of the hand without any hint of sarcasm or irony. "Even with you figuring it all out, you still lasted longer than the other patient. Katelyn said she was disappointed in her, given her reputation in the gaming world and all, but I guess her mental state was weaker than we'd anticipated. They're just getting ready to take her back to Vegas now."

Lewis tried to sit up. "Who's the other patient?"

Blackwell gave a big, annoying smile. "Oh, I'm not allowed to say. But I think you can guess."

"No, no," Lewis said, shaking his head in the water. "That's impossible, she was still in bed when I left."

The technician laughed. "I know, that's the beautiful irony about this thing! Had you stayed asleep instead of sneaking all the way back here, we would've come in and taken Jenna, then returned her by morning and you wouldn't have known the difference. If you'd woken up, we would've just sedated you and left you there. You were never the one we wanted, Lewis. You even figured that out in the dream world."

His blood pressure shot through the roof and he struggled in his restraints harder. The last of the Velcro on his right wrist wasn't undone just yet.

Blackwell laughed. "It was pretty funny. The team we sent out there, Jackson, Katelyn, and the others, were all wondering why you weren't in bed with her but they figured you'd gone off and had a late-night drink or something. Then, right after they got back, we found you snooping around here of all places!" He chuckled again. "But after your incident during the tour, it was clear you had played more *Rogue Horizon* than your girlfriend had. Not that that mattered, she didn't need the preliminary brainwashing to give in to the programming. But we figured we'd take it as a two-for-one special. Now you can both snap and kill each other when you get back to L.A.!"

"You need to work on your sales pitch."

The technician shrugged. "Eh, there's a reason I'm more of a behind the scenes guy." He turned back to the computer. "Now, unfortunately, comes the less fun part. Now that you know it's a simulation, there can be no narrative. When I put you under again, I'm afraid I'm going to have to use everything in the Dream Machine's power to break you. I will exploit every fear, every insecurity, and every traumatic memory until you become officially unstable enough to take you back to Vegas. You and your girlfriend will feel strange for a couple of days, but you're back in L.A. on Sunday and when and where you snap is irrelevant to the things we'll learn from *how* you each do it."

Lewis forced a laugh, still fumbling with the Velcro

underwater. "You people are mad. Completely. Fucking. Mad."

Blackwell opened a small metallic case and withdrew a syringe and a vial of sedative. "It's really all contextual, Lewis. It's not a *personal* thing. I've got nothing against you, your girlfriend, or any of the patients I get here. And it's not a business thing either, we're not profiting from this. At least, not in cash." He slid the needle into the bottle and drew the requisite amount.

Lewis's fingers kept slipping beneath the surface, the last bit of Velcro restraining his right wrist remaining stuck. "Alright then, at least tell me one last thing. I'm not going to remember, and like you said, I'll be dead soon anyway. Who actually funds all of this? The CIA? NSA? An organization so secret I'm not even supposed to know it exists?"

Blackwell approached him with the syringe and sat down in the seat with a sigh. "The thing is…I don't really know. It's above my pay grade. All I *do* know is that Andromeda Virtual Systems sends me a check every month and that that check clears." He held up the syringe and smiled. "But it doesn't really matter in the end, does it Lewis?"

Lewis stared up at the contraption that would soon begin beaming images directly into his mind. Reality would disappear, and he would slip into a nightmarish dreamscape from which he would never recover.

"No," he said, as if accepting it. "I guess it doesn't matter."

Then, as Blackwell bent down to administer the sedative, his freed right hand shot out of the water and grabbed the technician by the throat.

35

The syringe slipped from Blackwell's fingers as Lewis yanked him forward and he toppled into the pool. The man was not as nimble or quick-thinking in dangerous situations as his simulation counterpart. He immediately began floundering and pushing off Lewis as he scrambled for the other edge of the tank.

Lewis turned to his other wrist and tore the Velcro strap away, then spun around and wrapped his arms around the technician's waist just as he got half out of the water. He pulled back with all his might and both of them toppled backward and sank into the three-foot-deep pool, water cascading over the sides.

Blackwell struggled violently, but Lewis put him in a headlock and held him beneath the surface while he gasped for air above the water. He channeled the anger from everything he'd just experienced – the nightmarish chase through Vegas, witnessing his girlfriend's fake death, reawakening the trauma from his brother's tragic accident, tormenting him with the specter of the infected astronaut – and used it to push the technician deeper into the water.

He began struggling harder, nearly breaking free. Lewis thought of every person this sick fuck had tortured over the past half a year, the horrible deaths he had caused, the families that had been impacted, and forced Blackwell's head back down. The technician's right hand reached above the surface and began grabbing at Lewis's face. After a moment, the arm retreated underwater to assist its left counterpart in attempting to break Lewis's hold to little success.

It seemed to take forever, but finally, the last burst of bubbles escaped from Blackwell's lips, and with a few last twitches, the submerged body went still. Lewis let go and scurried back out of the water, wanting to get as far away from the corpse as possible. He fell onto the tile floor, turned over, and crawled away to the far wall where he sat breathing heavily for a good several minutes.

He looked at his hands, unable to believe he'd just killed a man. It didn't feel like slaying an enemy in a video game, not at all. There was something unnerving about the way Blackwell had finally stopped moving, his eyes remaining open aimlessly beneath the water. He didn't regret it though. The man had deserved to die.

Beside the desk with the monitors was a stool with his clothes from Friday folded neatly on top of it. A towel lay on the floor beside them. Still dripping water and being careful not to slip, Lewis made his way across the room, took the towel, and dried himself off. Still shaking and nervous, he got changed out of the haptic suit back into his own clothing. He saw his socks and shoes sitting beneath the stool, retrieved them, and slipped them on.

Once he was ready, he looked around the room for a

weapon. A pistol lay on the desk, its barrel pointing toward the wall. He picked it up and turned it over in his hand. It was weird holding one in real life; not even the simulation had prepared him for it. He was worried he wouldn't know how to use it correctly if the need arose. In games, firing was always triggered by a hand-held controller or the click of a mouse. Nothing like this.

However, he supposed that even aiming it at someone could be useful. They didn't know how good of a shot he was. There appeared to be a little switch on the side that he assumed was the safety, and he shifted it in the opposite direction. Well, at least he wouldn't make that rookie mistake.

He wasn't sure what his next move was at this point. Blackwell had said they were getting ready to take Jenna back to Vegas, that she'd already completed her brainwashing. But he hadn't; they weren't able to make him crack in time. If he could get out, he could alert the authorities. Maybe they could place Jenna in protective police custody to prevent her from hurting herself or others until they could get her psychiatric help to undo the psychological programming. There had to be a way.

He needed to get evidence and get out of here. There didn't appear to be any security cameras in here watching him, but they would probably have a guard do rounds once in a while just to make sure things were copacetic. Lewis's phone had been placed on the side of the desk next to his wallet, but the rental car keys were missing. They must've parked the vehicle in the lot; they were going to have to drive it back to Vegas when they left with him anyway. The keys had to be somewhere else, maybe in the reception of the Entertainment Center.

Lewis took out the phone, opened the camera app, and

began taking photos of the room, the Dream Machine equipment, images from the simulation still on the monitors, the haptic wetsuit, the syringe on the floor, even Blackwell's dead body in the pool. He took everything from multiple angles. He created a Google Drive folder to share them with Richter, but there was no signal here.

"Damn," he said, pocketing the phone. His primary goal was to get out of here now; he had the evidence he needed. But he'd have to get back into the main building to find car keys, whether they were his or one of the black Chevys parked out front. He went back to the tank, and, rolling up his sleeve, stuck his arm into the water to pull the technician's ID badge off his belt. He shook it to get some of the water off, then looked at it. The man's full name was Christopher Blackwell, and his official position was listed as "Director of Information Technology" at Andromeda Virtual Systems.

Lewis slowly opened the door and peered out into the hallway. There was a narrow corridor here that went off to a blank wall to his left with a fire extinguisher on it and came out into some kind of open area to his right. Taking one last look at the room, he shuddered and closed the door behind him.

He crept slowly toward the dimly-lit open area, staying close to the wall. When he reached the corner, he peered out. Nobody was there. At the other side, another hallway led off to what he assumed was the other Dream Machine room. Prominently displayed on the wall to his left was a black and white depiction of a galaxy and "AVS" in thin, black lettering below it.

And ahead of him, across the area, stood a set of double doors.

Lewis briskly strode toward them and pushed one open.

In the next room was an elevator and a double-landing staircase leading upward. Keeping the gun out in front of him, he started up the steps. As he turned to the next landing, he realized there was only one other level. The staircase was lit by bright white fluorescents as the lower level had been, but through the window on the door to the next floor, it looked pitch black.

He pressed his face to the window and looked inside. Stretching away from him were row after row of computer racks, each radiating red luminescence from lights along their sides.

It was the server room.

All of the data in Arcadia was stored here. The FBI would have a field day with this. Lewis suddenly remembered that he still had Gonzalez's business card in his wallet. He was certainly going to have a call with her about all this. Assuming he made it out alive.

Lewis opened the door and entered. It was chillier in here, but not uncomfortably so. He held his pistol at the ready as he began moving down the row that divided the server room in two. Each half was walled off behind thick glass on both sides of him. Electronics hummed and occasionally beeped as he passed by, the glare of the red LEDs shining in his peripheral.

He became even more tense as he reached the other side and saw a set of glass-paned double doors opening out into an empty white room. He pushed through them, walked through the room, and exited through a single door into the cold desert night air, a full moon shining in the sky.

Lewis found himself near the rear of the compound, at the entrance to the smaller building that he had seen Blackwell and the others taking Jenna toward earlier when she'd had the bag over her head. Directly in front of him, across a small paved road, were the solar panels he had crouched by. Immediately to his right stood the fencing around the construction site and diagonally to the right, across the road from him, was the largest building, the Entertainment Center.

Keeping low, he moved swiftly across the ground toward the safety of the solar panels. He was about halfway across the pavement when he heard a vehicle screech and turned his head to witness a black Chevy Suburban tearing out of Arcadia's front entrance and speeding south on Old Hwy 93.

They're taking Jenna back to the hotel, he thought. He had to move quickly.

Lewis forsook taking cover by the solar equipment and instead sprinted toward the back door of the Entertainment Center. He skidded to a halt and whipped out Blackwell's security badge, sliding it through the card reader beside a keypad. The light flicked from red to green and the heavy door unlocked beside him.

He kept the gun ready in his right hand while he gradually pulled the door open with his left. Lewis half expected one of the guards to jump out right then, but to his relief he managed to slip inside and close the door quietly behind him without interruption.

It actually began to make him worried. This was some kind of government installation. Where the hell was all the security?

Then, from the large main lobby far beyond the long stretch of dark, blue-lit corridor came the sound of voices.

Lewis flattened himself against the wall next to the door for Studio 3, the same space where he'd watched Jenna play *Retrowave Rampage* less than 24 hours before. It all seemed like an eternity ago. He couldn't believe it had been less than a week since this all started on the evening of her birthday.

He inched himself slowly along the hallway, the conversation steadily becoming more audible the closer he got. It sounded like two people were having an argument, one angrier and louder than the other.

Finally, he reached the end of the corridor and cautiously peered out into the entrance lobby. In the minimal illumination provided by the blue LEDs overhead, Lewis could make out three figures standing by the arcade machines obscured in enough shadow that he couldn't see their faces. Two of them appeared to be wearing suits, but the third, standing in the middle, wore a dark vest and khaki pants. He was pretty sure that was Jackson.

One of the two suited men raised his voice even louder. "…can't hide it from me any longer. *I* built this place and I demand to know what you people are really using it for. End of story."

The other man spoke. "Allow me to remind you who *paid* for your little playground, Mr. Zhao. My organization has funneled millions of dollars into this enterprise, and, as per our agreement, the research we do here is none of your concern. You had said you'd rather not know when we signed off on the deal. So *that's* the end of the story."

Lewis suddenly shrunk back from the corner. His body slid to the floor and his hands began shaking, a vise constricting his chest. He couldn't believe what he'd just heard with his own ears, but it was unmistakable.

The other man's voice belonged to Lance Bateman.

36

"The deal was always this," he continued. "Family First would pay for your dream VR attraction and fund it as it grew, but until our research was completed, it would not be advertised or exposed to press scrutiny. The visitors here all consented to be part of a psychological experiment."

"I know you've been re-jigging the stuff I developed for the CIA. Are you combining it with the Dream Machine prototype, is that it?" Zhao said.

Bateman held up his hands. "We want to run the definitive test of whether or not violence in video games creates violence in real life. That's all."

"That's one way of putting it."

They both spun around. Jackson reached for his gun, but Bateman motioned for him to put it away, a big smile coming across his face.

Lewis walked toward the three of them, his gun aimed at Jenna's father. "Didn't expect to see you here, Mr. Bateman. Seems a bit out of character for you."

He held up his hand and said, "Please, call me Lance."

"Shut the fuck up," Lewis said, switching the gun to one hand and pointing the barrel at the man's head.

Bateman chuckled. "You know Desmond, I'm sorry you had to get mixed up in all this. I truly am. It was never my intention. I mean, there was always the possibility that you were going to end up as collateral once Jenna went haywire, but that's nothing personal."

"What the hell is going on?" Zhao said, looking genuinely confused and backing away.

"Hey Victor," Lewis said bitterly, still glaring at Bateman. "Guess your buddy Lance here didn't tell you about his little brainwashing project, huh?"

"That's not exactly how I'd describe it," Bateman said. "But, I can see how that misconception would arise."

"This wasn't for knowledge or experimentation." The gun wavered slightly in his hand. "It was a carefully orchestrated smear campaign against violent video games, wasn't it? First, you identified prominent YouTube gaming icons, video game journalists, and e-sports competitors. Then you sent them copies of *Rogue Horizon*, a derivative sci-fi horror schlock-fest designed to make players' skin crawl. Its focus wasn't plot, gameplay, or character development like other games. No, its sole purpose was to disturb you with visceral, gory imagery, maybe with a little bit of subliminal imagery thrown in to spice it up.

"But in your early experiments, before you began sending out the game, that wasn't enough to make them crazy, was it Lance? You went to all that effort, and all the test subjects came away with were some bad dreams. Turns out even deliberately violent, disturbing games don't make people commit murder. There, your big question was solved."

"It's more than that, Desmond," Bateman snarled. "The games might not cause mass shootings or violent behavior, but it's *societal degradation*. The proliferation of bloody and explicit imagery, the mass devaluing of human life through the increased popularity of first-person shooters and criminal sandboxes like *Grand Theft Auto*..."

"But you didn't stop there, Lance. No, you had dedicated your entire life to the anti-violent media crusade. You weren't about to leave the arena empty-handed. So, you and your crazy fucking Family First friends decided to create something that would actually induce a homicidal rage. You spent millions of dollars creating advanced virtual reality neurotech so you could torture gamers' minds until it had the desired effect.

"But you couldn't move the Dream Machines around, so you had to bring the gamers to some remote location to brainwash them. You picked Las Vegas because it's a popular destination and because it's surrounded by desert, the perfect place to build an installation like this. You don't have to worry about random people walking in and your security costs would be less. That's why you had so few guards. In fact, I think Jackson is the only actual security guard."

"I'm more than enough," he grunted, his pistol still at his side.

"Wasn't talking to you, asshole," Lewis said. He turned back to Bateman. "Once this place was built and ready, *that's* when you began sending out the *Rogue Horizon* copies with the subliminal 'Arcadia awaits' message. You sent them to people like Charlie Wong and Jake Miller, even your own *daughter*. You probably even paid someone to write that *Atlantic* article."

"Didn't have to," Bateman said. "The author was a

regular donor to Family First. We simply asked her a favor."

"But then a couple things fucked up, didn't they? First, Jake began investigating you after you sent him a copy of the game. He suspected something about this place before he even got here, but the day he died, you tried to snag him back at his hotel."

"No," Jackson growled. "The normal procedure is to kidnap them while they're here during the day. He attempted to break in after-hours and I caught him in the main lobby. He managed to steal my gun and made it back to his car, which was parked in the desert just across the road. I chased him, but he got ahead and pulled aside at a gas station. I knew he'd have to take US-93 to get back to Vegas, so I ambushed him there. It worked better than I expected. I tried to ram him off the road, but he swerved off a hill without any damage to my car. Then I used a light rig to scare him and finished the job. Whole thing looked like an accident. We only ran a night op kidnapping you two tonight because you and your girlfriend left during the day before we could snag you – and Mr. Zhao was here."

"I knew about none of this," Zhao said, putting his hands up. He shot Bateman and Jackson angry looks. "They took my dream and turned it into a nightmare."

"Stop trying to be poetic," Bateman sneered. "You were a washed-up developer. We only picked you because of the serial killer simulator and the stint you did with the CIA."

Zhao sighed, turning to Lewis. "The original version of *Rogue Horizon* was a test project for the government. After the subjects began having violent dreams, it was shut down. I managed to keep some of the files…I mean, I'd worked hard on that game! But we all agreed it was for the best to end it. It never became a twisted psychological experiment like this."

Lewis directed his attention back to Bateman. "What kind of sick bastard sacrifices his own *daughter* for a social cause?"

He laughed. "That's where you're wrong, Desmond. You misinterpret my motivations. I'm not sacrificing Jenna for a failing social cause; my wife and I are sacrificing *ourselves* to save Jenna."

Now everybody looked confused.

Bateman continued. "I didn't dedicate these past years of my life to this project just because I hated violent video games. I believe they're a cultural cancer, but more importantly, they've irreparably damaged the mind of my daughter. They corrupted her innocence and distorted her brain, just like they did to the minds of millions of other children across this country, across the world. How many more parents have to suffer watching their sons and daughters devolve into violent savages, Desmond? How many more impressionable young minds have to be scarred by the violence of the media, and worst of all, violent *interactive* media?

"I knew Jenna was secretly buying violent games for her computer for many years. Patricia and I found them in a drawer. I played some of them myself while we debated whether or not to confront her about it. And you know what I thought? Some of them weren't half bad. They were pretty well made, and I almost started enjoying myself once I got the hang of the controls – that was always the worst part. But then…I realized what they were doing to me, playing off my baser animalistic instincts. The games were rated M for Mature, but the developers knew they would be played by children. They knew exactly what they were doing.

"Ultimately, we did confront her. We grounded her, took

the games away, and banned her from using the computer for several months. It was for her own good. But she went into withdrawal from those things and never recovered. By then she was off at USC, out of the house where we couldn't control her. She got diagnosed with borderline personality disorder, but I don't think the shrinks really knew what they were talking about. The mood swings, the sudden aggression…that had to be the games, Desmond. The games did it to her. There was no other explanation."

"So, because you refused to accept your failure as a parent, you conceived an elaborate murder scheme to get back at her?"

"No, no, no, to get back at *them* – the games, the developers, the society that promotes that kind of bullshit. That's why this is all coming to an end now. There are others we sent *Rogue Horizon* to, but since my daughter's completed her time in the Dream Machine, there's no need for more bloodshed. To cap off the past six months of violence by gamers, first-person shooter champion Jenna Bateman is going to violently butcher her two parents to death in their Beverly Hills home. She's then going to be arrested and institutionalized by police officers we've paid off to be close to the scene so that she'll be unable to kill herself in time.

"Don't you see it, Desmond? My daughter is finally going to get the help she needs! And she'll get to fulfill her lifelong dream: to kill her mother and I. She screamed at us when we grounded her, smashed plates and glasses on the floor. Patricia and I had never been so afraid in our lives. Jenna later said sorry, of course, but I had seen the real her in that moment, the version of my daughter that she hid from everyone else: violent, hateful, and aggressive. There had been outbursts before, but none that severe, and that's when it became clear to me that games were a complete menace, that *someone* had to stop them.

"So while Jenna is undergoing treatment, my wife and I will be martyred for the cause. Lance and Patricia Bateman, two anti-violent media activists who were murdered by their own crazed champion gamer daughter. The deaths over the past half a year were just the buildup. This is the main event. My friends at Family First are already preparing the biggest lobbying push in our history. They're going to start marches in D.C., Democrats and Republicans alike, all fighting for a new era of family-friendly entertainment, to control violent content and hold the film, television, and gaming industries accountable once and for all. My son James will probably take up my mantle once he graduates from college and use what video games did to his family to lead the charge. My only regret is that I won't live to see it."

Both Jackson and Zhao looked like sailors who had realized their captain had lost touch with reality and was currently steering them into a maelstrom.

"I think you're the one who needs help," Lewis said.

"No Desmond, this country is sick. And this is the bitter pill it needs to swallow."

Suddenly, he turned and grabbed the pistol out of the holster on Jackson's right hip and brought it up. The guard barely registered what was happening in time to turn his head in surprise, before Bateman pulled the trigger with the barrel less than a foot from the man's face. Blood and brains jetted from the back of Jackson's head as he fell back, a gaping dark hole torn through his right eye socket. Zhao turned and ran, but Bateman lined up a shot on him next and fired. He went down as a crimson spurt erupted from the back of his left shoulder.

He turned to Lewis next, who backed away with his gun still aimed. "Don't worry, I know you don't really know how to fire that thing. Otherwise, you would've shot me by now. It's time to clean up this mess. And unfortunately, Desmond…that includes you."

Bateman raised the pistol toward him and fired again.

37

Lewis ran as the bullet missed him by a wide margin. Fortunately, Bateman was a terrible shot. He'd only hit Jackson and Zhao because they'd been so close.

He sprinted down the corridor, loosing off a few shots behind him. The gun roared and kicked in his hand, and it hurt his wrist; he clearly wasn't holding it right. Then it clicked empty and he dropped it as he ran. Bateman leaned out from around a corner back where the hallway met the lobby, fired a couple more rounds after him, then darted forward to chase him on foot.

Lewis burst through the rear door and was hit with a gust of cold air, but it barely slowed him down as he turned on his heel and began running along the building toward the asphalt drive that divided the compound.

Even though Bateman's motives were insane, everything finally made sense. When he called after the incident with Charlie and asked Lewis if he'd noticed anything different in Jenna's behavior, he wasn't expressing a legitimate concern.

He had assumed his daughter had been playing *Rogue Horizon* and expected Lewis to tell him about the resulting changes in her actions. But Lewis hadn't noticed any changes because she'd only played the beginning of the game and hadn't gotten around to playing more of it since. He'd spent so much time wondering if she had been playing more and why she would be lying to him that he hadn't questioned the real reason her father would ask that. Jenna hadn't changed at all for the past several weeks.

Lewis turned on the road and began sprinting the length of the Entertainment Center. Bateman had been hot on his tail. He'd be right around the corner behind him any second now, the pistol kicking wildly in his hand. Lewis had to get back in the front entrance, snatch some keys off of either Jackson or Zhao, and then steal a car before Bateman could shoot him.

Suddenly, up ahead, a black Chevy Malibu swerved around the corner and gunned its engine straight toward him. Lewis froze. His vision darted left and right: he was trapped between the side wall of the building and the chain-link fencing that surrounded the construction site.

Quickly, he made his decision.

Lewis ran to the side and jumped up as he reached a gate in the fence, grabbing handholds and scrambling upward to find purchase with his feet. He flipped himself over the top, only to see the ground sloping downward, an entrance ramp for vehicles into the pit. He hit the dirt at an angle and rolled painfully down twenty-five feet to the base.

Up above, tires swerved and suddenly the front of the Malibu burst through the gate, metal swinging outward and clanging along the sides. Still lying in the dirt, Lewis rolled onto his back.

The car door opened and a figure stepped out.

"You've got to be fucking kidding me," he muttered.

Shutting the door and staring down at him from the top of the hill was the astronaut, the blue glow from within its helmet even harsher than it had been in the Dream Machine. It held a pistol in its right hand.

"Hi, Desmond," it said in a synthetic version of Lance Bateman's voice.

Then it aimed the gun at him.

Ignoring the pain he felt all over, Lewis got up and ran as a shot cracked behind him and whizzed by. The construction site was a large pit comprised of several large cargo containers scattered around and an area toward the corner diagonally across from him where a steel frame was being built. An excavator was parked next to it.

Lewis took cover behind one of the cargo crates and caught his breath. This couldn't be happening. It was Bateman chasing him, not the astronaut. He peered around the corner. At first, he just saw a blue light swinging around in the dark. Then something in his vision flickered and he saw it, the astronaut, clear as day.

"I know you're out here, Desmond," it said in its electronic voice.

He flinched back into his cover, his breathing uneven. *Get it together.* Staying focused, Lewis turned and crept along the side of the cargo crate. He had to think fast. The Malibu's engine purred softly at the top of the slope. Could he sneak around behind Bateman, steal it, and get out? It was possible, as long as his pursuer got far out enough into the construction site that he couldn't double back in time to stop him.

Lewis slipped around the back of the container and continued along the other side. He could see his goal about thirty feet away. The car's headlights shone out from the top of the slope and bathed the pit in bright light. The astronaut was nowhere in sight.

He had just begun to run forward when suddenly it jumped out from beside the crate, raising the gun and firing. Lewis slid to the ground in the nick of time just as the gun went off. It tried to fire the weapon again, but it clicked empty. The astronaut tossed the useless weapon aside and looked down, directing its blue light into his eyes.

Lewis brought up his hand to shield his face and blinked as it came closer. For a second he saw Lance Bateman, still in his black suit as he had been in the lobby, but with some kind of bright blue headlamp strapped around his forehead – then in the next blink, the astronaut stood before him again.

"Running only prolongs the inevitable," it said. "Haven't you suffered enough, Desmond?" The astronaut tilted its head to the side as it looked at him. "Aren't you ready to join your brother?"

Frantic now, Lewis got to his feet and ran away in the opposite direction. He dashed past two other cargo crates but had already made up his mind. There was only one more place that seemed safe here.

The excavator.

Parked up against the rear edge of the pit, it was big and yellow, with a large hydraulic bucket mounted to the right of the cockpit and two massive tank treads on each side. Lewis ran around and jumped up on the left tread, then grabbed the door and pulled. Thankfully, no one felt the need to lock it out here in the middle of the desert, and it swung wide open.

He climbed in, shut the door, and locked it, then began anxiously looking around the cockpit for keys. It wasn't too cramped in here, but there wasn't much extra space. Two joysticks sat on each side of the chair and a number of pedals lay at his feet that he didn't know what to do with. He looked up at the ceiling and saw there was a sun visor, just like in a car.

Lewis flipped it down and the key fell out, clanking to the floor. He bent down and felt around the floor for it with both hands. When he finally found it, he slid it into the ignition and turned the key just as a bright blue light appeared off to his left.

As the engine roared to life, he turned his head in time see the astronaut aggressively slam its elbow into the window with a loud *crack*. Lewis closed his eyes and raised his arm protectively as shards of broken glass pelted him, feeling many bounce off and rain down on the cockpit floor. The next thing he knew, the astronaut's arm wrapped around his throat and the attacker held him in a tight headlock.

"Just let it end, Desmond," the synthetic voice hissed.

Lewis could barely breathe. His left hand tried to pry the arm around him free while the other frantically slapped at the excavator controls. He hit a button and suddenly the entire thing lurched forward, the diesel engine grinding to life. The astronaut jumped upward, grabbing a handle inside the cockpit through the broken window to keep itself off of the treads. Its grip tightened around his neck.

"It's already begun," the voice continued. "Her programming is complete. Even if you stop me here, we've already won. So let it end."

Squinting in the harsh blue glare that shone over his shoulder, Lewis could just make out his and the astronaut's reflections on the unbroken right window. The astronaut was mostly obscured by the bright light, but no, he could see it, spacesuit and all.

Look harder.

Blackness crept around the edges of his vision, his lungs burning for breath. There wasn't much more of this he could take. He stared closely at the reflection and didn't let his mind fill in the gaps. He actually couldn't see his attacker's face at all. Just its arm, strangling him. A normal human arm, dressed in a black suit jacket. And there, just below the blue light, he finally saw it. A sinister smile, the leer of a deranged lunatic.

The astronaut was gone.

Summoning the last of his strength, Lewis reached past his head to the right and his fingers fumbled for a hold. Finally, they grasped the handle and with the last of his strength, he pulled it.

The door opened and the next thing he knew he was falling through space. His back hit the treads and he nearly rolled off, but something grabbed his left leg and a blue glow washed over him. He looked back. The door had swung Bateman out further; he'd landed near the front of the moving treads and had latched onto Lewis to pull himself back up. Beneath the bright light of the headlamp, his face contorted red with a mixture of rage and terror.

Lewis kicked Bateman in the shoulder as he began hauling himself closer and scrambled back as the older man's legs went over the edge. Jenna's father still had a death grip around Lewis's left ankle, preventing his escape, and it tightened as a stomach-turning *crunch* filled the air. Bateman's agonized scream tore through his ears as Lewis pulled his right leg back for a final kick. His opponent's lower torso completely disappeared from view just as Lewis slammed his heel into Bateman's forehead. He finally let go long enough for Lewis to roll off the side of the advancing treads and hit the ground.

He turned back just in time to see Lance Bateman's hand

reach for the heavens as it slipped out of sight, illuminated blue from the headlamp beneath it. Then the light shut off and the wet crunching noises abruptly came to an end. Dark blood seeped out from under the treads as the vehicle continued its forward motion, glistening in the light of the full moon.

Lewis got up and began walking around behind the excavator toward the Malibu's glaring headlights at the top of the entrance ramp.

In the darkness of the main lobby, Victor Zhao pulled himself up against the reception desk and began looking for a first-aid kit, only to find himself out of luck. The bullet was embedded deep in the back of his left shoulder, but he should be alright. Physically, at least. The truth he now knew about his employment and what had gone on here beneath his nose would scar his memory forever.

A pair of headlights swung around in front of the main glass doors, and a moment later Desmond Lewis stumbled in, covered in dirt and looking worse for wear.

"Bateman?" Zhao asked.

Lewis shivered. "Dead."

"Well, that solves one problem." He looked around the main lobby. This place had once been his pride and joy, but now it was just a bad dream. One that he couldn't wake up from. He should've known Family First's offer was too good to be true.

"I hoped that the bullet wouldn't have killed you. I need you to do us both a huge favor." Lewis ran up to him and handed him a business card. Zhao squinted at it in the dim light and barely made out the words "Sara Gonzalez", but definitely recognized the FBI insignia at the top.

"What is this?" he said.

"Call 9-1-1, get someone out here for your wound and to clean up the bodies. But you need to call this FBI agent, she's been assigned to the nationwide case. Tell her about the Dream Machine, the Batemans, *Rogue Horizon*, all of it. There are other Family First conspirators back in L.A. who she can bring down. This'll make national headlines."

"I'll get right on it," Zhao said. Lewis began running back to the doors. "Where are you going?"

"After Jenna. They still have her. Whatever happens to her or me, call that number." He disappeared out into the night.

Zhao leaned over the reception phone, picked it up with his blood-covered hand, and began rapidly dialing.

38

The open road stretched away before his headlights, yellow dashes rapidly flashing by on his left. The Malibu's speedometer ticked past a hundred, but he didn't worry about a stray cop at the side of the highway. The only thing that mattered to him was finding how far they'd gotten back to Vegas with their head-start. He was back on US-93 now, the Great Basin Highway; at this hour of the night, it was a lonely express back to civilization.

His bloodshot eyes watched the road curve softly through the desert, his body subconsciously leaning into each turn. Lewis knew he was exhausted, but adrenaline had taken over. It coursed through his veins and guided him as if he were a puppet. It and his determination were the only things keeping him running right now. Otherwise, after all that had happened, all he now knew, he probably would've collapsed back at Arcadia.

Then he saw something loom up ahead and slammed on the brakes. The car swiftly reduced its speed and came to a halt. Lewis blinked, shocked at the sight before him.

A black Chevy Suburban lay upside-down in the middle of the road. The body of a woman lay near it, face down.

Lewis threw open the Malibu's door and cautiously moved toward the wreck, turning on his phone's flashlight.

"Hello?" he called. Nothing answered him but the frigid nocturnal breeze. He approached the body and turned it over, jumping back in disgust. It was Katelyn Caruso, a shard of glass jammed deep into her trachea. Blood pooled beneath her, and her face was frozen in a look of abject terror.

Then another voice arose on the wind. "Please…oh please, don't darling, I love you–"

There was a quick scream, then it was over.

Lewis turned off the flashlight and advanced around the rear of the overturned SUV very, very slowly. Then he looked around the corner.

A figure was hunched over a dead body, stabbing it again and again. "Go away," they said. "I won't let you hurt me, I won't let you – no, no…" They broke down in sobs, their arms falling to their sides.

In the moonlight, Lewis saw a bloody glass shard clutched in the figure's right hand. Gradually, he began to approach them.

"Jenna," he said. "It's okay, they're not going to hurt you anymore."

The figure slowly stood up and turned around. Tears streaked down her face and her clothes, a white t-shirt and a pair of jeans, were covered in blood. Lewis saw that the body she'd been butchering was that of Patricia Bateman, whose eyes were still agape in shock.

He covered his mouth, taking a step back.

Jenna raised the makeshift weapon in a defensive

position. "Don't come closer. You're not gonna get me."

"Jenna, it's me, Desmond." Tears welled up in his eyes. "This isn't you. Come on, let's get you out of here."

They were completely alone. There wasn't another car visible for miles in either direction. It was just the two of them and the desert.

"Come on," he said, extending his hand. He could feel his knees wobbling. "Please..."

She launched herself at him, screaming as she slashed the shard like a blade. He jumped back and his phone clattered to the asphalt, his hands coming up protectively as she slashed again and again, driving him to the side of the road.

Jenna cut him along the forearm and he winced, ducking to avoid her next swing. The tears were making his vision blurry. "Please," he said again. She screamed and charged once more, bringing the blade down toward him in a stabbing motion.

He caught her arm with both hands. She was surprisingly strong and brought her left hand around to assist her right. The glass got closer and closer. Jenna leaned her entire body weight into it.

Tears poured down his face. "Please, please," he whispered.

Her eyes were frantic, like those of a scared animal lashing out in self-defense. The glass hovered mere inches from his face.

Lewis jerked his right leg up, kneeing her in the stomach. It drove the breath out of her and he used that moment to swivel around behind her, grab the glass shard, and wrench it from her hand. She gasped as it sliced her palm, but then it was gone, flung off into the night.

Jenna angrily turned around and clawed at him, tearing

his cheek, but he grabbed both of her arms and held them up. Her legs kicked at him, but he turned to the side and tensed his abs to lessen the damage.

"Listen Jenna, it's me, it's over."

"No, no, no," she muttered, still crying. Gradually, the struggling was replaced with uncontrollable sobbing. He pulled her close and hugged her tightly.

"It's okay," Lewis said, guiding her away from the wreck. "I've got you."

They stood there for several minutes as she slowly began calming down, but progress was abated when she looked over his shoulder at the corpse of her mother.

"Oh my God," she said, covering her mouth. "Did I…?"

"No-no-no-no-no," he whispered gently, turning her away. "Don't look back."

Together, they stumbled a good thirty feet from the carnage and sat by the side of the road, leaning against a metal railing. He pointed upward. "Look up there. Aren't they wonderful?"

Lewis saw her force a smile through the sobs. He hugged Jenna tightly and together they gazed up at the sky. Out here it was really something. No light pollution, no busy streets crowded with people, nor the distant ambiance of traffic. An endless cosmic painting revealed itself, all the constellations twinkling down from a breathtaking abyss. And as they sat there, neither of them ever taking their eyes off the stars, he leaned his head closer and whispered in her ear.

"Everything's gonna be alright."

VISIT

www.alexanderplansky.com

FOR UPDATES AND NEWSLETTERS

Made in the USA
Middletown, DE
13 December 2018